THE HUGO AWARD FINALIST

In the year 2550, premeditated murder is impossible in a society where surveillance of the citizens is almost universal. And a serial killer—completely out of the question!

And then the killings start. Even more shocking than the events themselves is the bizarre way in which they've been staged: the victims—all old men—are being eaten from within by specially bred plants and seeds, producing the "flowers of evil" ("les fleurs du mal") of an obviously deranged maniac. The question is: *why*.

Biotech artist Oscar Wilde, named for the infamous writer of the late nineteenth century, teams with U.N. detectives Charlotte Holmes and Hal Watson to unravel a futuristic nightmare in this masterful *tour de force*. Blending the best of science fiction prognostication with a dynamic and tense mystery, Brian Stableford has created one of his most compelling stories.

Borgo Press Books by BRIAN STABLEFORD

Against the New Gods and Other Essays on Writers of Imaginative Fiction
Algebraic Fantasies and Realistic Romances: More Masters of Science Fiction
Alien Abduction: The Wiltshire Revelations
The Best of Both Worlds and Other Ambiguous Tales
Beyond the Colors of Darkness and Other Exotica
Changelings and Other Metamorphic Tales
A Clash of Symbols: The Triumph of James Blish
Complications and Other Stories
The Cosmic Perspective and Other Black Comedies
Creators of Science Fiction
The Cure for Love and Other Tales of the Biotech Revolution
The Decadent World-View: Selected Essays
The Devil's Party: A Brief History of Satanic Abuse
The Dragon Man: A Novel of the Future
The Eleventh Hour
Exotic Encounters: Selected Reviews
Firefly: A Novel of the Far Future
Les Fleurs du Mal: A Tale of the Biotech Revolution
The Gardens of Tantalus and Other Delusions
Glorious Perversity: The Decline and Fall of Literary Decadence
Gothic Grotesques: Essays on Fantastic Literature
The Great Chain of Being and Other Tales of the Biotech Revolution
The Haunted Bookshop and Other Apparitions
Heterocosms: Science Fiction in Context and Practice
In the Flesh and Other Tales of the Biotech Revolution
The Innsmouth Heritage and Other Sequels
Jaunting on the Scoriac Tempests and Other Essays on Fantastic Literature
Kiss the Goat
Luscinia: A Romance of Nightingales and Roses
The Moment of Truth: A Novel of the Future
Narrative Strategies in Science Fiction, and Other Essays on Imaginative Fiction
News of the Black Feast and Other Random Reviews
An Oasis of Horror: Decadent Tales and Contes Cruels
Opening Minds: Essays on Fantastic Literature
Outside the Human Aquarium: Masters of Science Fiction, Second Edition
The Plurality of Worlds: A Sixteenth-Century Space Opera
Prelude to Eternity: A Romance of the First Time Machine
The Return of the Djinn and Other Black Melodramas
Salome and Other Decadent Fantasies
Slaves of the Death Spiders and Other Essays on Fantastic Literature
The Sociology of Science Fiction
Space, Time, and Infinity: Essays on Fantastic Literature
The Tree of Life and Other Tales of the Biotech Revolution
The Undead: A Tale of the Biotech Revolution
The World Beyond: A Sequel to S. Fowler Wright's The World Below
Yesterday's Bestsellers: A Voyage Through Literary History

LES FLEURS DU MAL

A TALE OF THE BIOTECH REVOLUTION

by

Brian Stableford

THE BORGO PRESS

An Imprint of Wildside Press LLC

MMX

CONTENTS

Author's Note... 7

Prologue: 14 April 2550... 13

Chapter One 17
Chapter Two.. 24
Chapter Three... 31
Chapter Four 38
Chapter Five.. 43
Chapter Six... 51
Chapter Seven 59
Chapter Eight 66
Chapter Nine 74
Chapter Ten... 84
Chapter Eleven.. 89
Chapter Twelve 96

About the Author 103

AUTHOR'S NOTE

The first version of this story was begun in December 1985, shortly after a four-and-a-half-year gap in which I had given up writing fiction in order to pretend to be an academic. (The pretence failed to convince me, and I returned to full-time writing in 1988.) It was the fourth story I began after that resumption to develop ideas that had been briefly broached in a futurology book that I had written in collaboration with David Langford, *The Third Millennium: A History of the World 2000-3000 A.D.*, which had been published earlier that year. In accordance with the common commercial practice of the day, I did not attempt to finish the story, which I envisaged as a novel, but prepared an outline of the whole narrative, for circulation to publishers along with three sample chapters.

It so happened that the newly-opened British offshoot of the US publisher Simon & Schuster had decided to initiate a science fiction line, and the editor responsible, Robyn Sisman, had indicated her willingness to consider a submission from me. *Les Fleurs du Mal* was the project I hope to sell, but in order to play safe, I also enclosed a copy of the only short story I had recently written that was not a "tale of the biotech revolution", together with an outline for its expansion to novel length. Because it had vampires in it, Robyn preferred the other submission—which eventually became *The Empire of Fear* (1988)—and continued to reject *Les Fleurs du Mal* whenever I broached the possibility of her taking it on thereafter, on the grounds that she wanted to maintain a certain consistency of product, although she did agree to publish a collection of stories in the series, as *Sexual Chemistry: Sardonic Tales of the Genetic Revolu-*

tion (1991), as a sweetener to the three-novel contract she was eager for me to sign in the wake of the success of *The Empire of Fear*.

Eventually despairing of Simon & Schuster (UK), I eventually decided to finish the novel version of *Les Fleurs du Mal* anyway, and completed it in 1992. I wrote the story to what seemed to be its natural length (68,000 words) but could not sell it, partly because publishers had changed their minds about the appropriate length for commercially-marketed novels. In the first phase of my career (1969-81), all the contracts I had signed had specified a maximum word-limit of 65,000 words, and it was only with great reluctance that publishers would issue genre novels of greater magnitude. By 1992, however, contracts issued for generic work tended to specify a minimum word-limit of 100,000, and shorter works were considered unmarketable. Despairing again, I decided to cut the text drastically and attempt to sell an abridged version of the story to one or other of the sf magazines as a novella. The present text is the 29,000-word result of that cut, although Gardner Dozois—who bought it for publication in the October 1994 issue of *Asimov's Science Fiction*—insisted on cutting out the gratuitous car chase, thus reducing the published version to 27,000 words.

Still desirous of getting the longer version into print, I formulated the ingenious plan of "hiding" it within a projected six-volume series of novels, all of which would be expansions of stories in the by-then extensive series of tales of the biotech revolution. It was projected as the fourth in the chronologically-ordered series, following expansions of "The Magic Bullet" (1989), "Inherit the Earth" (1995) another project circulated as an outline-and-sample in the late 1980s but subsequently redeveloped as a novella) and "Dark Ararat", a novel begun in the early months of 1981 but left incomplete when I had abandoned fiction writing for Academia. It was to be followed by expansions of "Mortimer Gray's History of Death", similarly written during the first burst of new creativity in the early months of 1987 but unpublished until Gardner Dozois bought a revised version for *Asimov's* in 1995, and an as-yet-unwritten novel that would round out the future history thus mapped out, taking it beyond the year 3000 that had marked the terminus of *The Third*

Millennium. The project attracted no takers in 1996, although one British editor offered to do a single-volume version in which all six sections retained novella length—an offer that vanished in a puff of smoke when he was made redundant, because his employer, like virtually every other publisher in the world, was abandoning science fiction as a moribund genre of no further commercial value.

In 1997, however, David Hartwell of Tor Books agreed to test the waters by issuing one of the novels, with a vague undertaking to try out another if the first proved profitable. He refused to start with the first in the projected series, however, preferring the expansion of "Inherit the Earth", which had already proven its reader-appeal when published in *Analog*, the sf magazine with the largest circulation. He sent back the novel for rewriting because my completed version was some way short of 100,000 words, but when the revised version was published it did make a small profit—probably because all Tor's rivals were in the process of abandoning the genre, thus creating a temporary imbalance of supply and demand within its gradually-dwindling readership. He then invited me to submit another item from the series, saying that he did not mind which one. As the whole point of the exercise, from my viewpoint, had been to achieve publication for *Les Fleurs du Mal*, I opted for that one, although I was obliged to do a further revision in order to inflate the 68,000-word text to 100,000 words. Suspecting that David would not be prepared to publish a novel with a title in French, I submitted it to him under the translated title of *The Flowers of Evil*, but he did not like that either and asked me to suggest some possible alternatives. I offered a couple that I quite liked, but he turned them down too. "I've just got the cover proof," he said, "and it has buildings on it, so we're going to call it *Architects of Emortality*." And he did.

Eventually, Tor did do all six volumes of the projected series, but only commissioned them one by one, leaving me perennially fearful that the axe might fall at any moment. I am still rather surprised that it didn't, given that the sales of titles in the series declined markedly over time, but it did fall immediately afterwards, and my career as a commercial writer effectively ended with the publication of the sixth volume, *The Omega Expedition* (2002)—

since which time I have been confined, for my sins, to the agonizing circles of the Dantean Hell that is small-press and print-on-demand publication.

(My suffering is, admittedly, utterly negligible by comparison to that endured by the great pioneer of science fiction, and the most inventive writer who ever lived, Edgar Poe, who died miserably of neglect at the age of forty, or those of the inspirational heroes of this narrative, Oscar Wilde and Charles Baudelaire, who both died in abject poverty, almost-universally despised, at the age of forty-six. My own version of *Les Fleurs du Mal*, although begun when I was a mere thirty-seven years of age, thus achieved publication at a propitious moment, shortly after my forty-sixth birthday—and I am still free to wonder at the fact that I have now lived longer than the fourth of my great literary heroes, Théophile Gautier, perhaps with a few years still in hand before poverty, misery and near-universal despite exact their final toll.)

The "original" 68,000-word version of *Les Fleurs du Mal* will never see print now, if only because all the typescripts and the electronic text have been lost. I do, however, still have a lingering affection for this 29,000-word version, whose slightly-abridged version came within a handful of votes of winning a Hugo (my one and only chance at that signal honor). The narrative it contains was, in a sense, the one that firmly established the quasi-decadent *weltanschauung* and set the flippantly ironic tone of the then-nascent series of tales of the biotech revolution, whose most recent and previously-unpublished product, as I write, is now paired with it for the sake of comparison.

Readers will observe a few changes in outlook between the two elements of this double volume, doubtless due to the fact that when I first set my fingers to the keyboard to write *Les Fleurs du Mal* I was still relatively young and in an unusually buoyant mood, having just found a seemingly-adequate replacement for the wife who had recently deserted and divorced me; whereas I am now manifestly old and irredeemably broken-down, having just been deserted and divorced by the replacement in question, with no plausible prospect of finding another. Hopefully, though, they will also observe the similarities that reflect and embody the essential core of my perverse personality, untouchable by elation and catastrophe alike. The road that connects the two narratives has not run straight, nor has it been particularly easy to travel, but it still extends before me, and I am still cycling along it as best I can on my penny-farthing, defiantly carrying a soiled and tattered banner whose legend is just about discernible as *Excelsior*.

—Brian Stableford
July 2010

PROLOGUE

14 April 2550

Oscar stood before the full-length mirror, carefully inspecting every detail of his face. He caressed the flawless flesh with sensitive fingertips, rejoicing in its gloss. "Ivory and rose-leaves," he murmured.

Oscar always addressed his own reflection in the most admiring terms while it remained full of youth. When it grew old, as it had three times before, it lost its capacity to inspire admiration, and became a mocking reminder of the hazards which he and all men of his era still faced: decay, senescence, decomposition.

His revitalized hair was a glossy chestnut brown. To describe his complexion in terms of ivory and rose-leaves was a trifle hyperbolic, but the skin was pale and even. Authentically young men never had skin as perfect as that, because they could not help accumulating petty flaws while growing to maturity; only the rejuvenated could attain perfection, thanks to the artistry of their cosmetic engineers.

It was a nice paradox, Oscar thought, that only those who had been old could look truly young. He had flown in the face of professional advice by attempting a third rejuvenation so soon, at the age of 133. Many older men than he had not yet undergone their second rejuvenation, refusing to risk deep somatic engineering while their bodies had not quite descended to the depths of decrepitude. Oscar was far less brave than they; his fear of personal dilapidation was pathological.

"It is only shallow people," he informed his reflection, confident in the knowledge that he had an appreciative audience, "who do not judge by appearances." He bathed in the luxury of his own narcissism, admiring his grey eyes, his soft lips, his pearly-white teeth.

He reached out to pluck a green carnation from the wall beside the mirror. He twirled it between his delicate fingers, admiring it with as much satisfaction as he admired his own image. The flower was his own creation. It was a joke, of course, but a serious joke. The games that Oscar played in consequence of his name—which had been given to him in all innocence by parents whose knowledge of the earlier Oscar Wilde was limited to a vague awareness that he had been a writer of note—were no mere matter of public relations. His identification with the ideas and ideals of his *alter ego* had long ago become a kind of fetish. He was not afraid to acknowledge that fact, or to take pride in it. Life, if it were to be lived to the full in modern conditions, required a definite style and aesthetic shape: a constant flow of delicate ironies, tensions, and innovations.

He placed the flower in the buttonhole of his neatly-tailored suit.

Furnishing hotel interiors was vulgar hackwork unbefitting a real artist, but a real artist had to make a living, and the commonplaceness of such commissions was offset by such flourishes of unorthodoxy as having it written into every contract that one suite of rooms should be fitted with green carnations instead of the more fashionable roses and amaranths. His clients did not mind his making such demands; they were, after all, paying for his fashionability as well as his technical dexterity, and he could not have been nearly so fashionable were it not for his extravagantly extrovert eccentricity.

He turned one way and then the other, shrugging his shoulders to make sure that his jacket hung perfectly upon on his remodeled body.

Oscar did not doubt for a moment, as his greedy eyes devoured the glory of his reflection, that he would be equal to the challenge of his third youth. He was no crass businessman, apt to fall back into the same old routines at the first opportunity, wearing a new face as if it were merely a mask laid over the old. Nor was he the kind of man who would go to the opposite extreme, reverting to the habits and follies of first youthfulness, playing the sportsman or the rake. He was an artist. Artists had always been the pioneers who led mankind into the psychological unknown, and the current technology of rejuvenation was, after all, little more than a century old. No one knew for sure how many times a man might be successfully restored to youth, although it was tragically obvious that many failed at the second or third attempt. Oscar was firmly resolved that if the only thing required to secure eternal life was the correct attitude of mind, then he would be the first man to live forever.

He closed his eyes for a moment while he savored the pleasures of anticipation, but his delicious reverie was shattered by the com-con bell. He sighed, and crossed the room to the nearest telescreen, pausing only to make sure that his cravat was in order before exposing himself to the unit's camera-eye. His precautions were unnecessary; no face appeared on the screen. There was only a teletext message, cold and impersonal.

It was a request that he should call on a man he knew only slightly, and did not like at all. It seemed an unromantic and unpromising beginning to the new phase of his life. He reached out to send a message refusing the invitation, but paused before his fingers could descend upon the keys. The fax light was blinking. He pressed the RECEIVE button. He expected a copy of the message displayed on the screen, but what emerged from the humming printer was a seat reservation for the midnight maglev to San Francisco. Oscar had no intention of going to San Francisco; no such thought had crossed his mind. He could not imagine why anyone, least of all Gabriel King, should send him such a gift, with or without an explanation.

"Curiouser and curiouser," he murmured.

He decided to obey the summons after all. He had never been able to resist temptation, and there was nothing in the world quite as tempting as a mystery.

CHAPTER ONE

While she waited for the forensic experts to conclude their examination of Gabriel King's apartment, Charlotte Holmes tried to collect her thoughts. This was by far the biggest case of her fledgling career. Routine police work was incredibly dull, at least for site-investigation officers, and there had been nothing in her training or experience to prepare her for anything half as bizarre as this. Murder was nowadays the rarest of crimes, and such murders that did happen usually occurred when rage or spite smashed through the barriers erected by years of biofeedback training. Premeditated murders had fallen out of fashion as soon as it became impossible for the perpetrators to avoid apprehension.

She went to the window at the end of the corridor and looked out over the city. She was on the thirty-ninth floor, and there was quite a view. Central Park looked much as it must have looked in the days before the Devastation, but the rotting skyline was a product of the moment, whose like would probably never be seen again. Charlotte assumed that Gabriel King must have taken up residence in New York so that he might bid for a lion's share of the work involved in the deconstruction of the city. He had always been bigger in demolition than in construction, because he controlled a number of key patents in decay biotechnology. The Decivilization Movement had been a great boon to his business, although its prophets detested Gabriel King as much as they detested all old-style entrepreneurs, especially wealthy multiple rejuvenates. King could easily have made enemies among the people whose crusade he was furthering, and among the business rivals who had competed with him for the contracts—but who among them could have thought up the murder weapon she had just been studying through a camera-eye?

Her waistphone buzzed, and she took the handscreen from its holster. No image appeared. Hal Watson rarely allowed his face to be seen; he was a dealer in data and preferred to remain invisible within the webs of information which he spun. "Two names," he said. As he spoke, the names appeared on the screen in capital letters: WALTER CZASTKA; OSCAR WILDE. "They're the top people involved in the engineering of flowering plants," the voice continued. "We'll need one of them as a consultant, to double-check the forensic investigation. Czastka's in Micronesia, on an island he's leased in order to build an artificial ecosystem. Wilde's here in New York but he's just gone through his third rejuvenation and may be incommunicado. Try Czastka first."

"I'll call him," said Charlotte. "What about the girl?"

"Nothing yet. Camscan's under way. Might be able to pick her up somewhere, figure out where she came from or where she went. Has the team come out of the apartment yet?"

"No," said Charlotte, glumly. "I'll stay until they do."

"Don't worry," Hal said. "It'll open up once we have the forensics. With luck, we might crack the case before the story leaks out."

Charlotte sighed, and began punching the buttons on the handset. She tried Czastka first, as instructed. The fact that he was on the other side of the world wasn't of any real consequence, because he'd have to use a camera to inspect the murder weapon anyhow, and probably wouldn't be able to do much more until the lab had turned up a geneprint. The image that came on to the screen was a grade A sim.

"Charlotte Holmes," she said, "UN Police. Sending authority." The privacy-breaking codes cut no ice. The sim told her that Czastka was temporarily unreachable. That probably meant that he was messing about somewhere on his island, without a bleeper. It wasn't worth the hassle of getting Czastka's house-system to send out a summoner while there was an obvious alternative.

This time she got a low-grade AI receptionist, which informed her that Oscar Wilde was not in his hotel room at present. She sent her authorization code. The pretty face flickered as the new subroutine was engaged. "Mr. Wilde is in a cab," said the higher-grade receptionist, her simulated voice still honey-sweet. "Sending contact code; destination Trebizond Tower."

Charlotte was just about to retransmit the contact code when she realized that Trebizond Tower was the building on whose thirty-ninth floor she was standing.

"What a coincidence," she murmured, reflectively. Before she had finished wondering what the coincidence might possibly signify, another voice-call came through. This one was from the uniformed officer she had posted at the bottom of the elevator shaft to keep the public at bay.

"There's an Oscar Wilde here," said the officer, laconically. "He says he got a message half an hour ago to come up to King's apartment."

Charlotte frowned. Gabriel King had been dead for quite some time, and no call could possibly have been made from his apartment. "Send him up," she said, tersely. She had an uncomfortable feeling of being out of her depth. She was only a legman, after all; Hal was the real investigator. She hesitated over calling Hal to tell him what had happened, but decided against it. Instead, she went to the elevator to meet the new arrival.

When the man emerged she felt a curious jolt of astonishment. Hal had mentioned that Wilde was a recent rejuvenate, but she hadn't adapted her expectations to take account of it. Expert witnesses and other consultants usually looked fairly old, but Oscar Wilde looked ten years younger than she did; in fact, he was quite the most beautiful man she had ever seen. He bowed gracefully, and then looked up, briefly, at the discreet plastic eye set in the wall, whose security camera recorded every face which passed by.

Public eyes and private bubblebugs were everywhere in a city like New York, and native New Yorkers were entirely used to living under observation; those who had grown up with the situation took it completely for granted. In some unintegrated nations it still wasn't common for all walls to have eyes and ears, but within the borders of the six superpowers citizens had long since been required to learn to tolerate the ever-presence of the benevolent mechanical observers that guaranteed their safety. Wilde was neither a native New Yorker nor a genuinely young man, but he didn't give the impression that he resented the presence of the eye at all. If anything, his self-consciousness suggested that he liked to be watched.

"Mr. Wilde?" she said, tentatively. "I'm Charlotte Holmes, UN Police Department."

"Please call me Oscar," said the beautiful man. "What exactly has happened to poor Gabriel?"

"He's dead," Charlotte replied, shortly. "I understand that you received a call from him, or his simulacrum?"

"The message came as text only, with a supplementary fax. It was an invitation—or perhaps a command. It was sufficiently impolite to warrant disobedience, but sufficiently intriguing to be tempting."

"That message wasn't sent from this apartment," she told him, bluntly.

"Then you must trace it," he replied, affably, "and discover where it did come from. It would be interesting to know, would it not, who sent it and why?"

They were interrupted by the emergence of the forensic team from the apartment. Charlotte waited patiently while they removed their sterile suits. Oscar looked curiously at all the protective gear, undoubtedly wondering why it had been necessary to use it.

"It's sealed," said the team-leader. "We set up a camera on remote control, and we stripped all the bubbled data there was. We connected his personal machines to the Net so that Hal can trawl the data."

Oscar wore a quizzical expression. Charlotte didn't want to enlighten him yet as to what had happened; she was anxious to see what his reaction would be when she showed him what was in the apartment. She led the way to the screen mounted in the wall outside the apartment door, and punched in the instruction codes.

The camera was still at the scene, but it had been left pointing tastefully away from the *corpus delicti*. The room was furnished in an unusually utilitarian manner; there was no decorative plant life integrated into the walls, nor any kind of inert decoration. There were mural screens on the blank walls, but they displayed plain shades of pastel blue. Apart from the food delivery point, the room's main feature was a particularly elaborate array of special-function telescreens. Charlotte juggled the camera while Oscar peered over her shoulder, raptly. On one of three sofas lay all that remained of the late Gabriel King. The "corpse" was no more than a skeleton, whose white bones were intricately entwined with gorgeous flowers. Charlotte zoomed in, and moved aside to let her companion look closely at the strange garlands and the reclining skeleton.

The stems and leaves of the marvelous plant were green, but the petals of each bloom were black. The waxy stigma at the centre of each bell was dark red, and had the form of a *crux ansata*. Oscar Wilde took over the controls, moving them delicately so that he could inspect the structure and texture of the flowers at the minutest level. He followed the rim of a corolla, then passed along a stem bearing huge thorns, paler in color than the flesh from which they sprouted. Each thorn was tipped with red, as if it had drawn blood. The stems wound around and around the long bones of the corpse, holding the skeleton together even though every vestige of flesh had been consumed. The plant had supportive structures like holdfasts, which maintained the shape of the whole organism and the coherence of the skeleton. The skull was very strikingly embellished, with a single stem emerging from each of the empty eye-sockets.

"Can you be certain that it's Gabriel?" asked Oscar, finally.

"Pretty certain," Charlotte said. "In the absence of retinas the analysts checked the skull-shape and the dental profile. A DNA scan on the bone marrow will confirm it. It seems that the flowers are composed of what used to be his flesh. You might say that their seeds devoured him as they grew."

"Fascinating," he said, in a tone which had more admiration in it than horror.

"Fascinating!" she echoed, in exasperation. "Can you imagine what an organism like that might do if it ever got loose? We're looking at something that could wipe out the entire human race."

"I think not," said Oscar, calmly. "These are single-sexed flowers from a dioecious species, incapable of producing fertile seed. How long ago did Gabriel die?"

"Between two and three days," she told him, grimly. "He seems to have felt the first symptoms about seventy hours ago; he was incapacitated soon afterwards, and died a few hours later."

Oscar licked his lips, as if savoring his own astonishment. "Those delightful flowers must have a voracious appetite," he said.

Charlotte eyed him carefully, wondering exactly what his reaction might signify. "You're something of a flower-designer yourself, I believe." Her gaze flickered momentarily to the green carnation in his lapel. "Could you make plants like those?"

Oscar met her eyes frankly. She was as tall as he, and their stares were perfectly level. He frowned as he considered the matter, then said: "Until I saw this marvel I would have opined that no man could. Clearly, I have underrated one of my peers." He seemed genuinely perplexed, although the level of his concern for the victim and for the fact that a crime had been committed left something to be desired.

Charlotte stared hard at the beautiful man, wondering whether anyone in the world were capable of committing an act like this and then turning up in person to confront and mock the officers investigating the crime. She decided that if he could be guilty of the first madness, the second might not be too hard to believe. "I can't help feeling that your appearance here is a very strange coincidence, Mr. Wilde," she said.

"It is indeed," said Oscar, blithely. "Given that it seems to be impossible that I was summoned by the victim, I can only conclude that I was summoned by the murderer."

"I find that hard to believe."

"It *is* hard to believe. But when we have eliminated the impossible, are we not committed to believing the improbable? Unless, of course, you think that I did this to poor Gabriel, and have come to gloat over his fate? I disliked the man, but I did not dislike him as much as that—and if I had decided to murder him, I certainly would not have revisited the scene of my crime in this reckless fashion. A showman I might be, a madman never." He turned back to the screen, and looked again at the deadly flowers, which were still displayed there in intimate close-up.

Charlotte did not want to be put off. "As it happens," she said, "we would have shown all this material to you anyway. We need an expert report on the nature and potential of the organism and I was given three possible names. I couldn't get through to Walter Czastka. I was trying to call you at your hotel while you were on the way over here."

"I'm offended by the fact that you tried Walter first," Oscar murmured, "but I forgive you."

"Mr. Wilde...," she began, feeling that her patience was being tested too far.

"Yes, of course," he said, "This is a serious matter—a murder investigation. I think I can hazard a guess as to why the summons was sent. I suspect that I was brought here to identify the murderer."

"How?" she demanded.

"By his style," he replied.

"That's ridiculous," she said, petulantly. "If the murderer had wanted to identify himself, all he had to do was call us. How would he know that you could recognize his work—and why, if he knew it, would he want you to do it?"

"Those are interesting questions," admitted Oscar. "Nevertheless, I can only suppose that I was sent an invitation to this mysterious event in order that I might play a part in its unraveling." He paused, and looked at her reproachfully, radiating injured innocence. "You really do suspect that I'm responsible for this, don't you?" he said.

"If not you," she countered, "then who?"

He opened his arms wide in a gesture of exaggerated helplessness. "I cannot claim to be absolutely certain," he said, "but if appearances and my expert judgment are to be trusted, these flowers are the work of the man who has always been known to me as Rappaccini!"

CHAPTER TWO

Charlotte called Hal Watson. "Oscar Wilde's here," she said, making an effort to be business-like. "Can you trace the call that was made to his hotel room asking him to come? He says the flowers might have been made by a man named Rappaccini."

"Of course," Oscar added, with annoying casualness. "Rappaccini is not his real name. Some long-standing members of the Institute of Genetic Art still prefer to exhibit their work pseudonymously—a hangover from the days of prejudice."

"Are you one of them?" she asked.

Oscar shook his head. "I am fortunate enough to have a real name that sounds like a pseudonym—my identity thus becomes a kind of double bluff."

"Perhaps," she said, "your identification of Rappaccini as the man who made the flowers is also a double bluff."

Oscar shook his head. "I fear that I have an ironclad alibi. Three days ago I was in hospital, and the flesh of my outer tissues was unbecomingly fluid. I had been there for some time."

"That doesn't prove anything," Charlotte pointed out. "You might have made the seeds months ago, and made sure that they were delivered—or began to take effect—while you were in hospital."

"I suppose I might have," said Oscar, wearily, "but I assure you that your investigation will proceed more smoothly if you forget about me and concentrate on Rappaccini."

"Why should a man take the trouble to summon someone capable of identifying him to the scene of the crime?" she asked, with a trace of asperity. "Why didn't he simply leave his calling card?"

"Why didn't he simply shoot Gabriel King with a revolver?" countered the geneticist. "Why go to the effort of designing and making this fabulous plant? There is something very strange going on here, my dear Charlotte."

There certainly is, she thought, staring at him, as if by effort she could penetrate the lovely mask to see the secret self within. Oscar, seemingly unalarmed by her scrutiny, began to play with the keys that controlled the camera in the apartment. He zoomed in on something that lay on the glass-topped table. It was a small cardboard rectangle. It had been lacquered over as a safety-measure, but it was still possible to read what was written on it. The words were in French, but Oscar effortlessly read out what Charlotte took to be a translation.

"'Stupidity, error, sin and poverty of spirit,'" he said, "'possess our hearts and work within our bodies, and we nourish our fond remorse as beggars suckle their parasites.' Perhaps the murderer did leave his calling card, Inspector Holmes. A man like Gabriel King would hardly make a note of such lines as those."

"Do you recognize them?" asked Charlotte.

"A poem by Baudelaire. *Au lecteur*—that is, 'To the Reader'. From *Les Fleurs du Mal*. A play on words, I think."

Charlotte's audio-link to Hal Watson was still open. "Did you catch that, Hal?" she asked.

"I checked the words already," Hal replied. "He's right."

Charlotte wondered how many men there were in the world who could recognize seven-hundred-year-old poems written in French. Surely, she thought, Oscar Wilde must be the person behind all this. But if so, what monstrous game was he playing?

"What significance do you attach to the card?" she asked him, sharply.

"If my earlier reasoning was correct, it must be a message directed to me," replied Oscar. "All this is communication—not merely the card, and the message that summoned me, but the flowers, and the crime itself. The whole affair is to be read, and hence understood. I am here because Rappaccini expects me to be able to interpret and comprehend what he is doing."

Charlotte tried to remain impassive, but she knew that her amazement was showing. She was grateful when the phone in her hand crackled.

"I'm blocked on Rappaccini for the moment," said Hal. "His real name is recorded as Jafri Biasiolo, but there's hardly any official data on Biasiolo at all beyond his birth date, way back in 2420. It's all old data, of course, and may be just a sketchy construction of disinformation."

Old data tended to be incomplete, often corrupted by all kinds of errors—although she noticed that Hal had said "disinformation", which meant lies, rather than "misinformation". In Hal's view, old data was senile data, too decrepit to be of much use in a slick modern police inquiry. But Gabriel King had been nearly a hundred and fifty years old, and Oscar Wilde—in spite of appearances—must be well over a hundred. If Rappaccini really had been born in 2420, the motive for this affair might go all the way back to the final years of the Aftermath. The Net had been full of holes in those days.

"What about the call that summoned Wilde here?" she asked.

"Placed three days ago from a blind unit, time-triggered to arrive when it did. I've got nowhere with the woman yet. No picture-match, no route to or from the apartment-house. This is going to take longer than I hoped."

Charlotte digested this information. She was not unduly surprised by the news that the real person behind "Rappaccini" might be difficult to identify. It was easy enough nowadays to establish electronic identities whose telescreen appearances could be maintained and controlled by AI simulacra. Virtual individuals could play so full a role in modern society that their real puppet-masters could easily remain hidden—until they came under the scrutiny of a highly skilled investigator. Hal could get through any conventional information-wall, and work his way through any data-maze, but it would take time. She had a gut feeling telling her that the creator of "Rappaccini" was right in front of her, taunting her with his presence, but she didn't dare say so to Hal. He was no respecter of gut feelings.

"Can you patch the security tape through to the wallscreen here?" she said. "I'd like Mr. Wilde to see it. He seems to know everything else—perhaps he can tell us who the woman is."

"Ah," said Oscar, softly. "*Cherchez la femme*! Without a woman, the crime could not be deemed complete."

"Hal Watson's a top cracksman," Charlotte told him, trying to shake his casual composure. "He can get into all the little electronic backwaters, all the locked-up mines of information. It's impossible to hide anything from him. It's only a matter of time before we get to the bottom of this."

Wilde did not seem in the least intimidated. "I'm delighted to find the two of you working in partnership," he said. "It demonstrates that even the higher echelons of the International Bureau of Investigation are home to a sense of humor and a sense of tradition."

He was trying to be clever again, but this time she knew what he meant. Everyone made jokes about it.

On the biggest of the display screens on the far wall there appeared an image of the corridor outside the apartment. The tape had already been edited; no sooner had it started than a young woman came into view, reaching out to activate the door chime. Her lustrous brown hair was worn unfashionably long. She had clear blue eyes and finely-chiseled features. Even in this day and age, when cosmetic engineers could so easily remold superficial flesh, her beauty was striking. It was not merely the shape of her face, but the indefinable presence that she brought to it. Charlotte could not quite make up her mind whether she was authentically young, or whether she was a successful product of rejuvenative engineering, whose perfection of manner arose from long and careful practice. The woman stepped forward as the door opened, and passed beneath the eye.

The viewpoint abruptly shifted to the second security camera in the hall. King was visible now, with his back to the camera, and Charlotte watched carefully as the girl moved forward, her eyes gazing into his, and raised her head slightly so that he could kiss her on the lips. King did not seem surprised, and he responded to the unspoken invitation. The kiss did not seem particularly passionate; it might, Charlotte thought, have been a polite greeting between people who had some history of intimacy, but were meeting now as friends, or it might have been a friendly kiss exchanged in hopeful anticipation of future intimacy. There was no sound-track on the tape, but few words were spoken before King stood aside to let his visitor precede him into the sitting room. The tape cut again, and they saw the woman re-emerge from the doorway. She was alone, and seemed quite composed as she walked to the main door of the apartment, opened it, and went out.

"She was inside for about half an hour," said Charlotte, dryly. "King was still perfectly healthy when she left, and it wasn't until some twelve or thirteen hours later that he called up a diagnostic program. He never had a chance to hit his panic button—the progress of the plant was too swift. We'll know more when we've decanted his bubblebugs, but we won't know what went on in the bedroom. The girl might have nothing at all to do with it, but she was the last person to see him alive. We don't know how she fed him the seeds, if indeed she did feed them to him. Do you recognize her?"

"I'm afraid not," said Oscar. "I can only offer the obvious suggestion."

"Which is?"

"Rappaccini's daughter."

Charlotte said nothing, but simply waited for clarification.

"It's another echo of the nineteenth century," said Oscar, with a slight sigh. "Rappaccini borrowed his pseudonym from a story by Nathaniel Hawthorne entitled 'Rappaccini's Daughter'. You don't know the period, I take it?"

"Not very well," she said, awkwardly. "'Hardly at all' would have been nearer the truth."

"Then it's as well that I'm here. Otherwise, this exotic performance would be entirely wasted."

"You think that the man you know as Rappaccini is acting the part of his namesake—just as you make a show of acting the part of yours?"

Oscar shrugged. "In the story, Rappaccini committed no murder—but he did cultivate fatal flowers: *fleurs du mal*. Our Rappaccini has signed his work, for those who have the wit to read the signature. I have a strong suspicion that we have probably seen the murder committed, by means of the gentle kiss that our mysterious visitor delivered. She, of course, would have to be immune to them."

"This is too much," Charlotte complained.

"I quite agree. As lushly extravagant as a poem in prose by Baudelaire himself. But we have been instructed to expect a Baudelairean dimension. I can hardly wait for the next installment of the story."

"You think this is going to happen again?"

"I'm almost sure of it," said the beautiful but infuriating man, calmly. "If Rappaccini intends to present us with a real psychodrama, he will hardly stop when he has only just begun. The next murder, by the way, might well be committed in San Francisco."

"Why San Francisco?"

"Because the item that was faxed through to me when I was summoned here was a reservation for the midnight maglev to San Francisco." So saying, he took a sheet of paper from his pocket, and held it out for her inspection. She took it from him, and stared at it dumbly.

"Why didn't you show me this immediately?" she said.

"My mind was occupied with other things. Anyhow, your colleague Dr. Watson must have obtained a copy of the message when he tried to trace it. Perhaps he has already begun to investigate. I do hope that you won't try to prevent my using the ticket—and that you will allow me to assist you throughout the investigation."

"Why should I?" she replied. She was uncomfortably aware of the fact that she could not prevent his going anywhere in the world he pleased.

"Because the person who committed this murder has gone to extraordinary lengths to make me a party to the investigation. If I am supposed to go to San Francisco, there must be a reason. This is only the beginning, dear Charlotte, and if you wish to get to the end with all possible speed, you must stay with me. You can, of course, count on my complete co-operation and my absolute discretion."

And you, Charlotte said, silently, while she stared into his lovely eyes, *can count on being instantly arrested, the moment Hal digs up anything that proves your involvement in this unholy mess.*

CHAPTER THREE

IBI headquarters in New York were in the "new" UN complex built in 2431. There had once been talk of the UN taking over the whole of Manhattan Island, but that had gone the way of most dream-schemes during the troubled years of the Aftermath. Now, an even more grandiose plan to move the core of the UN bureaucracy to Antarctica was well-advanced. The same sentence of death had been passed on the IBI complex that had been passed on the whole of New York City, but Gabriel King's brand of controlled rot had not yet been allowed to set in.

"How well did you know Gabriel King?" Charlotte asked Oscar, while they were en route in the police car. He had suggested that he come with her until the time appointed for his departure, and she had been quick to agree although she knew that Hal would not approve.

"I supply his company with decorative materials for various building projects. I haven't met him for more than twenty years. He and I are by no means kindred spirits."

"And how well do you know Rappaccini?"

"I know the work far better than the man, but there was a period before and after the Great Exhibition when we met regularly. We were often bracketed together by critics who observed a kinship in our ideas, methods and personalities, but I was never convinced of the similarity. Our conversations were never intimate; we discussed art and genetics, never ourselves. It was a long time ago."

She would have pursued the line of questioning further, but the distance between the Trebizond Tower and the UN complex was short, and they arrived before she had a chance to do any serious probing. She asked Oscar to wait in her office while she consulted her colleague in private. "I brought Wilde with me," she told Hal, brusquely.

Even in the dim light, she was easily able to see the expression of distaste that flitted across Hal's face, but all he said was: "Why?"

"Because he knows too much about this business," she said, wishing that it didn't sound so feeble, so intuitive. "I know it sounds crazy, but I think he set this whole thing up, and then turned up in person to watch us wrestle with it."

"So you think his introduction of Rappaccini's name is just a red herring?"

"Yes I do. It's all far too convenient. Is it possible that Rappaccini is entirely his invention?"

"I'll check it out," Hal said. "But we don't need him here."

"He wants to go to San Francisco on the midnight maglev."

"Let him. What difference does it make? We can find him, if need be, in San Francisco or on the moon."

"Suppose he were to murder someone else," said Charlotte, desperately. It was pointless. Modern detective work was sifting data, carefully sorting the relevant from the irrelevant, and the real information from misinformation and disinformation. Talking to people, being a real-time activity, was generally considered to be an inordinately wasteful use of IBI time, to be kept to an absolute minimum even by lowly scene-of-crime officers. "Can I bring him down here?" Charlotte asked, defensively. "I'd like you to see for yourself what he's like—then perhaps you'll understand what I mean."

Hal shrugged in world-weary fashion.

Charlotte collected Oscar from her office, and brought him down into Hal's Underworld. The room was crowded with screens and comcons, but there were enough workstations for them to sit reasonably comfortably.

"Oscar Wilde—Hal Watson," she said, with awkward formality. "Mr. Wilde thinks that his unique insight may be of some help in the investigation."

"I hope so," said Oscar, smoothly. "There are times when instant recognition and artistic sensitivity facilitate more rapid deduction than the most powerful analytical engines. I am an invader in your realm, of course—and I confess that I feel like one of those mortals of old who fell sleep on a burial mound and woke to find himself in the gloomy land of the fairy folk—but I really do feel that I can help you. I have some hours in hand before the midnight mag-lev leaves."

"I'm always grateful for any help I can get," said Hal, not bothering to feign sincerity. Charlotte saw that her colleague was unimpressed by Oscar Wilde's recently-renewed handsomeness. Hal, whose machine-assisted perceptions ground up all the richness and complexity of the social world into mere atoms of data, had not the same idea of beauty as common men. The cataract of encoded data pouring through his screens was his reality, and for him beauty was to be found in patterns woven out of information or enigmas smoothed into comprehension, not in the hard and soft sculptures of stone and flesh. Unfortunately, the unshadowy world of hard and superabundant data had yet to be persuaded to explain how it had produced the eccentric masterpiece of mere appearances that was the murder of Gabriel King.

"Rappaccini is proving evasive," Hal told Charlotte, while his eyes continued to scan his screens. "His business dealings are fairly elaborate, but he holds a flag-of-convenience citizenship in the Kalahari Republic and has no recorded residency. His telephonic addresses are black boxes and he conducts all his affairs through the medium of AIs. The Rappaccini name first became manifest in 2480, when he registered with the Institute of the Genetic Arts in Sydney. He participated in a number of public exhibitions, including the Great Exhibition of 2505, sometimes putting in personal appearances. Unlike other genetic engineers specializing in flowering plants, he never got involved in designing gardens or in the kind of interior decoration that provides you with a living. He seems to have specialized in the design of funeral wreaths."

"Funeral wreaths?" echoed Charlotte, incredulously. The manufacture of funeral wreaths seemed an absurd profession for anyone to follow, even in the guise of a part-time persona. Now that serial rejuvenation supposedly guaranteed everyone an extended lifespan, funerals were not the everyday occurrences they once had been. On the other hand, their very rarity meant that the ceremony devoted to the commemoration of revered public figures was usually very lavish.

"Rappaccini's flowers have always been grown under contract by middlemen in various parts of Australia," Hal went on, while his fingers roamed in desultory fashion over his keyboards. "I'm checking the routes by which seeds used to be delivered, trying to backtrack them to the laboratories of origin, but he hasn't put out anything new in thirty years. His agents are still making up wreaths and crediting him with royalties, but they've had no personal contact since 2520. He still has a considerable credit balance, and he probably has more in accounts I haven't identified yet. His last manifestation as an active electronic persona was in 2527. Incoming telephone calls have been handled since then by a simulacrum which doesn't seem to have referred enquiries elsewhere. Our best hope of discovering the real person behind the network of sims is a thorough interrogation of the financial records. The real person has to have some means of recovering or redirecting credit accumulated by the dummy. I also have AIs trawling out the data relating to every recorded public appearance Rappaccini has ever made. We'll pin him down, even if it takes a week. I have all the data in the world to work with—I just need time to find, extract and combine the relevant items. If your artistic intuition throws up any other helpful suggestions, Mr. Wilde, just let me know, and I'll let loose another pack of data-hounds."

"Mr. Wilde hasn't been able to guess why Rappaccini should want to murder Gabriel King," said Charlotte. "Do we have anything on a possible motive?"

"I'm investigating King's background," said Hal. "If there's a motive there, I'll find it. For the time being, I'm more interested in the method. We know that the murderer has to be a first-class genetic engineer, so I've got AIs looking at the people who have the necessary expertise, trying to eliminate them one by one. It's not easy, of course—there are too many commercial engineers whose work involves the relevant technical skills. Even a structural engineer like Gabriel King might be able to adapt what he knew."

"I don't think so," Oscar said, dubiously.

"Maybe not," said Hal. "Naturally, we'll start with the people whose expertise is most relevant. Walter Czastka—and yourself, of course, Dr. Wilde.

"My life," said Oscar, airily, "is an open book. I fear that the sheer profusion of data will test the stamina of your programs—but that might make it all the easier for them to eliminate me from consideration. The idea that Walter Czastka might be Rappaccini is too absurd to contemplate."

"Why?" asked Charlotte.

"A matter of style," said Oscar. "Walter never had any."

"According to the database, he's the top man in the field—or was."

"I presume you mean that he has made more money than anyone else out of engineered flowers. Walter is a mass-producer, not an artist. I fear that if Rappaccini is leading a double life, you will not find his secret identity among the ranks of flower-designers. You'll have to cast your net further afield. He might be an animal engineer, perhaps a human engineer...but there are thousands of experts in the each category."

"My AIs are indefatigable," Hal assured him. He was interrupted by a quiet beep from one of his comcons. His fingers raced back and forth across the relevant keyboard for a few seconds while he stared thoughtfully at a screen half-hidden from Charlotte's view. After half a minute or so, he said: "You might be interested to see this, Dr. Wilde." He pointed to the biggest of his display screens, mounted high on the wall directly in front of them.

A picture appeared on the left of the screen. It showed a tall man with silver hair, a dark beard trimmed into a goatee, and a prominent nose. "Rappaccini in 2481," Hal said. "Taken at the offices of his growers during an early meeting." He pressed more keys, and another image appeared in the centre of the screen, showing two men side by side. One of them was clearly the same man whose image already on the screen.

"Isn't that...?" Charlotte began.

"I fear that it is," said Oscar, regretfully. "I looked a lot older then, of course. Taken in 2505, I believe, at the Sydney Exhibition."

It proves nothing that they've been photographed together, Charlotte thought. *That might only be an actor, hired to lend flesh to the illusion.* Somehow, though, she couldn't quite believe it.

"It was 2505," agreed Hal. A third picture appeared, again showing Rappaccini alone. "2520," Hal said. "His last public appearance."

Charlotte compared the three pictures. There was hardly any difference between them. The man had not undergone a full rejuvenation between 2481 and 2520, although he had probably employed light cosmetic reconstruction to maintain the appearance of dignified middle age.

"If he really was born in 2420, he seems to have delayed rejuvenation far longer than usual," said Hal, pensively. "He must have had a full rejuve very soon after the last picture was taken—I'll get a program to trawl the records. A picture-search program might be able to connect up the face, but that kind of data's very messy. It's proving difficult to track the woman who visited Gabriel King's apartment—there are plenty of cameras on the streets, but a bit of everyday make-up and a wig can cause a good deal of confusion. Faces aren't as widely different as they used to be, now that so many people use light cosmetic engineering to follow fashion-trends. We'll trace her eventually, but...again, it's a matter of time."

As he spoke, three signals began bleeping and blinking within the space of a second's hesitation, and his attention was instantly diverted. Charlotte and Oscar left the computer-man to the company of his assiduous AIs.

"It's good to know," observed Oscar, as the elevator carried them up, "that there are so many patient recording angels sorting religiously through the multitudinous sins of mankind. Alas, I fear that the capacity of our fellow men for committing sins may still outstrip their best endeavors."

"On the contrary," Charlotte retorted. "The crime rate keeps going down and down as the number of spy-eyes and bubblebugs scattered around the world goes up and up."

"I spoke of sins, not crimes," said Oscar. "What your electronic eyes do not see the law may not grieve about, but the capacity for sin will lurk in the hearts of men long after its expression has been banished from their actions."

"People can do what they like in the privacy of their virtual realities," she said. "There's no sin in that."

"If there were no sin in our adventures in imagination," Oscar replied, evidently determined to have the last word, "there would be no enjoyment in them. It is mainly our sense of sin that sustains our appetite for virtual experience. No matter how perfect an image we present to the world, in our appearances and our actions, we are as vicious at heart as we have ever been. If you cannot understand that, my dear, I fear that you will never be a real detective."

CHAPTER FOUR

While he still had time to spare, Charlotte took Oscar to dinner in the IBI's restaurant, where he decided that his appetite demanded was Tournedos Béarnaise and a bottle of St. Émilion. IBI food technology was easily adequate to the task of meeting these requirements. Its beef was grown from a celebrated local tissue-culture which had long rejoiced in the pet name of Baltimore Bess: a veritable mountain of muscle, "rejuvenated" a hundred times or more by means of the techniques whose gradual perfection in the last two centuries had paved the way for the rejuvenation of human beings. The St. Émilion was authentic, although the whole region extending between Bordeaux and Burgundy had been replanted as recently as 2430, when connoisseurs had decided that the native root-stocks had suffered too much deterioration due to environmental degradations of the Third Biotech War.

"This crime," said Charlotte, as soon as she felt the time was ripe for talk of business, "is the work of a very remarkable mind."

"Very," Oscar agreed. "I have, of course, a very remarkable mind myself, but genius is always unique. I wear my genius openly, and can barely understand the temperament that would hide away an entire life behind a series of electronic masks, but the man who has invented Rappaccini is clearly a dissimulator. I suspect that this crime has been planned for a very long time. The fictitious Rappaccini might have been invented with this murder in mind, and every detail of him tailored to its requirements. Absurd as it may seem, I cannot help by wonder whether my involvement as a witness was planned along with the crime."

Charlotte studied his face soberly. She wondered whether he had designed his own features. It was rare to see such flamboyant femininity in the lines of a male's face, but she had to admit that it suited him.

"What was your impression of the man who posed as Rappaccini?" she asked

"I liked him. He had an admirable hauteur—as if he considered himself a more profound person by far than the other exhibitors at the Great Exhibition. He was a man of civilized taste and conversation. He appeared to like me, and we shared a taste for all things antiquarian—particularly relics of the nineteenth century, to which we were both linked by our names."

"Do you remember anything useful?" asked Charlotte, with some slight impatience. "Anything which might help us to identify the man behind the name."

"I fear not. We never became friends. We were both solitary workers, deeply interested in the purely aesthetic aspects of our work. One could not say that of all the exhibitors at Sydney, or even of the majority. Walter Czastka is more typical—he has always worked with an army of apprentices, far more interested in industry than art."

"You don't seem to like Walter Czastka," she observed.

Oscar hesitated briefly before replying. "I don't dislike Walter," he said, "although I find him rather dull. He's an able man, in his way, but a hack. Whereas I aspire to perfection in my work, he aims to be prolific. He certainly has Creationist ambitions—he has taken out a lease on a small island in the Pacific, just as I have—but I can't imagine what on earth he is doing with it."

"Walter Czastka knew Gabriel King very well," Charlotte observed, having scanned several pages of data copied to her by Hal Watson while they ate. "They were both born in 2401, and they attended the same university. Czastka has done a great deal of work for King's companies—far more than you. Most murders, you know, involve people who know one another well."

"Walter does not have sufficient imagination to have committed this crime," said Oscar, firmly, "even if he had a motive. I doubt that he did; he and Gabriel are—or were—cats of a similar stripe."

"What do you mean by that?"

"I mean that they were both hacks. A modern architect, working with thousands of subspecies of gantzing bacteria, can raise buildings out of almost any materials, shaped to almost any design. The integration of pseudo-living systems to provide water and other amenities adds a further dimension of creative opportunity. A true artist could make buildings that would stand forever as monuments to contemporary creativity, but Gabriel King's main interest was always in productivity—razing whole towns to the ground and re-erecting them with the least possible effort. His business was the mass-production of third-rate homes for second-rate people."

"I thought the whole point of bacterial cementation processes is that they facilitate the provision of decent homes for the very poor," said Charlotte.

"That is the utilitarian view," agreed Oscar. "But it is two hundred years out of date. Future generations will look back at ours with pity for the recklessness with which we have wasted our aesthetic opportunities. One day, the building of a home will be part of a person's cultivation of his own personality. Making a home will be one of the things every man is expected to do for himself, and there will be no more Gabriel King houses with Walter Czastka subsystems."

"We can't all be Creationists," objected Charlotte.

"Oh, but we can," retorted Oscar. "We can all be everything we want to be, or we should at least make every effort to do so. Even men like me, who were born when rejuvenation technology was still in its infancy, should do their utmost to believe that the specter of death is impotent to set a limit upon our achievements. The children of tomorrow will surely live for centuries, if only they have the will to do so. You and I, Charlotte, must be prepared to set them a good example. The men of the past had an excuse for all their failures—that man born of woman had but a short time to live, and full of misery—but only cowardice inhibits us now. There is no excuse for any man who fails to be a true artist, and declines to take full responsibility for both his mind and his environment. Too many of us still aim for mediocrity, and are content with its achievement. You don't intend to be a policewoman all your life, I hope?"

Charlotte was slightly discomfited by this question. "I'm continuing my education," she said. "My options are still open." Her waistphone began to buzz. She plucked it from its holster and accepted the call. She held it close to her ear so that Oscar would not be able to eavesdrop, assuming that Hal had ferreted out some further morsel of information about Rappaccini. What he actually had to say was rather more disturbing. When she had replaced the phone she looked at her companion, trying to control the bleakness of her expression

"Do you know a man named Michi Urashima?" she asked, as blandly as she could.

"Of course I do," said Oscar. "I hope you aren't going to tell me that he's dead. He was a better man by far than Gabriel King."

"Not everyone would agree with you," she said, shortly. Urashima was an expert in computer graphics and image-simulation, famed for the contributions to synthetic cinema he had made before becoming involved in outlawed brainfeed research—which had led to a much-publicized fall from grace.

"How was he killed?" Oscar asked, sadly. "The same method?"

"Yes," she said, tersely. "In San Francisco. There's no need for you to take the maglev now."

"On the contrary," he said. "There is every reason. This affair is still in its early stages, and if we want to witness the further stages of its unfolding we must follow the script laid down for us. You will come with me, I hope?"

"Scene-of-crime officers don't operate nationwide," she said. "Police work isn't done that way in this day and age." She knew even as she said it, though, that she still wanted—and still intended—to cling to her suspect.

"Police work may not be," he replied, with an infuriating wave of his hand, "but psychodrama is. The mystery in this, my dear Charlotte, is not who has done it, but why. I am the man appointed by the murderer himself to the task of following the thread of explanation to the heart of the maze. If you want to understand the crime as well as solving it, you must come with me."

"All right," she said, hypocritically. "You've convinced me. I'll stick with you till the bitter end."

CHAPTER FIVE

Charlotte rose earlier than was her habit; the maglev couchette was not the kind of bed that encouraged one to lie in. She called Hal to get an update on the investigation, and then wandered along to the dining car to dial up some croissants, coffee and pills. It was a pity, she thought, that there was no quicker way than the maglev to travel between New York and San Francisco. She had an uncomfortable feeling that she might end up chasing a daisy-chain of murders all around the globe, always twenty-four hours behind the breaking news. But the maglev was the fastest form of transportation within the bounds of United America since the last supersonic jet had flown four centuries before. The power crises of the Aftermath were ancient history now, but the inland airways were so cluttered with private flitterbugs and helicopters, and the green zealots so avid in their crusades against large areas of concrete, that commercial aviation had never really got going again. Even intercontinental travelers tended to prefer the plush comfort of airships to the hectic pace of supersonics. Electronic communication had so completely taken over the lifestyles and folkways of modern man that most business was conducted via concom.

By the time Charlotte had finished her breakfast, the train was only four hours out of San Francisco. Oscar joined her then, looking neat and trim although the green carnation in his buttonhole was now rather bedraggled. "Such has been the mercy of our timetable," he observed, "that we have slept through Missouri and Kansas."

She knew what he meant. Missouri and Kansas were distinctly lacking in interesting scenery since the re-stabilization of the climate had made their Great Plains prime sites for the establishment of vast tracts of artificial photosynthetics. Nowadays, the greater part of the Midwest looked rather like sections of an infinite undulating sheet of a dull, near-black violet, which offended unpracticed eyes. The SAP-fields of Kansas always gave Charlotte the impression of looking at a gigantic piece of frilly corrugated cardboard. Houses and factories alike had retreated beneath the dark canopy, and parts of the landscape were almost featureless. By now, though, the maglev passengers had the more elevating scenery of Colorado to look out upon. Most of the state had been returned to wilderness, and its centers of population had taken advantage of the versatility of modern building techniques to blend in with their surroundings. Chlorophyll green was infinitely easier on the human eye than SAP-violet, presumably because millions of years of adaptive natural selection had helped to make it so.

While Oscar ordered eggs duchesse for breakfast, Charlotte activated the wallscreen beside their table and called up the latest news. The fact of Gabriel King's death was recorded, but there was nothing as yet about the exotic circumstances. The IBI never liked to advertise crimes until they were solved, but the exotic circumstances of King's death would make it a hot topic of gossip, and she knew that it was only a matter of time before bootleg copies of the security tapes leaked out.

"My dear Charlotte," said Oscar, "you have the unmistakable look of one who woke too early and has been working too hard."

"I couldn't sleep," she told him. "I took a couple of boosters with breakfast. They'll clear my head soon enough."

Oscar shook his head. "No one who looks twenty when he is really a hundred and thirty-three can possibly be less than worshipful of the wonders of medical science, " he said, "but in my experience, the use of drugs to maintain one's sense of equilibrium is a false economy. We must have sleep in order to dream, and we must dream in order to discharge the chaos from our thoughts, so that we may reason effectively while we are awake. Now, what about the second murder? Any progress?"

She frowned. She was supposed to be the one asking the questions. "Did you know Urashima personally, or just by reputation?" she countered, determined not to let him get the upper hand.

"We met on several occasions," said Oscar, equably. "He was an artist, like myself. I respected his work. Although I didn't know him well, I would have been glad to count him a friend."

"He'd been inactive of late," she said, watching her suspect closely. "He hadn't worked commercially since his conviction for illegal experimentation thirteen years ago. He served four years' house arrest and control of communication. He was probably still experimenting, though, and he may well have been engaged in illegal activities."

"His imprisonment was an absurd sentence for an absurd crime," Oscar opined. "He placed no one in danger but himself."

"He was playing about with brainfeed equipment," she said. "Not just memory boxes or neural stimulators, but mental cyborgization. And he didn't just endanger himself; he was pooling information with others."

"Of course he was," said Oscar. "What on earth is the point of hazardous exploration unless one makes every effort to pass on the legacy of one's discoveries?"

"Have you ever experimented with that sort of stuff?" Charlotte asked, vaguely. Like everyone else, she bandied about phrases like "psychedelic synthesizer" and "memory box", but she had little or no idea of the way such legendary devices were supposed to work. Ever since the first development of artificial synapses capable of linking up human nervous systems to silicon-based electronic systems, numerous schemes for hooking up the brain to computers had been devised, but almost all the experiments had gone disastrously wrong, often ending up with badly brain-damaged subjects. The brain was the most complex and sensitive of all organs, and disruption of brain-function was the one kind of disorder that twenty-sixth century medical science was impotent to correct. The UN had forced a worldwide ban on devices for connecting brains directly to electronic apparatus, for whatever purpose, but the main effect of the ban had been to drive research underground. Even an expert fisherman like Hal Watson would not have found it easy to figure out what sort of work might be going on, where, and why.

"You've just heard me express my dislike of everyday chemical boosters," Oscar pointed out. "There is nothing I value more than my genius, and I would never knowingly risk my clarity and agility of mind. That does not mean that I disapprove of what Michi Urashima did. He was not an infant, in need of protection from himself. His perennial fascination was the simulation of experience, and for him, the building of better visual images was only a beginning. He wanted to allow his audience to live in his illusions, not merely to stand outside and watch. If we are ever to make a proper interface between natural and artificial intelligence, we will need the genius of men like Michi. Now, have you anything to tell me about his death which may help to unravel the puzzle which confronts us?"

"Perhaps," she said, grudgingly. "Did you know that Michi Urashima was at college with Gabriel King—and, for that matter, with Walter Czastka?" She permitted herself a slight smile of satisfaction when Oscar raised an interested eyebrow.

"I did not," he said. "Was Rappaccini, perhaps, also at this particular institution of learning? Has he been harboring some secret grudge for a hundred and thirty years? Where was this remarkable college, where so many of our great men first met?"

"Wollongong, in Australia."

"Wollongong!" he exclaimed, in mock horror, "If only it were Oxford, or the Sorbonne, or even Sapporo...but it is an interesting coincidence."

Charlotte regarded him speculatively. "Hal transmitted a copy of the scene-of-crime tape," she said. "Urashima's last visitor was a woman. She'd changed her appearance quite considerably, but we're pretty sure that she's the same one who visited Gabriel King."

Oscar nodded. "Rappaccini's daughter," he said. "I expected it."

"The main thrust of Hal's investigation is to identify and track the woman," Charlotte went on. "He's set up programs to monitor every security camera in San Francisco. If she's already gone, we might to be able to pick up her trail. The problem is that she left

Urashima's house more three days ago; if she moved fast, she may have delivered more packages in the interim."

"We must certainly assume that she did," Oscar agreed. "Did she leave another calling card, by any chance?"

"Not this time. But she kissed Michi Urashima, exactly as she kissed Gabriel King." She had decanted the tape on to a disc, so she only had to slot it in. Like the tape she had displayed for Oscar outside Gabriel King's apartment, it had been carefully edited from the various spy-eyes and bubblebugs that had been witnesses to Michi Urashima's murder.

The similarity between the two records was almost eerie. The woman's hair was silvery blonde now, but still abundant. It was arranged in a precipitate cataract of curls. The eyes were the same electric blue but the cast of the features had been altered subtly, making her face thinner and apparently deeper. The changes were sufficient to deceive a standard picture-search program, but, because Charlotte knew that it was the same woman, she could see that it was the same woman. There was something in the way her eyes looked steadily forward, something in her calm poise that made her seem remote, not quite in contact with the world through which she moved. She was wearing a dark blue costume now, which hung loose about her seemingly fragile frame. It was the kind of outfit that would not attract much attention in the street. As before, the woman said nothing, but moved naturally into a friendly kiss of greeting before preceding her victim into an inner room beyond the reach of conventional security cameras. Her departure was similarly recorded by the spy-eye. She seemed perfectly composed and serene.

There were more pictures to follow, showing the state of Urashima's corpse as it had eventually been discovered. There were long, lingering close-ups of the fatal flowers. The camera's eye moved into a black corolla as if it were venturing into the interior of a great greedy mouth, hovering around the *crux ansata* tip of the blood-red style like a moth fascinated by a flame. There was, of course, a sterile film covering the organism, but it was quite transparent; its presence merely served to give the black petals a weird sheen, adding to their supernatural quality.

Charlotte let the tape run through without comment, and then flipped the switch. "The flowers aren't genetically identical to the ones used to kill King. Our lab people think that the germination of the seeds may have been keyed to some trigger unique to the victim's genotype—that each species was designed to kill a specific victim, while being harmless to everyone else. That would explain how the girl can carry the seeds around. She traveled to San Francisco on a scheduled maglev. The card she used to buy the ticket connects to a credit account held in the name of Jeanne Duval. It's a dummy account, of course. She didn't use the Duval account to reach New York, and she'll presumably use another to leave San Francisco."

"You might set the search programs you're using to find her to pick up the names Daubrun and Sabatier," Oscar advised. "Jeanne Duval was Baudelaire's mistress, and it's possible that she has other intimate friends of his on her list of *noms de guerre*."

Charlotte transmitted this information to Hal. The maglev was taking them down the western side of the Sierra Nevada now, and she had to swallow air to counter the pressure on her eardrums.

"By the time we get to San Francisco," she said, "there won't be anything to do there except to wait for the next phone call."

"Perhaps not," said Oscar. "But even if she's long gone, we'll be in the right place to follow in her footsteps."

The buzzer on Charlotte's waistphone sounded, and she snatched it up.

"One of Rappaccini's bank accounts became active," Hal told her. "A debit went through ten minutes ago. The credit was drawn from another account, which had a guarantee arrangement with the Rappaccini account."

"Never mind the technical details," she said. "What did the credit buy? Have the police at the contact point managed to get the user?"

"I'm afraid not. The debit was put through by a courier service. They don't collect until they've actually made delivery. We've got a picture of the woman from their spy-eye, looking just the same as she did when she went to Urashima's apartment, but it's three days old. It must have been taken before the murder, immediately after she arrived in San Francisco."

Charlotte groaned softly. "What did she send, and where to?"

"A package she brought in. We don't know what's in it. It was addressed to Oscar Wilde, Green Carnation Suite, Majestic Hotel, San Francisco. It's there now, waiting."

"We don't have the authority to open that package without your permission," Charlotte told Oscar. "Can I send an instruction to the San Francisco police, telling them to inspect it immediately?"

"Certainly not," Oscar said, without hesitation. "It would spoil the surprise. We'll be there in less than an hour."

Charlotte frowned. "You're inhibiting the investigation," she said. "I want to know what's in that package. It could be a packet of seeds."

"I think not," said Oscar, airily. "If Rappaccini wished to murder me, he surely wouldn't treat me less generously than his other victims. If they're entitled to a fatal kiss, it would be unjust and unaesthetic to send my *fleurs du mal* by mail."

"In that case," she said, "it's probably another ticket. If we open it now, we might be able to find out where her next destination is in time to stop her making her delivery."

"I fear not," said Oscar. "The delayed debit was timed to show up after the event. The third victim is probably dead already. The package is addressed to me and I shall open it. That's what Rappaccini intended. I'm sure he has his reasons."

"Mr. Wilde," she said, in utter exasperation, "you seem to be incapable of taking this matter seriously."

"On the contrary," he replied, with a sigh. "I believe that I am the only one who is taking it seriously enough. You seem to be unable to look beyond the mere fact that people are being killed. If we are to come to terms with this strange performance, we must take all its features as seriously as they are intended to be taken. I am as deeply involved in this as the victims, although I cannot as yet understand why Rappaccini has chosen to involve me."

"You'd better make sure that nothing you do fouls up our investigation," said Charlotte, ominously, "because we won't hesitate to throw the book at you if we find a reason."

"I fear," said Oscar, sadly, "that Rappaccini has already thrown more than enough books into this affair himself."

CHAPTER SIX

The promised package lay on a table in the reception room of the Green Carnation Suite. It was round, about a hundred centimeters in diameter and twenty deep. Charlotte had taken the precaution of arming herself with a spraygun loaded with a polymer which, on discharge, formed itself into a bimolecular membrane and clung to anything it touched.

Oscar reached out to take hold of the knot in the black ribbon securing the emerald green box. It yielded easily to his nimble fingers, and he drew the ribbon away. He lifted the lid and laid it to one side. As Charlotte had half-expected since seeing the shape of the container, it contained a Rappaccini wreath: an intricate tangle of dark green stalks and leaves. The stalks were thorny, the leaves slender and curly. There was an envelope in the middle of the display, and around the perimeter were thirteen black flowers like none that she had ever seen before. They looked like black daisies.

Oscar Wilde extended an inquisitive forefinger, and was just about to touch one of the flowers when it moved.

"Look out!" said Charlotte.

As though the first movement was a kind of signal, all the "flowers" began to move. It was a most alarming effect, and Oscar reflexively snatched back his hand as Charlotte pressed the trigger of the spraygun and let fly. When the polymer hit them, the flowers' movements became suddenly jerky. They thrashed and squirmed in obvious distress. The limbs that had mimicked sepals struggled vainly for purchase upon the thorny green ring on which they had been mounted. Now that Charlotte could count them, she was able to see that each of the creatures had eight hairy legs. What had seemed to be a cluster of florets was a much-embellished thorax.

"Poor things," said Oscar, as he watched them writhe. "They'll asphyxiate, you know, with that awful stuff all over them."

"I might have just saved your life," observed Charlotte, dryly. "Those things are probably poisonous."

Oscar shook his head. "This was no attempted murder. It's a work of art—probably an exercise in symbolism."

"According to you," she said, "the two are not incompatible."

"Not even the most reckless of dramatists," said Oscar, affectedly, "would destroy his audience at the end of act one. We are perfectly safe, my dear, until the final curtain falls. Even then Rappaccini will want us alive and well. He surely will not risk interrupting a standing ovation and cutting short the cries of *encore!*"

Charlotte reached out to pick up the sticky envelope at the centre of the ruined display, and contrived to open it. She took out a piece of paper. It was a car-hire receipt, overstamped in garish red ink: ANY ATTEMPT TO INTERROGATE THE PROGRAMMING OF THIS VEHICLE WILL ACTIVATE A VIRUS THAT WILL DESTROY ALL THE DATA IN ITS MEMORY. It was probably a bluff, but she didn't suppose that Oscar Wilde would let her call it—and she still didn't have any legal reason to overturn his decisions.

As soon as she had updated Hal she got through to the car hire company and demanded all the information they had. They told her that they had delivered the car to the hotel three days earlier, and that they had no knowledge of any route or destination which might have been programmed into its systems after dispatch. Hal quickly ascertained that the account which had been used to pay for the car had enough credit to cover three days' storage and a journey of two thousand kilometers.

"That could take you as far north as Juneau or as far south as Guadalajara," Hal pointed out, unhelpfully. "I can't tell how many more accounts there might be on which Rappaccini and the woman might draw, but I've traced several that are held under other names; it's possible that one of them is his real name.

"What are they?" Oscar asked.

"Samuel Cramer, Gustave Moreau and Thomas Griffiths Wainewright."

Oscar sighed heavily. "Samuel Cramer is the protagonist of a novella by Baudelaire," he said. "Moreau was a French painter. Wainewright was the subject of a famous essay by my namesake called 'Pen, Pencil and Poison'. It's just a series of jokes, presumably intended to amuse me."

The car which awaited them was roomy and powerful. Once it was free of the city's traffic control computers, it would be able to zip along the transcontinental at two hundred KPH. If they were headed for Alaska, Charlotte thought, they'd be there some time around midnight.

As soon as they were both settled into the back seat, Oscar activated the car's program. It slid smoothly up the ramp and into the street. Then he called up a lunch menu from the car's synthesizer, and looked it over critically.

"I fear," he said, "that we are in for a somewhat Spartan trip."

Charlotte took out her handscreen and began scrolling through some pages of data that one of Hal's AIs had compiled from various dossiers. It had found many links between Gabriel King and Michi Urashima—more links than anyone could reasonably have expected. It seemed that the construction engineer and the graphic artist had remained in close touch throughout their long lives. Many of Urashima's experiments had been funded by King, and the two of them had embarked upon several ventures in partnership. Charlotte could see that the AI searches had only just begun to get down to the real dirt. No one whose career was as long as King's was likely to be completely clean, but a man in his position could keep secrets even in today's world, just as long as no one with state-of-the-art equipment actually had a reason to probe. It was only to be expected that his murder would expose a certain amount of dirty linen, but this particular collection seemed overabundant. It seemed entirely probable that Gabriel King had been a major stockholder in the clandestine brainfeed business, and that he had not only funded Urashima, but had established all kinds of shields to hide his work and its spin-off. Was there a motive for multiple murder in there? But if there was, where did Rappaccini and Oscar Wilde fit in? Why all the bizarre frills? And who was the mystery woman?

When Charlotte had digested the dossier's contents, she plugged her waistphone into the car's transmitter and phoned Hal.

"Anything new on the woman?" Charlotte inquired.

"No identification yet," said Hal. "We haven't picked up a visual trace since she left Urashima's apartment. I've loosened up the match criteria, but she must have done a first-rate job of disguising herself. Where are you?"

Charlotte realized, guiltily, that she had not even bothered to take note of the direction in which they were headed. She squinted out of the window, but there was nothing to be seen now except the eight lanes of the superhighway.

"We're headed south," said Oscar, helpfully.

"She may have gone south," Charlotte said to Hal. "Better check all plausible destinations between here and Mexico City." She signed off.

"It might be as well," Oscar said, ruminatively, "if I were to have a word with Walter Czastka."

"No you don't," Charlotte said, suddenly remembering that she should have called Czastka herself, several hours ago. "That's my job. Walter Czastka may be a suspect."

"I know Walter," said Oscar. "He was a difficult man even in his prime, and he's not in his prime now. It really would be better if I did it. You can listen in."

She weighed up the pros and cons. It might, she thought, be interesting to see what Oscar Wilde and Walter Czastka had to say to one another. "You're a free man," she said, in the end. "Go ahead." She moved to the edge of her seat, out of range of the tiny eye mounted above the car's wallscreen. She watched Oscar punch out the codes on the keyboard. He didn't need to call a directory to get the number.

She could see the image on the screen even though she was out of camera-range. She knew immediately that the face which appeared there was that of Walter Czastka himself. No one would ever have programmed so much ostentatious world-weariness into a simulacrum.

"Hello, Walter," said Oscar.

Czastka peered at the caller without the least flicker of recognition. He looked unwell. Charlotte could not imagine that he had ever been handsome, and he obviously thought it unnecessary to compromise with the expectations of others by having his face touched up by tissue-control specialists. In a world where almost everyone was beautiful, or at least distinguished, Walter Czastka was an anomaly—but there was nothing monstrous about him. His sad eyes were faded blue, and his stare had a rather disconcerting quality. Charlotte knew that Czastka was exactly the same age as Gabriel King and Michi Urashima, but he looked far worse than either of them. Perhaps rejuvenation hadn't taken properly.

"Yes?" he said.

"Don't you know me?" asked Oscar, in genuine surprise.

For a moment, Czastka simply looked exasperated, but then his stare changed as enlightenment dawned. "Oscar Wilde!" he said, his tone redolent with awe. "My God, you look.... I didn't look like that after my last rejuvenation! But that must be your third—how could you need...?"

Oddly enough, Oscar did not swell with pride in reaction to this display of naked envy. "Need," he murmured, "is a relative thing. I'm sorry, Walter; I didn't mean to startle you."

"You'll have to be brief, Oscar," said Czastka, curtly. "I'm expecting the UN police to call—they tried to get past my AI yesterday, but didn't bother to leave a message to say what they wanted. They're taking their time about getting back to me. Damn nuisance."

"The police can break in on us if they really want to," said Oscar, gently. "Have you heard the news about Gabriel King?"

"No. Is it something I should be interested in?"

"He's dead, Walter. Murdered by illegal biotechnics—a very strange kind of flowering plant."

Charlotte couldn't read Czastka's expression. "Murdered by a plant?" he repeated, disbelievingly.

"I've seen the pictures," said Oscar. "The police might want you to take a look at the forensic reports. They have a suspicion that you or I might have designed the murder-weapon, but I'm morally certain that it's Rappaccini's work. Do you remember Rappaccini?"

Charlotte began to regret having given Oscar Wilde permission to make this call. Perhaps it would have been better to ask Czastka to make a separate judgment. If both of them, without collusion, identified Rappaccini as the designer...but how could she be sure that they weren't in collusion already?

"Of course I remember Rappaccini," snapped Czastka. "I'm not senile, you know. Specializes in funeral wreaths—a silly affectation, I always thought. I dare say you know him better than I do, you and he being birds of a feather. Are you saying that he murdered Gabriel King."

"Michi Urashima is dead too," Oscar said. "He and Gabriel were killed by seeds that grew inside them and consumed their flesh. This is important, Walter. Genetic art may have come a long way since the protests at the Great Exhibition, but the green zealots wouldn't need much encouragement to put us back on their hate list. Neither of us wants to go back to the days when we had petty officials looking over our shoulders while we worked. When the police release the full details of this case there's going to be a lot of adverse publicity. I'm trying to help the police find Rappaccini. I wondered whether you might remember anything that might provide a clue to his real identity."

Czastka's face had a curious ocherous pallor as he stared at his interlocutor. "King and Urashima—both dead?" He didn't seem to be keeping up with Oscar's train of thought.

"Both dead," Oscar confirmed. "I think there might be others. You knew Gabriel and Michi from way back, didn't you?"

"So what?" said Czastka, grimly. "I didn't know Urashima as well as you did, and all my dealings with King were strictly business. We were never friends—or enemies." Charlotte noted that Czastka's eyes had narrowed, but she couldn't tell whether he was alarmed, suspicious, or merely impatient.

"No one's accusing you of anything," said Oscar, carefully. "I've told the police that you couldn't possibly be the man behind Rappaccini—and I think they're more inclined at present to suspect that I might be. We all need to find out who he really is. Can you help?"

"No," said Czastka, without hesitation. "I never knew him. I've had some dealings with his company, but I haven't set eyes on him since the Great Exhibition."

"What about his daughter?" said Oscar, abruptly.

If he intended to surprise the other man, it didn't work. Czastka's stare was as stony as it was melancholy. "What daughter?" he said. "I never met a daughter—not that I remember. It was all a long time ago. I can't remember anything at all. It's nothing to do with me. Leave me alone, Oscar—and tell the police to leave me alone."

Charlotte could see that Oscar Wilde was both puzzled and disappointed by the other man's reaction. As Czastka closed the connection Oscar's face wrinkled into a frown.

"That wasn't much help, was it?" she said, unable to resist the temptation to take him down a peg. "He doesn't even like you."

"As soon as I told him about the murders he froze," Oscar said, thoughtfully. "He's hiding something, but I can't imagine what—or why. I would never have thought it of him. There's something very strange about this. Perhaps your clever associate and his indefatigable assistants should start attacking the problem from the other end."

"What's that supposed to mean?" she demanded.

"The Wollongong connection. We ought to find out how many other people there are in the world who were at Wollongong at the relevant time. Walter and the two victims are uncommonly old men, even in a world where serial rejuvenation is commonplace. It's possible that such a list might contain the name of other potential victims—and the university records might offer a clue as to a possible motive."

Charlotte called Hal to relay the suggestion, but he scornfully informed her that he had already put two AIs to work on it. "One more thing," he added. "Rappaccini's pseudonymous bank accounts have been used over the years to purchase materials that were delivered for collection to the island of Kauai, in Hawaii. They were collected by boat. There are fifty or sixty islets west and south of Kauai, natural and artificial. Some are leased to Creationists for experiments in the construction of artificial ecosystems." Charlotte had already turned to look at Oscar, and was on the point of forming a predatory grin when Hal continued: "Oscar Wilde's island is half an ocean away in Micronesia—but Walter Czastka's is nearby. All the supplies that Czastka purchases in his own name are picked up from Kauai, by boat."

CHAPTER SEVEN

Charlotte winced as the car lurched slightly, throwing her sideways. They had left the superhighway and were climbing into the hills along roads which did not seem to have been properly maintained. This had been a densely populated region in the distant past, but California had suffered several plague attacks in the Second Biotech War, and rural areas like this one had been so badly hit as to cause a mass exodus of refugees. Most of those who had survived had never returned, preferring to relocate to more promising land. Three-quarters of the ghost towns of the Sierra Madre were ghost towns still, even after three hundred years. The car had not been designed for climbing mountains and it had slowed considerably when it first began to follow the winding road up into the foothills of the mountain range, but now it was picking up speed again. Charlotte called up a map of the region on to the car's wallscreen, but it was stubbornly unhelpful in the matter of providing clues as to where they might be going or why.

"The region up ahead is real wasteland," she told Oscar. "Nobody lives there. Nothing grows except lichens and the odd stalk of grass. The names on the map are just distant memories."

"Something must be up there," Oscar said, shifting uncomfortably as the car took another corner. "Rappaccini wouldn't bring us up here if there were nothing to see."

Charlotte wiped the map from the screen, and replaced it with a list which Hal had beamed through to her. There were twenty-seven names on it: the names of all the surviving men and women who had attended the University of Wollongong while Gabriel King, Michi Urashima and Walter Czastka had been students there. The names, that is, of all the supposed survivors; Hal's patient AIs had so far only managed to obtain positive confirmation of the continued existence of twenty-three. The business of trying to contact them all was proving uncommonly difficult; they all had high-grade sims to answer their phones and most of the sims had been programmed for maximum unhelpfulness. IBI priority codes were empowered to demand maximum co-operation from every AI in the world, but no AI could do more than its programming permitted.

"These people are crazy!" she complained.

"They're all old," Oscar pointed out. "Every single one of them is a double rejuvenate. They were born during the Aftermath, when the climate was still disturbed, the detritus of the plague wars hadn't yet finished claiming casualties, the Net was still highly vulnerable to software sabotage, and cool fusion and artificial photosynthesis were brand new. All of them were conceived by living mothers, and I doubt if one in five was carried to term in an artificial womb. They're strangers in today's world and many of them don't have any sense of belonging any more. Half of them have nothing left to desire except to die in peace, and more than half—as your associates must have found out in trying to cross-examine them—have no memory at all of the long-gone years they spent at the University of Wollongong."

She looked at him curiously. "But you're not much younger than they are," she said, "and you're a triple rejuvenate. You obviously don't feel like that?"

"The fact that I do not," he said, dryly, "is the greatest proof of my genius. I am a very unusual individual—as unusual, in my way, as Rappaccini. Does it not seem to you that the AI driving this vehicle is being a little incautious?"

Charlotte had not bothered to look out of the windows for some time. Now that she did, it seemed to her that he was understating the case. AI drivers were programmed to the highest safety standards, and everyone fell into the habit of trusting them absolutely, but the road seemed to be far too rough and curvaceous to warrant their present speed. There was no guard-rail on their right-hand side, and the scree slope fell away precipitously. She called the AI and queried the speed, suddenly moved to wonder what other surprises the car's hirer might have tucked away in its memory along with the secret of their destination and the alleged virus.

The AI displayed a message on the screen: INCREASED SPEED NECESSITATED BY PROXIMITY OF PURSUING VE-HICLE.

Charlotte blinked, then tapped in an instruction to open a view-point in the rear of the cabin. She and Oscar both turned to look through it. The vehicle behind them was not an ordinary car. It was smaller, squarer, and looked as if it were armored. It was also far closer to their rear end than normal safety regulations permitted. It must have had an AI driver because its windscreen was quite opaque, but the AI in question had obviously been programmed in defiance of the law.

"It's trying to force us off the road!" said Charlotte, hardly able to believe her eyes. In all her years in the police force she had never encountered anything so outrageous. As she pressed the car's PANIC button her waistphone buzzed, and she lifted it from its hol-ster reflexively.

"You can take Paul Kwiatek off your list," Hal's voice said, dully. "They just found him dead. Same method, same visitor."

"Hal!" she squawked. "Someone's trying to kill us!"

"What?" said Hal, disbelievingly.

"There's some kind of jeep trying to smash into us from be-hind!"

The car round a bend, and the resultant lurch threw Charlotte and Oscar together. As they bumped heads, a combination of sur-prise and pain made Charlotte cry out.

"Charlotte!" said Hal, his disbelief turning to alarm. "What's happening?"

Charlotte wanted to shout instructions to the men who ought by now to be monitoring their situation through the car's sensors. *Scramble a helicopter*! she wanted to scream. *Send a smart bomb*! As she straightened up again she looked out of the side-window at the drop that awaited them, if their driver were to be careless enough to let a wheel slide over the edge.

It was a very long drop.

She let out a wordless cry as they soared around another bend, and she turned back to the rear viewport, clutching her throbbing head as she did so, hoping that the pursuing vehicle might not make it around the bend. It did make it, but it fell back eight or ten meters in so doing, and Charlotte felt her heart surge as she wondered whether some preventative signal had got through—but then there was a curious rattling noise at the rear end of their own vehicle.

"Hal!" she cried, again, "They're shooting at us, Hal!"

"I've got visual!" came the reply. "I've got—*corruption and corrosion*!"

Charlotte had never heard Hal use such words before, except in an uninflected and strictly literal fashion. Had she been able to find words herself she would have found even more profound obscenities. They had just taken yet another bend. This time, the pursuing vehicle failed to make the turn—in fact, it went straight over the edge and into empty air. For almost a second it seemed to hang there, like some absurd character in a synthomovie who would not start to feel the effects of gravity until he became conscious of being unsupported. Then, with a peculiar gracefulness, it began to fall. When it finally hit the rocky slope two hundred meters below it exploded like a bomb, sending shards in all directions.

Their own AI driver was dutifully slowing down now that the threat of a damaging collision was no longer moving it to recklessness. Charlotte shut her eyes and breathed deeply, while the pain in her head ebbed slowly away. When she opened her eyes again, Oscar Wilde had turned his own side-window into a mirror, and he was inspecting his own head very carefully. There was a noticeable bluish bump above the right eyebrow. She could not find it in her heart to regret the temporary damage done to his outrageous good looks, although he obviously felt differently.

"What do you make of that?" she asked him.

"Another vignette in the unfolding psychodrama," he said, dryly. "Rappaccini evidently feared that the journey might be a trifle boring, and laid on a measured dose of excitement."

She stared at him for a few seconds. "You mean," she said, slowly, "that the person who hired this car also hired that one—as a practical joke!"

"He's right," said Hal, over the phone link. "The information's coming through now. The jeep was hired at the same time, paid for from the same account. The local police have no reason to think anyone was aboard, but they'll send a crew to check the debris. It wasn't carrying a gun—that rattling you heard was produced by your own car's AI."

Charlotte was speechless. Oscar leaned over to speak into the mouthpiece of her waistphone. "What were you saying when we were so rudely interrupted?" he asked Hal. "Who's dead?"

"Paul Kwiatek. Another Wollongong graduate, born 2401."

Charlotte snatched up the phone again, sorely annoyed with herself. Determined to be businesslike, she said: "Where?"

"Bologna, Italy."

"Bologna! But...when?"

"Some time last week. It looks as though he was killed before King. The woman probably flew to New York on an intercontinental flight from Rome. I'll try to figure out where she was before that—there might be other bodies we haven't found yet. We're stepping up our attempts to contact and question the others on the list, but I don't know how to work out which of them are potential victims, let alone potential murderers."

"Czastka knows something." said Charlotte. "He might be the key."

"We've just talked to him," Hal said, in his infuriating fashion. "He denies knowing anything at all that would connect him with King, Urashima and Kwiatek, and he denies having received the equipment and supplies paid for by the Rappaccini accounts. So far, there's no proof that he's lying. We're worried about another name on the Wollongong list—Magnus Teidemann. He's supposed to be out in the wilderness somewhere in mid-Africa, but he's been ominously silent for some time. If he's dead, it could take us a week to find the body. I've ordered a search. That's all for now." He broke the connection, without waiting for Charlotte to respond.

Charlotte had already recalled the list, and had begun tracing a path through the back-up information. "Paul Kwiatek," she said to Oscar. "Software engineer. Should I call up a more detailed biog, or do you know him?"

"No," said Oscar, "but I know Teidemann by repute. He was a major force in the UN a hundred years ago, one of the inner circle of world-planners. Gabriel King probably knew him personally. The unfolding network of cross-connections is going to deluge your friend's AIs with data. There's too much of it to sort out and un-ravel, unless we can somehow cut the Gordian knot at a stroke."

"It doesn't work like that," she told him, although she wasn't entirely convinced. "The machines are so fast that profusion of data doesn't trouble them. The real problem is the age of the data. If the motive for the murders really does go back a hundred and fifty years...but if it does, why wait until now to carry them out? Why murder men who are already on the threshold of extinction?"

"Why indeed?" echoed Oscar Wilde.

"It's insane," Charlotte opined, being unable to see any other explanation. "It's some weird obsession." Such things were not un-heard of, even in these days of chemical retuning and biofeedback training. The brain was no longer the great mystery it once had been, but it kept stubborn and jealous guard over many of its secrets.

"Obsession might sustain memories that would otherwise fade away," Oscar admitted. "If there were no obsession involved, no murderer could nurse a plan as elaborate as this for as long as Rap-paccini must have nursed this one."

Charlotte returned to her contemplation of the list displayed on the screen. Apart from Teidemann's, none of the names meant any-thing at all to her. Only a handful were listed as genetic engineers of any kind, and none seemed to have the right kind of background to be Rappaccini—except, of course, for Walter Czastka. As she scanned the subsidiary list of addresses, though, her eye was caught by the word "Kauai". She stopped scrolling. One Stuart McCan-dless, ex-Chancellor of the University of Oceania, had retired to Kauai. She was tempted to call Hal and trumpet her discovery, but she knew what his response would be. His AIs would have turned up the coincidence; investigation of the data-trail would be in hand. She wished, briefly, that she were back in New York. There, at least, she would be involved in the routine pursuit of enquiries, making calls. What was she accomplishing out here, in the middle of nowhere?

She glanced out of the side-window as the car swung slowly and carefully around a bend into one of the ghost-towns, whose names were still recorded on the map in spite of the fact that no one had lived in them for centuries. The ancient stone buildings had been weathered by dust-storms, but they still retained the sharp angles which proudly proclaimed their status as human artifacts. The land around them was quite dead, incapable of growing so much as a blade of grass, and every bit as desolate as an unspoiled lunar landscape, but the shadowy scars of human habitation still lay upon it.

In the long-gone days when the earth had lain temporarily unprotected by an ozone layer, this would have been a naked place. Even then, it would probably have been almost empty; this part of America, being outside the old fifty-state Union, had been very hard hit even by the first and least of the three plague wars—whose victims, not knowing that there was far worse to come, had innocently called it the Great Plague War.

CHAPTER EIGHT

The wallscreen blanked out. While Charlotte was still wondering what the interruption signified, the car's AI relayed a message in large, flamboyant letters: WELCOME, OSCAR: THE PLAY WILL COMMENCE IN TEN MINUTES. THE PLAYHOUSE IS BENEATH THE BUILDING TO YOUR RIGHT.

"Play?" said Charlotte, bitterly. "Have we come all this way just to watch a play?"

"It appears so," said Oscar, as he opened the door and climbed out into the sultry heat of the deepening evening. "Do you carry transmitter-eyes and bubblebugs in that belt you're wearing?"

"Of course," she said, moving to inspect the place where bullets had seemed to strike the car. There were no marks; the sound of the shots striking home had indeed been manufactured by the car's AI. *Very amusing*, she thought. *We could still have been killed if we'd gone off the road.*

"I suggest that you place a few about your person," said Oscar. "I have only one bubblebug of my own, which I shall mount on my forehead."

Charlotte turned to stare at the building to their right. It did not look in the least like a theater. It might once have been a general store. It was roofless now, nothing more than a gutted shell.

"Why bring us out here to the middle of nowhere?" she demanded, angrily. "Why didn't he just record it on tape for transmission in a theater in San Francisco or New York?" As she spoke, she planted two electronic eyes above her own eyebrows.

Oscar quickly located a downward-leading flight of stone steps inside the derelict building. Charlotte planted head-high nanolights every six or seven steps to illuminate their passage, which had been hollowed out using bacterial deconstructors far more modern than the building itself. By the time they reached the bottom of the stair, there were several meters of solid rock separating her from the car; she knew that her transmitter-eye would only function as a re-cording-device. At the bottom there was a door made from some kind of synthetic organic material; it had no handle but when Oscar touched it with his fingertips it swung inwards. "All doors in the world of theater are open to Oscar Wilde," he muttered, sarcasti-cally.

Beyond the doorway was a well of impenetrable shadow. Char-lotte automatically reached up to the wall inside the doorway, plac-ing another nanolight there, but the darkness seemed to soak up its luminance effortlessly, and it showed her nothing but a few square centimeters of matt-black wall. The moment Oscar took a tentative step forward, however, a small spotlight winked on, picking out a two-seater sofa upholstered in black.

"Very considerate," said Oscar, dryly. He invited her to move ahead of him, and she did. Five seconds after they were seated the spotlight winked out. Charlotte could not suppress a small gasp of alarm. The nanolight she had set beside the door shone like a single distant star in an infinite void.

When light returned, it was cleverly directed away from them; Charlotte could not see Oscar, or her own body. It was as if she had become a disembodied viewpoint, like a bubblebug, looking out upon a world from which her physical presence had been erased. She seemed to be ten or twelve meters away from the event which unfolded before her eyes, but the distance was illusory. Cinematic holograms of the kind to which Michi Urashima had devoted his skills before turning to more dangerous toys were adept in the se-ductive art of sensory deception.

The "event" was a solo dance. The performer was a young woman, whose face was made up to duplicate the appearance that the image's living model had presented to Michi Urashima's spy-eyes. Only her hair and costume were different; the hair was now long, straight and jet black, and she was dressed in sleek, translucent chiffons, which were gathered in multi-colored profusion about her lissome form, secured at strategic points by gem-faced catches. The music to which she danced, lithely and lasciviously, was raw and primitive. Charlotte's knew by now that the original Oscar Wilde had written a play called *Salomé*. Forearmed by that knowledge, she quickly guessed what she was to watch.

As the virtual Salomé began the dance of the seven veils, the first impression Charlotte formed was that the dance was utterly artless. Modern dance, with all the artifice of contemporary biotechnology as a resource, was infinitely smoother and more complicated than this—but she judged that its primitive quality was deliberate. In the nineteenth century, Charlotte knew, there had been something called 'pornography'. Nowadays, in a world where most sexual intercourse took place in virtual reality, with the aid of clever machinery, the idea of pornography was redundant; everyone now accepted that in the realm of mechanized fantasy nothing was perverse and nothing was taboo. Charlotte thought she understood, dimly, the historical implications of Salomé's silly prancing, but she found it neither stimulating nor instructive. The gradual removal of the veils was simply a laborious way of counting down to a climax she was already expecting. She waited for Salomé to acquire a mute partner for her mesmerized capering.

The dancer did look as if she were mesmerized. She looked as if she were lost in some kind of dream, not really aware of who she was or what she was doing. Charlotte remembered that the young woman had given a similar impression during the brief glimpse of her which Gabriel King's cameras had caught. The dance slowed, and finally stopped. Salomé stood with bowed had for a few moments, and then reached out into the shadows which crowded around her, and brought out of the darkness a silver platter, on which sat the decapitated head of a man. Charlotte was not surprised, but she flinched. The virtual head looked more startlingly real than a real head would probably have done, by virtue of the artistry which had gone into the design of its horror-stricken expression and the bloodiness of the crudely-severed neck. She recognized the face that the virtual head was wearing: it was Gabriel King's.

The dancer plucked the head from its resting-place, entwining her delicate fingers in its hair. The salver disappeared, dissolved into the shadow. The dance began again.

How differently, Charlotte wondered, was Oscar Wilde seeing this ridiculous scene? Could he see it as something daring, monstrous, and clever? Would he be able to sigh with satisfaction, in that irritating way of his, when the performance was over, and claim that Rappaccini was indeed a genius?

The macabre dance now seemed mechanical. The woman appeared to be unaware of the fact that she was supposedly brandishing a severed head. She moved its face close to her own, and then extended her arms again, maintaining the same distant and dreamy expression. Then the features of the severed head changed. It acquired an Oriental cast. Charlotte recognized Michi Urashima, and suddenly became interested again, eager for any hint of further change. She fixed her gaze steadfastly upon the horrid head. She had seen no picture of Paul Kwiatek, so she could only infer that the third appearance presented by the luckless Baptist was his, and she became even more intent when the third set of features blurred and shifted. The number and nature of the metamorphoses might well be crucial to the development of the investigation. She felt a surge of triumph as she realized that this revelation might vindicate her determination to stay with Oscar Wilde. She did not recognize the fourth face, but she was confident that the bubblebug set above her right eye would record it well enough for computer-aided recognition. How many more would there be?

The fifth face was darker than the fourth—naturally dark, she thought, not cosmetically melanized. She did not recognize this face, either, but she knew the sixth. She had seen it within the last few hours, looking considerably older and more ragged than its manifestation here, but unmistakably the same. It was Walter Czastka.

There was no seventh face. Salomé slowed in her paces, faced the sofa where Oscar and Charlotte sat watching, and took her bow. Then the lights came on. Charlotte had assumed that the performance was over, and its object attained, but she was wrong. What she had so far witnessed was merely a prelude. The lights which came on brought a new illusion, infinitely more spectacular than the last.

Charlotte had attended numerous theatrical displays employing clever holographic techniques, and knew well enough how a black-walled space which comprised no more than a few hundred cubic meters could be made to seem far greater, but she had never seen a virtual space as vast and as ornate as this. Here was the palace in which Salomé had danced, painted by a phantasmagoric imagination: a crazily-vaulted ceiling higher than that in any reconstructed Medieval cathedral, with elaborate stained-glass windows in mad profusion, offering all manner of fantastic scenes. Here was a polished floor three times the size of a sports-field, with a crowd of onlookers that must have numbered tens of thousands. But there was no sense of this being an actual place: it was an edifice born of nightmarish dreams, whose awesome and impossible dimensions weighed down upon a mere observer, reducing Charlotte in her own mind's eye to horrific insignificance.

Salomé, having bowed to the two watchers who had watched her dance at closer range than any of the fictitious multitude, turned to bow to another watcher: Herod, seated upon his throne. There had never been a throne like it in the entire history of empires and kingdoms; none but the most vainglorious of emperors could even have imagined it. It was huge and golden, hideously overburdened with silks and jewels, an appalling monstrosity of avaricious self-indulgence. It was, Charlotte knew, intended to appall. All of this was a calculated insult to the delicacy of effective illusion: a parody of grandiosity; an exercise in profusion for profusion's sake.

The king on the throne had drawn himself three times life-size, as a bloated, overdressed grotesque. The body was like nothing any longer to be seen in a world which had banished obesity four hundred years before, but the face, had it only been leaner, would have been the face that Rappaccini had worn in the photographs that Hal Watson had shown her the day before.

Oscar took her wrist in his hand and squeezed it. "Tread carefully," he whispered, his invisible lips no more than a centimeter from her ear. "This simulation may be programmed to tell us everything, if only we can question it cunningly enough."

Herod/Rappaccini burst into mocking laughter, his tumultuous flesh heaving. "Do you think that I have merely human ears, Oscar? You can hardly see yourselves, I know, but you are not hidden from me. Your friend is charming, Oscar, but she is not one of us. She is of an age that has forgotten and erased its past."

Mad, thought Charlotte. *Absolutely and irredeemably mad.* She wondered whether she might be in mortal danger, if the man beside her really was the secret designer of all of this.

"Moreau might have approved," Oscar said, off-handedly, "but his vision always outpaced his capacity for detail. Michi Urashima would not have been satisfied so easily, although I detect his handiwork in some of the effects. Did Gabriel King supply the organisms that hollowed out this Aladdin's cave, perchance?"

"He did," answered Rappaccini, squirming in his huge uncomfortable seat like a huge slug. "I have made art with his sadly utilitarian instruments. I have taken some trouble to weave the work of all my victims into the tapestry of their destruction."

"It's overdone," said Oscar, bluntly. "As a show of apparent madness, it's too excessive to be anything but pretence. Can we not talk as civilized men, since that is what we are?"

Rappaccini smiled. "That is why I wanted you here, dear Oscar," he said. "Only you could suspect me of cold rationality in the midst of all this. But you understand civilization far too well to wear its gifts unthinkingly. You may well be the only man alive who understands the world's decadence. Have the patient bureaucrats of the United Nations Police Force discovered my true name yet?"

"No," said Oscar.

"We soon will," Charlotte interposed, defiantly. The sim turned its bloodshot eye upon her, and she flinched from the baleful stare.

"The final act has yet to be played," Rappaccini told her. "You may already know my true names, but you will have difficulty in identifying the one that I presently use as my own." The sardonic gaze moved again, to meet Oscar's invisible stare. "You will thank me for this, Oscar. You would never forgive me if I were not just a little too clever for you."

"The car chase was gratuitous," said Oscar. "A jarring note in the performance, I thought."

"Consistency is the hallmark of a narrow mind," replied the fat man.

"If you wanted to kill six men," said Oscar, "why did you wait until they were almost dead? At any time in the last seventy years fate might have cheated you. Had you waited another month, you might not have found Walter Czastka alive."

"You underestimate the tenacity of men like these," Rappaccini replied. "You think they are ready for death because they have ceased to live, but longevity has ingrained its habits deeply in the flesh. Without me to help them, they might have protracted their misery for many years yet. But I am nothing if not loyal to those deserving of my tenderness. I bring them not merely death but glorious transfiguration! The fact of death is not the point at issue here. Did you think me capable of pursuing mere revenge? It is the manner of a man's death which is all-important in our day and age, is it not? We have rediscovered the ancient joys of mourning, and the awesome propriety of solemn ceremony and dark symbol. Wreaths are not enough—not even wreaths that consist of spiders in disguise. The end of death itself is upon us, and how shall we celebrate it, save by making a new compact with the Grim Reaper? Murder is almost extinct, and it should not be. Murder must be rehabilitated, made romantic, flamboyant, gorgeous and glamorous. What have my six victims left to do but set an example to their younger brethren? And who but I should appoint himself their deliverer, their ennobler, the proclaimer of their fame?"

"I fear," said Oscar, coldly, "that this performance might not make the impact that you intend. It reeks of falsity."

Rappaccini smiled again. "You know better than that, Oscar," he said. "You know in your heart that this marvelous appearance is real, and the hidden actuality a mere nothing. This is no cocoon of hollowed rock; it is my palace. You will see a finer rock before the end."

"Your representations are deceptive, Dr. Rappaccini," Charlotte put in. "Your daughter showed us Gabriel King's head first and foremost, but Kwiatek died before him, and Teidemann was probably dead even before Kwiatek. It was optimistic, too—we've already warned Walter Czastka, and if the other one can still be saved, we'll save him too."

Rappaccini's sim turned back to her. She had not been able to deduce, so far, how high a grade of artificial intelligence it had. She did not expect any explicit confirmation of her guess that Magnus Teidemann was a victim, or that the woman really was Rappaccini's daughter, but she felt obliged to try.

"All six will go to their appointed doom," the sim told her.

She wanted to get out now, to transmit a tape of this encounter to Hal Watson, so that he could identify the fifth face, but she hesitated.

"What can these men possibly have done to you?" she asked, trying to sound contemptuous although there was no point. "What unites them in your hatred?"

"I do not hate them at all," replied the sim, "and the link between them is not recorded in that silly Net which was built to trap the essence of human experience. I have done what I have done because it was absurd and unthinkable and comical. Great lies have been banished from the world for far too long, and the time has come for us not merely to tell them, but to live them also. It is by no means easy to work against the grain of synthetic wood, but we must try."

And with that, darkness fell, lit only by the tiny star marking the door through which they had entered the Underworld.

CHAPTER NINE

Night had fallen by the time Charlotte and Oscar emerged into the open, but there was a three-quarter moon and the stars shone very brightly through the clear, clean air. The car had gone. Charlotte's hand tightened around the bubblebugs that she had carefully removed from their stations above her eyebrows. She had been holding them at the ready, anxious to plug them into the car's systems so that their data could be decanted and relayed back to Hal Watson. She murmured a curse.

"Don't worry," said Oscar, who had come out behind her. "Rappaccini will not abandon us. A vehicle of some kind will be along very shortly to carry us on our way."

"Where to?" she asked, unable to keep the asperity out of her voice.

"Westwards. We may have one more port of call *en route*, but our final destination will surely be the island where Walter Czastka is. His death is intended to form the climactic scene of this little drama."

"Let's hope it's not too late to prevent that," said Charlotte bitterly. "And let's hope the fifth man is still alive when we get a chance to find out who he is. He may be dead already, of course—your ghoulish friend displayed his victims in the order in which their bodies were discovered, not the order in which they were killed."

"He was never my friend," Oscar objected, "and I am not sure that I like his determination to involve me in this. There is an element of mockery in it."

"Mockery," she said, tersely, "isn't a crime. Murder is." She took out her waistphone and tried to send a signal. There was a chance that the power-cell had enough muscle to reach a relay-station. Nothing happened. She turned back to her enigmatic companion.

"Did you understand all that stuff?" she asked him, point-blank.

"I think so," Oscar admitted. "My ancient namesake's *Salomé* provided the format, but the set owed more to Gustave Moreau's paintings than Oscar Wilde's humble play...." He broke off. His words had gradually been overlaid by another sound, whose monotonous drone now threatened to drown him out entirely.

"There!" said Charlotte, pointing at a shadow eclipsing the stars. It was descending rapidly towards them, growing hugely as it did so. It was a VTOL airplane, whose engines were even now switching to the vertical mode so that it could land helicopter-fashion. Charlotte and Oscar hurried into the shelter of the building from which they had come, to give it space to land.

The plane had only an AI pilot. While Oscar climbed in behind her Charlotte plugged her waistphone into the comcon and deposited her bubblebugs in the decoder. "Hal," she said, as soon as the connection was made. "Data coming in: crazy message from Rappaccini, delivered by sim. Conclusive proof of Rappaccini's involvement. Pick out the face of the fifth victim and identify it. Send an urgent warning to Walter Czastka. And tell us what course this damn plane is following, when you can track it." The plane had already taken off again.

Hal acknowledged, but paused only briefly before saying: "I'm sure all this is very interesting, but I've closed the file on Rappaccini. We're concentrating all our efforts on the woman."

"What?" said Charlotte, dumbfounded. "What do you mean, closed the file? The tape is proof of Rappaccini's involvement. Have you found out his real name?" Hal was too busy decanting the data and setting up programs to deal with it; there was a frustrating pause. Charlotte looked around. The airplane was a small one, built to carry a maximum of four passengers; there was a second comcon and a second pair of seats behind the one into which she and Oscar had climbed. Behind the second row of seats there was a curtained section containing four bunks. Oscar was busy inspecting the menu on the food-dispenser, frowning.

"It all depends what you mean by a real name," said Hal, finally. "He really was born Jafri Biasiolo. The dearth of information about Biasiolo is the result of poor data-gathering towards the end of the Aftermath. After his first rejuvenation—which changed his appearance to the one which we saw earlier—he began to use the name Rappaccini for all purposes. Later, as he approached his second rejuve, he established half a dozen fake identities under various pseudonyms, including Gustave Moreau. After the rejuve, when he had his appearance considerably modified again, he began using the Moreau name as a primary, and Rappaccini became exclusively virtual. Moreau leased an islet west of Kauai, where he's spent most of the last twenty-five years, never leaving for more than four or five weeks at a time. There's no evident connection between Moreau and the victims, except that Walter Czastka's his nearest neighbor. So far as we know, Biasiolo never had any connection with the university at Wollongong."

"I don't understand," said Charlotte. "Surely we have enough to arrest Moreau, with all the stuff I've just sent through. Why close the file?"

"Because he's dead," Hal replied, smugly. "Ten weeks ago in Honolulu. Details of his birth might be lost in the mists of obscurity, but every detail of his death was scrupulously recorded. There's no doubt that it was him. The comcon links to his island were closed down before that—he's been shipping equipment and material back to Kauai for over a year. There's nothing there now except the ecosystem that he built. The island's off-limits until the UN can get an inspection team in."

"But he's still responsible for all this," Charlotte protested. "He must have set it all up before he died. He and the girl—his daughter."

"Moreau never had a daughter in any of his incarnations. He was sterilized before his first rejuve—even though it wasn't actually a legal requirement back then, it was a point of political principle.

He made the customary deposits in a reputable sperm bank, but they've never been touched."

"Oh, come on, Hal! He's a top-class genetic engineer—his sterilization doesn't mean a thing. Look at the tape. She's playing Salomé to his Herod!"

"That's not evidence," said Hal, sharply. "Anyhow, the exact relationship of the girl to Moreau is neither here or there. The point is that she's the active mover in all this. She's the only one we can put on trial, and she's the one we need to find before the newscasters start billing this mess as the Crime of the Century. If there's any real help you can give me, I'd be grateful, but all this theatrical stuff is just more news fodder, which we can do without. Okay?"

Charlotte could understand why Hal was edgy. News of how Gabriel King and the others had died must have leaked out, and he was very sensitive about cases being publicized before arrests had been made. It wasn't his image or his reputation within the department that he was worried about; it was a point of principle, a private obsession.

"We are helping, aren't we?" she whispered, after the inset had disappeared. The question, by necessity, was addressed to Oscar Wilde.

"He won't find her before we do," Oscar said, softly. "We've been given the fast track to the climax of the psychodrama. And she is his daughter—if not a literal daughter, then a figurative one. I see now why the simulacrum said that we'd have difficulty identifying his true name. Moreau was his true name, by then, but he knew that the coincidence would make me assume that it was a mere pseudonym. I must talk to Walter again."

Before he could touch the keyboard, however, another call came in.

"The fifth face is Stuart McCandless," said Hal's voice. "We've spoken to him once but we're trying to get through to him again; his house AI's sent out a summoner. Your plane's heading west, on course for Kauai. You might be able to speak to him in person soon."

Charlotte placed her fingers on the rim of the keyboard, but Oscar put his hand on top of hers, gently insistent. "I have to call Walter," he said. "Dr. Watson will have priority on the call to McCandless.

She let him go ahead, although she knew that she shouldn't let her authority to slip away so easily. She, after all, was the investigator. She no longer thought that Oscar was a murderer, but that didn't affect the fact that he was the one who was only along for the ride.

Oscar's call was fielded by a sim, which looked considerably healthier than the real Walter had. "Oscar Wilde," he said, curtly. "I need to talk to Walter urgently."

"I'm not taking any calls at present," said the simulacrum, flatly.

"Don't be ridiculous, Walter," said Oscar, impatiently. "This is no time to go into a sulk."

The sim flickered, and its image was replaced by Czastka's actual face. "What do you want?" he said, his voice taut with aggravation.

"You're a player in this game whether you like it or not, Walter," Oscar said, soothingly. "We really do have to try to figure it out."

"I'm not in any danger," said Walter, tiredly. "There's no one else on the island, and no one can land without the house systems knowing about it. I'm perfectly safe. I never heard of anyone called Biasiolo, I've never met Moreau, and I know of no connection between myself and the other names the police gave me that could possibly constitute a motive for murder."

"I don't think the motive is conventional," said Oscar. "This whole business is a publicity stunt, a weird artistic statement, but there must be some kind of connection—something that happened at Wollongong."

Czastka looked ominously pale. "I told your friends, Oscar—I don't remember. Nobody remembers what they were doing a hundred and thirty years ago. Nobody."

"I don't believe that, Walter," said Oscar, softly. "We forget almost everything, but we can always remember the things that matter most, if we try hard enough. This is something that matters, Walter. It matters now, and it mattered then. If you try, you can remember."

"I can't." The word was delivered with such bitterness and anguish that Charlotte flinched.

"What about you and Gustave Moreau, Walter?" Oscar asked. "Didn't you know he was your neighbor?"

"I've never even seen the man," said Czastka. "All I know about him is the joke the wise guys on Kauai keep repeating. The island of Dr. Moreau, get it? You must—you've probably even read the damn thing. You must know, too, that we keep ourselves to ourselves out here. All I want is to keep myself to myself. I just want to be left alone."

Oscar paused for thought. "Do you want to die, Walter?" he asked, finally. His inflection suggested that it was not a rhetorical question.

"No," said Czastka, sourly. "I want to live forever, just like you. I want to be young again, just like you. But when I do die, I don't want flowers by Rappaccini at my funeral, and I don't want anything of yours. When I die, I want all the flowers to be mine. Is that clear?"

"I think we're on our way to see you," said Oscar, placidly. "We can talk then."

"Damn you, Wilde," said the old man, vehemently. "I don't want you on my island. You stay away, you hear? Stay away!" He broke the connection without waiting for any response.

Oscar turned sideways to look at Charlotte. His face looked slightly sinister in the dim light of the helicopter's cabin. "Your turn," he said. His smile was very faint.

It didn't take as long to get through as Charlotte had expected. Evidently, whoever had called on Hal's behalf had been brisk and businesslike. Stuart McCandless wasn't answering his phone in person, but when Charlotte fed his sim her authority codes it summoned him without delay.

"Yes?" he said, his dark and well-worn face peering at her with slightly peevish surprise. "I've hardly begun on the data you people dumped into my system. It's going to take some time to look at it all."

"I'm Charlotte Holmes, Dr. McCandless," she said. "I'm in an airplane that has apparently been programmed by Gustave Moreau, alias Rappaccini. He seems intent on providing my companion—Oscar Wilde—with a good seat from which to observe this unfolding melodrama. We're heading out into the ocean from the Mexican coast. We're heading your way and I thought we ought to talk. Have you ever met Moreau?"

McCandless shook his head vigorously. "I've already answered these questions," he said, irritably.

"Have you looked at the tapes of the girl who visited Gabriel King and Michi Urashima? Do you recognize her?"

"I'd be able to study your tapes more closely if you'd allow me time to do it, Ms. Holmes. I'm looking at them now, but in these days of changing appearances it's almost impossible to recognize anyone. I don't know whether the person in those pictures is twenty years old or a hundred. I've had dozens of students who were similar enough to be able to duplicate her appearance with a little effort. There's a visitor here now who would only need a little elementary remodeling."

Charlotte felt Oscar Wilde's hand fall upon hers, but she didn't need the hint. She was already trying to work out how to phrase the next question. "Who is your visitor, Dr. McCandless?" she asked, in the end.

"Oh, there's not the slightest need to worry," McCandless replied. "I've known her for some time. Her name is Julia Herold. I told your colleague in New York all about her."

"Could you ask her to come to the phone?" asked Charlotte. She glanced sideways, very briefly, at Oscar.

"Oh, very well," McCandless said. He turned away, saying, "Julia?"

Moments later he moved aside, surrendering his place in front of the camera to a young woman, apparently in her early twenties. The woman stared into the camera. Her abundant hair was golden red, and very carefully sculptured and her eyes were a vivid green. *A wig and a bimolecular overlay*, Charlotte thought. "I'm sorry to disturb you, Miss Herold," she said, slowly. "We're investigating a series of murders, and it's difficult to determine what information might be relevant."

"I understand," said the woman, calmly.

Charlotte felt a strange pricking sensation at the back of her neck. *It's her*, she thought. *It has to be her.* Hal Watson was undoubtedly checking the woman out at this very moment, with all possible speed, and if he found anything to justify action, he would act swiftly—but until he did, there was nothing she could do. *She's playing with us*, Charlotte thought. *She has McCandless in the palm of her hand and there's no way we can save him. But she'll never get away. She can't make another move without our knowing about it.*

"May I talk to Dr. McCandless again?" she asked, dully.

They switched places again. Charlotte wanted to say *Whatever you do, don't kiss her!* but she knew how stupid it would sound. "Dr. McCandless," she said, uncomfortably, "we think that something might have happened, when you were a student yourself. Something that links you, however tenuously, with Gabriel King, Michi Urashima, Paul Kwiatek, Magnus Teidemann and Walter Czastka. We desperately need to know what it was. We understand how difficult it is to remember, but...."

McCandless controlled his irritation. "I'm checking back through my records, trying to turn something up," he said. "I hardly know Czastka, although he lives close by. The others I know only by repute. I didn't even know that I was contemporary with Urashima or Teidemann. There were thousands of students at the university. We didn't all graduate in the same year. We were never in the same place at one time, unless...."

"Unless what, Dr. McCandless?" said Charlotte, quickly.

The dark brow was furrowed and the eyes were glazed, as the man reached for some fleeting, fugitive memory. "The beach party...?" he muttered. Then, the face became hard and stern again. "No," he said, firmly. "I really can't remember."

Charlotte saw a slender hand descend reassuringly upon Stuart McCandless's shoulder, and she saw him take it in his own, thankfully. She knew that there was no point in asking what he had half-remembered. He was shutting her out.

It's happening now, she thought, *before our very eyes. She's going to kill him within the next few minutes, and we can't do a thing to stop it. But we can surely stop her before she gets to Walter Czastka.*

"Dr. McCandless," she said, desperately. "I have reason to believe that you're in mortal danger. I advise you to isolate yourself completely—and I mean completely, Dr. McCandless."

"I know what you mean," he retorted, testily. "I know how the mind of a policeman works. But I can give you my absolute assurance that I'm in no danger whatsoever. Now, may I get on with the work that your colleague asked me to do?"

"Yes," she said. "I'm sorry." She let him break the connection; she didn't feel that she could do it herself.

When the screen blanked she turned and said: "He's as good as dead, isn't he?"

"The seeds may already be taking root in his flesh," said Oscar, gently. "It might have been too late, no matter what anyone could have said or done."

"What was it that he started to say?" she asked. "And why did he stop?"

"Something that came to mind in spite of his resistance. Something, perhaps, that Walter might half-remember too, if only he wanted to...."

Charlotte shook her head, tiredly. She called Hal. "Julia Herold," she said, shortly. "Have you tied her in with Moreau yet?"

"No," said Hal, simply. "She's a student. Her career seems quite ordinary, all in order. According to the Net, she wasn't in New York when Gabriel King received his visitor, nor in San Francisco when Urashima was infected. I'm double-checking—if it's disinformation, I'll get through it in a matter of hours."

"She was there," said Charlotte. "Whatever the superficial data-flow says, she was there. It's all in place, Hal—everything except the reason. You've got to stop her leaving the island. Whatever else happens, you mustn't let her get to Czastka."

"Who's her father?" Oscar put in. "Whose child is she?"

"Egg and sperm were taken from the banks," said Hal. "Both donors long-dead. Six co-parents filed the application—no traceable link to anyone involved in this. The sperm was logged in the name of Lothar Kjeldsen, born 2355, died 2417. The ovum was Maria Inacio's, born 2402, died 2423. No duplicate pairing registered, no other posthumous offspring registered to either parent. I'm checking for disinformation input, in case the entire Herold identity is virtual."

"The mother was born at the same time as the men on the victim list. Could she have known them?"

"It's possible. She was an Australian resident at the appropriate time. There's no trace of her in the University records, but she might have been living next door. What would it prove if she was? She's been dead for a hundred and thirty years. She drowned in Honolulu—presumed accidental, possibly a suicide. This isn't getting us anywhere, Dr. Wilde, and I have a whole panel lighting up on me—I'm cutting off."

The screen went blank yet again.

"She's Rappaccini's daughter," said Oscar, softly. "I don't know which bit of the record's been faked, or how, but she's Rappaccini's daughter. And she'll get to Walter, even if she has to swim."

CHAPTER TEN

Charlotte stared out of the viewport beside her. Behind them, in the east, the dawn was breaking. Ahead of them, in the west, the sky was still dark and ominous. Beneath them, the sea was only just becoming visible as fugitive rays of silvery light caught the tops of lazy waves. In these latitudes, the sea was almost unpolluted by the vast amount of synthetic photosynthetic substances that was pumped out daily from the artificial islands of the Timor Sea; even by day it did not display the defiant greenness of Liquid Artificial Photosynthesis. Even so, this region of the ocean could not be reckoned a marine wilderness. The so-called seven seas were a single vast system, now half-gentled by the hand of man. The Continental Engineers, despite the implications of their name, had better control of evolution's womb than extinction's rack. Even the wrathful volcanoes that had created the Hawaiian Islands were now sufficiently manipulable that they could be forced to yield upon demand the little virgin territories that the likes of Walter Czastka and Oscar Wilde had rented for their experiments in Creation.

"In my namesake's novel, *The Picture of Dorian Gray*," Oscar said, ruminatively, "the eponymous anti-hero made a diabolical bargain, exchanging fates with a portrait of himself, with the consequence that his picture was marred by all the afflictions of age and dissolution while the real Dorian remained perpetually young. He cast aside all conventional ideas of morality, determined to savor the entire gamut of pleasurable sensation."

"I'm sure it's great fun," said Charlotte, ironically.

Oscar ignored the remark. "At that time, of course," he said, "the story of Dorian Gray was the purest of fantasies, but we live in a different era now. It is perhaps too early to declare that yours is the last generation that will be subject to the curse of aging, but I am living proof of the fact that even my generation has set aside much of the burden with which ugliness, disease and the aging process afflicted us in days of old. We are corruptible, but we also have the means to set aside corruption, to reassert in spite of all the ravages of time and malady the image which we would like to have of ourselves. Nowadays, everyone who has the means may have beauty, and even those of limited means have a right of access to the elementary technologies of rejuvenation. I am young now for the fourth time, and no matter how often doctors and doubters tell me that my flesh is too weak to weather a fourth rejuvenation, I will not be prevented from attempting it. Nothing will induce me to become like Walter Czastka when I might instead gamble my mortality against the chance of yet another draught from the fountain of youth.

"So what?" said Charlotte. "Why tell me?"

"Because," he said, tolerantly, "that's why Rappaccini expects me to understand what sort of artwork he is designing. That's why he expects me to become its interpreter and champion, explaining to the world what it is that he has done. Because I am Oscar Wilde— and because I am Dorian Gray. Men like the first Oscar Wilde and the first Gustave Moreau were fond of likening their own era to the days of the declining Roman Empire, when its aristocracy had grown effete and self-indulgent, so utterly enervated by luxury that its members could find stimulation only in orgiastic excess. They argued that the ruling class of the nineteenth century had been similarly corrupted by comfort, to the extent that anyone among them who had any sensitivity at all lived under the yoke of a terrible ennui, which could only be opposed by sensual and imaginative excess. All that remained for men of genius to do was mock the meaninglessness of conformity and enjoy the self-destructive exultation of moral and artistic defiance.

"They were right, of course. Theirs was a decadent culture, absurdly distracted by its luxuries and vanities, unwittingly lurching towards its historical terminus. The 'comforts' of the nineteenth century—hygiene, medicine, electricity—were the direct progenitors of what we now call the Devastation. Few men had the vision to understand what was happening, and even fewer had the capacity to care. Addicted to their luxuries as they were, even terror could not give them foresight. Blindly and stupidly they laid the world to waste, and used all the good intentions of their marvelous technology to pave themselves a road to Hell. In the Aftermath, of course, the work of renewal began. Collective control of fertility was achieved, and the old world of hateful tribes was replaced by the world of the Net, which bound the entire human race into a single community. And we were able once again to cultivate our comforts...to the extent that Rappaccini seemingly believes that the revolution is complete, and that the wheel has come full circle."

"But that's nonsense!" said Charlotte. "There's no way that there could be another Devastation. There couldn't possibly be another population explosion, or another plague war."

"That's not what Rappaccini fears," said Oscar. "What he's trying to make us see, I think, is the horror of a world inhabited entirely by the old: a world made stagnant by the dominion of minds that have lost their grip on memory and imagination alike, becoming slaves to habit, imprisoned by their own narrow horizons. He's telling us that, in one way or another, we must kill our old men. The argument of his artwork is that if we can't liberate our renewable bodies from the frailty of our mortal minds, then the technological conquest of death will be a tragedy and not a triumph. He has undertaken to murder six men who are nearing a hundred and fifty years of age, not one of whom has dared to risk a third rejuvenation, even though it would seem that they have little or nothing to lose—and he has chosen for his audience a man who has taken that gamble, hopefully soon enough to avoid the kind of mental sclerosis which has claimed his victims. Can you begin to see what he's about?"

"I can see that he's stark, staring mad," said Charlotte.

Oscar smiled wryly. "Perhaps he is," he said. "His fear is real enough—but perhaps the threat isn't as overwhelming as he seems to think. Perhaps the old men will never take over the world, no matter how many they are or how old they grow. Old age is, after all, self-defeating. Those who lose the ability to live also lose the will to live. But the creative spark can be maintained, if it's properly nurtured. The victory of ennui isn't inevitable. If and when we really can transform every human egg-cell to equip it for eternal physical youth, those children will discover ways to adapt themselves to that condition by cultivating eternal mental youth. My way of trying to do that is, I admit, primitive—but I am here to help prepare the way for those who come after me. They will be the true children of our race: the first truly human beings."

Charlotte felt her eyes growing heavy; she felt drained. If only she had been more alert, she thought, she might have obtained a firmer grasp on Oscar Wilde's arguments. After all, she too retained an echo of the 1890s in her name. Could the small phonetic step that separated 'Charlotte' from 'Sherlock' really signify such a vast abyss of incomprehension? She knew that she needed sleep, but she felt in need of a soporific. Unfortunately, she was four thousand kilometers away from the ingenious resources of her intimate technology. She looked uncertainly at Oscar Wilde. He was watching her, with a serious expression in his liquid, luminous eyes.

"We ought to get some sleep," Charlotte said. "It'll be late tomorrow before we get to Hawaii." She hesitated, wondering how to proceed, her gaze drifting to the curtain which screened the cabin's bunk space.

"How my namesake's heart would have warmed to our Virtual Realities and the wonders of our intimate technology!" Oscar said, as though continuing his reverie. "I fear, though, that we have not yet learned to use our intimate technologies as fully or as consciencelessly as we might. Even in a world of artificial wombs and long-dead parents we cling to the notion that sexual intercourse is essentially a form of communication, or even communion, rather than an entirely personal matter, whose true milieu is the arena of fantasy, where all idiosyncrasies may be safely unfettered."

Charlotte couldn't help blushing, although she presumed that he had pre-empted her proposition mainly in order to spare her blushes.

"Thanks for telling me," she said, sharply. "I suppose that if Rappaccini had you on his list of victims, you'd be in no danger."

"Not so," he said. "A kiss is, after all, just a kiss—and I can appreciate a lovely face as well as any man. It is only in matters of true passion that I am an exclusive and unrepentant Narcissus."

CHAPTER ELEVEN

When Charlotte awoke the sun was high, but Oscar had darkened the viewports in order to conserve a soft crepuscular light within the cabin of the speeding plane. She sat up and drew the curtain aside to look over the backs of the seats. Her waistphone was still plugged in to the concom; data was parading across the main screen at the command of Oscar's deft fingertips.

"Good morning," he said, instantly aware of her movement although he had not turned. "It is still morning, thanks to the time-harvesting effects of westward travel. We're less than half an hour from Kauai, but I fear that we'll be unable to do much there except bear witness to the completion of the fifth phase of Rappaccini's grand plan."

Because she was slightly befuddled by sleep, it took her a second or two to work out what he meant. "McCandless is dead!" she said, finally.

"Quite dead," he confirmed. "The local police had him removed to an intensive-care unit as soon as he showed signs of illness, but there was absolutely nothing to be done for him. The progress of his devourers will be tracked with infinite patience by a multitude of observers—the doctors have sent a fleet of nanocameras into his tissues—but to no avail. What remains of Teidemann's body has been found too."

Charlotte donned the tunic of her police uniform. "What about Julia Herold? Have they got her in custody?"

"Alas, no."

Charlotte knew that she ought to have been astonished and outraged, but all that she really felt was a sense of bitter resignation.

"How could they possibly fail to intercept her?"

"She had already left when McCandless began to show signs of distress," said Oscar, who did not seem overly disappointed. "She went for a moonlight swim, and never surfaced again. The eyes set to follow her were mounted on flitterbugs, and by the time suitable submarine eyes entered the water she was beyond reach. Flying eyes are, of course, watching avidly for her to surface, but she must have had breathing apparatus secreted off-shore, and some kind of mechanized transport."

"A submarine?" said Charlotte, incredulously.

"More likely a towing device of some kind. The officer in charge of the failed operation pointed out that there was little more he could have done without a warrant for her arrest. One has now been issued. The Kauai police have sent helicopters to lie in wait for her, but Walter has forbidden them permission to land, and they're not empowered to override his wishes unless and until they actually see her. There's one more police helicopter awaiting our arrival on Kauai."

"Have you talked to Czastka?"

"No. He's refusing all calls. He presumably still thinks that all he needs to do is keep his house sealed. 'Julia Herold', by the way, is a fiction of disinformation. Your Dr. Watson has proved that the person in McCandless's house was indeed the same one who visited Gabriel King in New York and Michi Urashima in San Francisco. He is confident that he will be able to prove that she delivered the fatal flowers to Teidemann and Kwiatek too. He assures me that it is only a matter of time before he discloses an authentic personal history."

"Is that everything?"

"By no means. It required all my skills as an organizer to present these edited highlights so economically."

Charlotte looked resentfully at the bright and beautiful young man, who seemed unafflicted by the least sign of weariness. She switched the nearest viewport to reflector mode so that she could straighten her hair, and studied the faint wrinkles that were becoming apparent in the corners of her eyes. They could be removed easily enough by the most elementary tissue-manipulation, but they still served as a reminder of the biological clock that was ticking away inside her. *Thirty years to rejuve number one*, she thought, *and counting*. It was not a kind of paranoia to which she was usually prone, but she could not help comparing her flawed features with Oscar's fully-restored perfection.

As soon as they had set down at the Kauai heliport, Charlotte opened the door, and leapt down to the blue plastic apron. The promised helicopter was waiting less than a hundred meters away. Its police markings were a delight to her eyes, holding the promise of control. From now on, she would no longer be a passenger but an active participant: a pursuer, an active instrument of justice. Oscar kept pace with her in spite of the fact that his gait seemed much lazier.

"I should leave you here," she said, while climbing aboard. "I can, you know—this isn't public transport."

"You wouldn't be so cruel," he said. He was right

The helicopter lifted as soon as they were strapped in. Charlotte reached into the equipment-locker under the seat, and brought forth a handgun. She checked the mechanism before clipping it to her belt.

"You're not thinking of using that, I hope?" said Oscar.

"Now the proof's in place," Charlotte answered, tautly, "I can employ any practical measure which may be necessary to apprehend her. The bullets are non-lethal. We're the police, remember."

They were traveling at a lower speed than they had previously, but flew so low that their progress seemed more rapid. The downdraft of their blades carved the roiling waves into all manner of curious shapes. High in the sky above them, a silver airship was making its stately progress from Honolulu to Yokohama. Oscar tuned in a broadcast news report. There were pictures of Gabriel King's skeleton, neatly entwined with winding stems bearing black flowers in horrid profusion. This was only the beginning; the AI voice-over promised that details of several more murders would soon be revealed. Charlotte knew that an operation of the size that was now being mounted would attract the attention of half the newshawks in

United America and a good few in not-very-united Eastasia. Flocks of flying eyes would be migrating this way from every direction. The privacy which Walter Czastka so passionately desired to conserve was about to be rudely shattered.

Oscar blanked the newscast as soon as it moved on to more mundane matters, and his fingers punched out Walter Czastka's telephone code. The AI sim that answered had clearly been reprogrammed since Charlotte had last seen it.

"Damn you, Oscar Wilde," it said, without bothering with any conventional identification or polite preliminary. "Damn you and Rappaccini to the darkest oblivion imaginable."

Charlotte turned the camera-eye so that her own image filled the viewfield. "Dr. Czastka," she said, "this is Charlotte Holmes of the UN Police. I need to speak to you, urgently.

"Damn you, Oscar Wilde," replied the sim, stubbornly. "Damn you and Rappaccini to the darkest oblivion imaginable."

Charlotte looked at Oscar, whose face had creased into an anxious frown. "I have a horrible suspicion," he said, "that we might be too late." Charlotte looked at her wristwatch. They were still twenty minutes away from the island. She punched in another code, connecting herself to the commander of the task-force which had surrounded it.

"What's happening?" she demanded.

"No sign of her yet," the answer came back. "If anything happens, Inspector, you'll be the first to know." There was nothing to do but wait, so she sat back in her seat and stared down at the agitated waves. They were still a few minutes away when the voice came back on line. "We have camera contact," it said. "Relaying pictures."

The screen showed a female figure in a humpbacked wetsuit walking out of the sea, looking for all the world as if she were enjoying a leisurely stroll. She paused at the high tide line to remove the suit and its built-in paralung, then knelt beside the discarded wetsuit and removed something from an inner pocket. Over the voice-link they could hear the officer who had spoken to them instructing her to desist.

Suddenly, the air around the girl was filled by a dense smoke, which swirled in the breeze as it dispersed.

"Alate spores," Oscar guessed. "Millions of them."

Julia Herold stood still, with her arms upraised in a gesture of seeming surrender. She had apparently done what she came to do.

"Stay in the copters," Charlotte instructed. "The stuff she's released is probably harmless to anyone but Czastka, but there's no need for everyone to take the risk. I'll pick her up myself."

"As you wish," said the other officer, sourly. He evidently thought that Charlotte was intent on appropriating what little glory there might be in making the arrest."

"I think we might have mistaken the exact form that the final murder was intended to take," said Oscar, quietly. "It's not Walter those spores are after—it's his ecosystem. She came here to destroy his private Creation."

As the helicopter swept in to land Charlotte scanned the trees which fringed the beach. Lush undergrowth nestled about the boles of palm-like trees. She half-expected to see the green leaves already flecked with darker colors but nothing was happening yet.

"Nothing can stop it," said Oscar, softly, his voice reduced now almost to a whisper. "Each murderer is one hundred per cent specific to its victim. Walter's own body is safe inside the house, but that's not what he cares about...it's not what he is. Rappaccini's instruments are going to devour his entire ecosphere—every last molecule."

For the first time, Charlotte realized, Oscar Wilde was genuinely horrified. The equanimity that had hardly been rippled by the sight of Gabriel King's hideously-embellished skeleton was ruffled now. For the first time, Oscar was identifying with one of Rappaccini's victims, seeing Rappaccini as a criminal as well as an artist. But even as Charlotte observed his outrage, Oscar's expression was changing.

"Look!" he said. "Look what kind of demi-Eden Walter Czastka has been endeavoring to build here." The helicopter had set down some thirty meters from the woman, who was still standing in the same spot, with her arms upraised. She was taking no notice of them or the other hovering machines; her green eyes were quite blank. Charlotte climbed down, keeping one eye on the woman while she obeyed Oscar's instruction to look inland. She could not see anything surprising or alarming.

"Poor Walter," said Oscar, sadly. "What a petty Arcadia this is! Immature and incomplete though it undoubtedly is, its limitations already show. Here is the work of a hack trying desperately to exceed his own potential—but here is the work of a man who has not even the imagination of blind and stupid nature. I can see now why Walter tried to keep me away. The mysterious Julia does not have to kiss poor Walter, because Walter is already dead, and he knows it. Even if his heart still beats within his withered frame, he is dead. Rappaccini's worms are feeding on his carcass."

"It looks perfectly ordinary to me," said Charlotte, staring up at the uneven line made by the crowns of Walter Czastka's palm-like trees, as they extended their ample canopies to bask in the life-giving light of the sun.

"Precisely," said Oscar Wilde, with a heavy sigh.

Charlotte moved to confront the woman, who stood statue-still, looking up into the brilliant blue sky.

"Julia Herold," she began, "I arrest you for...."

She heard a strange squawking sound behind her, and guessed that someone was trying to attract her attention by shouting over the voice-link to the helicopter's concom. She picked up her waistphone impatiently. "It's okay," she said. "I've got her. It's all over."

"Look behind you!" said the voice from the other end, trying to shout at her although the volume control on her waistphone compensated automatically. "*Corrosion and corruption, woman, look behind you!*"

Uncomprehendingly, Charlotte looked behind her.

Falling towards her from the vivid brightness of the early afternoon sun was a black shadow. At first she could judge neither its size nor its shape but as it swooped down the truth became abundantly and monstrously clear. She could not believe the evidence of her eyes. She knew full well that what she was seeing was flatly impossible, and her mind stubbornly refused to accept the truth of what she saw.

It was a bird, but it was a bird like none that had ever taken to the skies of earth in the entire evolutionary history of flight, bigger by far than the helicopters whose automatic pilots were taking evasive action to avoid it. The pinion-feathers of its black wings were the size of samurai swords, and its horrible head was naked, like a vulture's. Its beak was agape, and it cried out as it swooped down upon her. Its cry was a terrible inhuman shriek, which made her think of the wailing of the damned in some Dantean Hell.

Wise panic took hold of her and threw her aside like a rag doll, lest she be struck by the diving impossibility. She had no time to fire her gun, or even to think about firing it. Her reflexes rudely cast her down, tumbling her ignominiously on to the silvery sand.

Julia Herold didn't move a muscle. Charlotte understood, belatedly, that the raising of her arms had not been a gesture of surrender at all. With confident ease, the girl interlaced her fingers with the reaching talons of the huge bird, and was lifted instantly from her feet.

According to all the best authorities, Charlotte knew, no bird could lift an adult human being from the ground—but this bird could. It was climbing again now, beating its fabulous night-black wings with extravagant majesty, circling back into the dazzling halo of brilliance surrounding the tropical sun.

Charlotte reached up her own hand to take the one that Oscar Wilde was extending to her. "Do you remember when Rappaccini's simulacrum said to us, 'This is no cocoon of hollowed rock; it is my palace. You will see a finer rock before the end'?" he asked, resignedly. "The second 'rock' was actually 'roc'. A cheap shot, in my judgment."

"Get back in the helicopter," she said, grimly. "I don't know how far or how fast that thing can fly, but she is not going to get away."

"I don't think she's even trying," said Oscar, with a sigh. "She's merely escorting us to the much-joked-about island of Dr. Moreau, so that we may cast a critical eye over her father's Creation."

CHAPTER TWELVE

Moreau's island was more or less identical in size and shape to Walter Czastka's. By the time it was in view Charlotte had Hal Watson on the line, watching the drunken flight of the giant bird through the helicopter's camera-eyes. Huge though it was, the woman's weight was burden enough to make flight very difficult, and Charlotte wondered whether the creature had sufficient strength left to make landfall.

"It is clear," said Oscar, "that the murders were committed partly in order to lay a trail. We shall be the first to reach its end, but by no means the last. Every news service in the world must have dispatched spy-eyes by now. We are about to attend an exhibition, dear Charlotte—one that will put the so-called Great Exhibition of 2505 to shame."

"We picked up enough body-cells at McCandless's house to produce a DNA-spectrum," Hal put in. "The lab people didn't expect any kind of correlation with the people who were registered as Julia Herold's parents, but they found one. According to her genes Herold *is* Maria Inacio, saving some slight somatic modifications compatible with cosmetic transformation. Inacio's alleged death in 2423 must be disinformation."

"No," said Oscar, softly. "Maria Inacio was born in 2402; there's no way that she could be Rappaccini's daughter. You won't find Julia Herold's birth recorded anywhere, Dr. Watson. She was born from an artificial womb on the island, not more than twenty years ago."

"A clone!" said Charlotte. "An unregistered clone! But she's not his daughter. You were wrong about that."

"In the literal sense, yes," admitted Oscar, as the bird summoned the last vestiges of its strength for one last surge towards the silver strand where the waves were breaking over Dr. Moreau's island, "but he has raised her from infancy within the confines of his own Garden of Eden, and I'll wager that he has exactly the same degree of genetic relatedness to her as he would have to a daughter: fifty per cent."

"You mean," said Charlotte, "that she's his sister!"

"No," said Oscar, clenching his fist in a tiny gesture of sympathetic triumph as the bird dropped the girl into the sand and lurched exhaustedly to a sprawling landing twenty meters further on. "I mean that Maria Inacio was Rappaccini's mother."

"I suppose you've worked out who his father was, as well?" said Charlotte, as the helicopter zoomed in to land. The helicopter's safety-minded AIs gave the beached roc a wide berth, putting them down sixty meters away from the point where the woman had been dropped; she had already picked herself up and disappeared into the trees fringing the beach. Charlotte unplugged her waistphone from the comcon. She didn't bother unshipping any transmitter-eyes. Hal would soon have plenty of eyes with which to see. The whole world was coming to this party.

"We can narrow it down to one of six," said Oscar, as he opened the door and climbed out of the slightly-tilted helicopter. "Perhaps that's as far as Rappaccini cared to narrow it down. It's possible, if McCandless's half-recollection of a beach-party at which all six of the victims might or might not have been present means anything at all, that Maria Inacio was uncertain which of them was the father of her child. I strongly suspect, though, that a genetic engineer of Rappaccini's skill and dedication could not have been content with any such uncertainty."

Charlotte looked uneasily along the strand at the chimerical creature which was peering at them dolefully from an unnaturally large and bloodily crimson eye. "It was Walter Czastka," she said, knowing that she could claim no credit simply for filling in the blank.

"It was Walter Czastka," he echoed. "Poor Walter! To harbor such genius in his genes, and such mediocrity in his poor mortal body."

Charlotte wasn't about to waste time feeling sorry for Walter Czastka—not, at any rate, for that reason—but she couldn't help feeling a pang of sympathy for poor Maria Inacio, dead before her life had really begun, leaving nothing behind but a child of uncertain parentage. Such things couldn't happen nowadays, when all children were sterilized as a matter of course—and only a tiny minority ever applied for desterilization in order to exercise their right of reproduction while they were still alive—but Maria Inacio had been a child of the Aftermath. Hers had been the last generation of women victimized by their own fertility.

Charlotte and Oscar walked side by side to the place where Rappaccini's mother/daughter had disappeared. They kept a wary eye on the roc, but the bird made no move towards them. It seemed to be in considerable distress. As they paused before moving into the trees, Charlotte saw the bloodshot eyes close. They moved into the forest, following a grassy pathway that had all the appearance of an accident of nature, but which had in fact been designed with the utmost care, as had every blade of grass.

The trunk of every tree had grown into the shape of something else, as finely-wrought in bronze-barked wood as any sculpture. No two were exactly alike: here was the image of a dragon rampant, here a mermaid, here a trilobite and here a shaggy faun. Many were the images of beasts that natural selection had designed to walk on four legs, but all of those stood upright here, rearing back to extend their forelimbs, separately or entwined, high into the air. The upraised forelimbs provided bases for spreading crowns of many different colors. Some few of the crowns extended from an entire host of limbs rather than a single pair, originating from the maws of krakens or the stalks of hydras.

The animals whose shapes were reproduced by the trunks of the trees all had open eyes, which seemed always to be looking at Charlotte no matter where she was in relation to them, and although she knew that they were all quite blind, she could not help feeling discomfited by their seeming curiosity. Her own curiosity, however, was more than equal to theirs. Every tree of the forest was in flower, and every flower was as bizarre as the plant which bore it. There was a noticeable preponderance of reds and blacks. Butterflies and birds moved ceaselessly through the branches, each one wearing its own coat of many colors, and the tips of the branches moved as if stirred by a breeze, reaching out towards these visitors as though to touch their faces. There was no wind: the branches moved by their own volition, according to their own mute purpose.

Charlotte knew that almost all of what she saw was illicit. Creationists were banned from engineering insects and birds, lest their inventions stray to pollute the artwork of other engineers, or to disrupt the domestic ecosystems of the recently-renewed world-at-large. When the final accounting was complete, and all of Rappaccini's felonies and misdemeanors had been tabulated by careful AIs, he would probably turn out to have been the most prolific criminal who had ever lived upon the surface of the earth. Rappaccini had given birth to an extraordinary fantasy, fully aware that it would be destroyed almost as soon as others found out what he had done—but he had found a way to show it off first, and to command that attention be paid to it by every man, woman and child in the world. Had he, perhaps, hoped that his contemporaries might be so overawed as to reckon him a god indeed, far above the petty laws of humankind? Had he dared to believe that they might condone what he had done, once they saw it in all its glory?

Rappaccini's creative fecundity had not been content with birds and insects. There were monkeys in the trees, which did not hide or flee from the visitors of their demi-paradise, but came instead to stare with patient curiosity. The monkeys had the slender bodies of gibbons and lorises, but they had the wizened faces of old men. Nor was this simply the generic resemblance which had once been manifest in the faces of long-extinct New World monkeys; these faces were actual human faces, writ small. Charlotte recognized a family of Czastkas and an assortment of Kings and Urashimas, but there were dozens she did not know. She felt that her senses were quite overloaded. The moist atmosphere was a riot of perfumes, and the murmurous humming of insect wings composed a subtle symphony.

Is it beautiful? Charlotte asked herself, as she studied the sculpted trees staring at her with their illusory eyes, marveling at their hectic crowns and their luminous flowers. *Or is it mad?*

It *was* beautiful: more beautiful than anything she had ever seen or ever hoped to see. It was much more beautiful than the ghostly echoes of Ancient Nature that modern men called wilderness, doubtless more beautiful than Ancient Nature itself—even in all its pre-Devastation glory—could ever have been. Charlotte could see, even with her unschooled eyes, that it was the work of a young man. However many years Rappaccini had lived, however many he had spent in glorious isolation in the midst of all this strange fecundity, he had never grown old. This was not the work of a man grown mournful in forgetfulness; this was the work of a man whose only thought was of the future that he would not live to see: its novelty, its ambition, its progress. This was Moreau's island, by which its creator meant morrow's island.

It was mad, too, but its madness was essentially divine.

In the heart of the island she expected to find a house, but there was none. There was only a mausoleum. She knew that Moreau's body could not be inside it, because he had died in Honolulu, but it was nevertheless his tomb. It was hewn from a white marble whose austerity stood in imperious contrast to the fabulous forest around it. It bore neither cross, nor carven angel, nor any inscription.

"Like you and me, dear Charlotte," Oscar said, "Jafri Biasiolo was delivered by history to the very threshold of true immortality, and yet was fated not to live in the Promised Land. How he must have resented the fading of the faculties which had produced all this! How wrathful he must have become, to see his fate mirrored in the faces and careers of all those who might—had the whim of chance dictated it—have been his father. When the true immortals emerge from the womb of biotechnical artifice, they will no longer care about who their fathers were or might have been, for they will indeed be designed, by men like gods, from common chromosomal clay. He, alas, was not."

Charlotte looked around curiously as she spoke, wondering where the woman might be. "He may be dead," she reminded Oscar, grimly, "but his accomplice and executioner will have to stand trial."

"Yes, of course" he murmured. "She must settle her own account with the recording angels of the Celestial Net." So saying, he walked around the massive mausoleum. Charlotte followed him.

The woman was sitting on the pediment on the further side of the tomb, facing a crowd of leaping lions and prancing unicorns, vaulting hippogriffs and rearing cobras, all hewn in living wood beneath a roof of rainbows. Hundreds of man-faced monkeys were solemnly observing the scene. Her vivid green eyes were staring vacuously into space. It was as if she could not see the fantastic host that paraded itself before her. She was quite bald, and the dome of her skull was starred with a thousand tiny contact-points, glistening in the sunlight. The golden red wig that she had worn lay like stranded sea-weed between her feet. In her left hand she held a flower: a gorgeously gilded rose. In her right hand was a curious skull-cap, made of exceedingly fine metal mesh.

Oscar Wilde picked up the gilded rose, and placed it carefully in his buttonhole, where he was accustomed to wear a green carnation. Charlotte picked up the skull-cap, and turned it over in her hands, marveling at its thinness, its lightness, and its awesome complexity.

"What is it?" she asked, as her eyes dutifully compared its shape to the contours of the girl's strangely-decorated skull.

"I imagine," said Oscar, "that it is your murderer's accomplice and executioner: Rappaccini's daughter. The Virtual Individual that has moved this Innocent Eve through the world, fascinating her appointed victims and luring them to the acceptance of her fatal kisses, is the vengeful ghost of Rappaccini, left behind to settle all his accounts on earth. When your Court of Judgment sits, that will be the only guilty party that can be summoned to appear before it. No part of this project originated within the mind and purpose of the girl herself. You may add trafficking in illegal brainfeed equipment to the seemingly-endless list of Dr. Moreau's crimes."

Charlotte let out her breath in a long, deep sigh that sounded exactly like one of Oscar Wilde's. She looked up into the little tent of blue sky above the mausoleum, which marked the clearing in which they were standing. Already, the sky was full of flying eyes.

This is Rappaccini's funeral, she thought, *and all of this was his last gift to himself: his last and finest wreath. It's a great symbolic circle woven out of life and death, laying claim to the only kind of immortality he could design for himself. Everybody in the world has been invited, to mock or mourn or marvel as they please.*

The eyes, she knew, had ears as well. The words that she and Oscar spoke could be heard by thousands of people all over the world, and would in time be relayed to billions. Oscar was looking upwards too, with a curious smile on his face.

"It was, after all," he said, wryly, "a perfect murder."

ABOUT THE AUTHOR

BRIAN STABLEFORD was born in Yorkshire in 1948. He taught at the University of Reading for several years, but is now a full-time writer. He has written many science fiction and fantasy novels, including *The Empire of Fear, The Werewolves of London, Year Zero, The Curse of the Coral Bride, The Stones of Camelot* and *Prelude to Eternity*. Collections of his short stories include a long series of *Tales of the Biotech Revolution*, and such idiosyncratic items as *Sheena and Other Gothic Tales* and The *Innnsmouth Heritage and Other Sequels*. He has written numerous nonfiction books, including *Scientific Romance in Britain, 1890-1950, Glorious Perversity: The Decline and Fall of Literary Decadence, Science Fact and Science Fiction: An Encyclopedia* and *The Devil's Party: A Brief History of Satanic Abuse*. He has contributed hundreds of biographical and critical entries to reference books, including both editions of *The Encyclopedia of Science Fiction* and several editions of the library guide, *Anatomy of Wonder*. He has also translated numerous novels from the French language, including several by the feuilletonist Paul Féval and numerous classics of French scientific romance by such writers as Albert Robida, Maurice Renard, and J. H. Rosny the Elder.

TURN THIS BOOK
OVER FOR A
SECOND GREAT READ!

A BIZARRE CRIME

In the world of the future, the newest rage among the rich and aged is to purchase computer-generated biotech simulations of their personalities before they die—and thus to become, after their passing, "Undead," immobile personalities trapped within the tombstones erected in their honor, only able to communicate with the outside world by voice and through texting.

But religious fanatics, and the relatives who thought they would inherit the Undeads' wealth, are outraged, regarding the sims as abominations. And then a cluster of four tombstones is vandalized in the night, the first of several such attacks; and cemetery Chief Security Officer Tann Hicks must find the perpetrator(s) and stop the crimes.

But are the sims alive or dead? And is the motive for the desecrations religious, personal, or a just a matter of greed? As the controversy grows and the media and police become involved, Tann finds himself squeezed on all sides. Can he solve the mystery before the Undead become the next flashpoint of a highly polarized society?

Borgo Press Books by BRIAN STABLEFORD

Against the New Gods and Other Essays on Writers of Imaginative Fiction
Algebraic Fantasies and Realistic Romances: More Masters of Science Fiction
Alien Abduction: The Wiltshire Revelations
The Best of Both Worlds and Other Ambiguous Tales
Beyond the Colors of Darkness and Other Exotica
Changelings and Other Metamorphic Tales
A Clash of Symbols: The Triumph of James Blish
Complications and Other Stories
The Cosmic Perspective and Other Black Comedies
Creators of Science Fiction
The Cure for Love and Other Tales of the Biotech Revolution
The Decadent World-View: Selected Essays
The Devil's Party: A Brief History of Satanic Abuse
The Dragon Man: A Novel of the Future
The Eleventh Hour
Exotic Encounters: Selected Reviews
Firefly: A Novel of the Far Future
Les Fleurs du Mal: A Tale of the Biotech Revolution
The Gardens of Tantalus and Other Delusions
Glorious Perversity: The Decline and Fall of Literary Decadence
Gothic Grotesques: Essays on Fantastic Literature
The Great Chain of Being and Other Tales of the Biotech Revolution
The Haunted Bookshop and Other Apparitions
Heterocosms: Science Fiction in Context and Practice
In the Flesh and Other Tales of the Biotech Revolution
The Innsmouth Heritage and Other Sequels
Jaunting on the Scoriac Tempests and Other Essays on Fantastic Literature
Kiss the Goat
Luscinia: A Romance of Nightingales and Roses
The Moment of Truth: A Novel of the Future
Narrative Strategies in Science Fiction, and Other Essays on Imaginative Fiction
News of the Black Feast and Other Random Reviews
An Oasis of Horror: Decadent Tales and Contes Cruels
Opening Minds: Essays on Fantastic Literature
Outside the Human Aquarium: Masters of Science Fiction, Second Edition
The Plurality of Worlds: A Sixteenth-Century Space Opera
Prelude to Eternity: A Romance of the First Time Machine
The Return of the Djinn and Other Black Melodramas
Salome and Other Decadent Fantasies
Slaves of the Death Spiders and Other Essays on Fantastic Literature
The Sociology of Science Fiction
Space, Time, and Infinity: Essays on Fantastic Literature
The Tree of Life and Other Tales of the Biotech Revolution
The Undead: A Tale of the Biotech Revolution
The World Beyond: A Sequel to S. Fowler Wright's The World Below
Yesterday's Bestsellers: A Voyage Through Literary History

THE UNDEAD

A TALE OF THE BIOTECH REVOLUTION

by

Brian Stableford

THE BORGO PRESS

An Imprint of Wildside Press LLC

MMX

CONTENTS

Chapter One 9
Chapter Two.. 21
Chapter Three.. 35
Chapter Four 50
Chapter Five.. 66
Chapter Six... 78
Chapter Seven 86
Chapter Eight 101
Chapter Nine 116
Chapter Ten.. 128

About the Author 134

DEDICATION

FOR BLACKIE

CHAPTER ONE

As he turned his car into the parking lot outside the gates of the Bracknell site of Virgil's Elysium, Tann Hicks wasn't sure whether to be grateful or annoyed that Sam Scarlett, the senior guard on night duty, hadn't phoned him as soon as he'd discovered the damage to the headpieces. Tann was all too well aware of the fact that his position as the Elysium's "Chief Security Officer" was largely nominal, with little real authority attached to it, and he was aware, too, that Sam was a trifle resentful of his being appointed to wear the title, given that Sam had twice as much experience under his belt. Given that Tann *was* the man primarily responsible for the Elsyium's security, however, he thought that he really ought to have been apprised of the incident without delay. On the other hand, Meg certainly wouldn't have appreciated it if they'd both been woken up at four o'clock in the morning and Tann had then had to desert her in order to go into work, with the midnight shift only half over and a full shift plus overtime still to do.

The car glided silently into its reserved spot and Tann climbed out, anxiously surveying the members of the little crowd gathered outside the Elysium's gate, searching for signs of excitement and agitation. The demonstrators were a little more numerous than they usually were before eight A.M., and they were talking to one another in hushed tones rather than simply standing around with banners reading THE UNDEAD ARE AN INSULT TO GOD or SACRED GROUND SHOULD NOT BE PROFANED, but they were not manifesting the kind of fervor that might have been expected had they believed that anything of major importance had transpired. They were, after all, residents of deepest suburbia, accustomed to a polite and quiet life.

As Tann made his way to the little side-gate, keycard in hand, the unofficial leader of the protest—a white-haired hobbyist named Seymour Conway who had taken up tub-thumping to while away the years of his retirement—blocked his path, and said: "Is it true, Mr. Hicks, that four of the Undead have been destroyed by an Avenging Angel?"

"So far as I know," Tann told him, pausing briefly before pushing his way past, "any damage sustained by the memorials is minor—and the perpetrator was certainly no Avenging Angel. Wasn't it one of your little flock?"

Conway smiled sardonically as he said: "My friends and I are careful to obey the law against trespass, Mr. Hicks, although we resent your employers' refusal to allow us to pay our respects to the dead." He stood aside, though, when Tann did ease past him, offering no resistance. None of his followers attempted to follow Tann through the gate, in defiance of the Elysium's "relatives only" policy, which was nowadays strictly observed.

Tann didn't hurry as he walked along the path that led to the office complex; he didn't want to give the demonstrators the satisfaction of thinking that he was at all anxious or disturbed. The graves lined up to either side of the path were all old, with crosses or headstones that were utterly mute and inert. The smarter monuments, inorganic and organic alike, were all on the far side of the administration center, shielded from the road as if huddled behind a barricade, acutely aware of their revolutionary status.

There really wouldn't have been any point in Sam waking Tann up when the incident had occurred, given that the perpetrator had fled the scene before Sam got there, and there was nothing at all that Tann could have done about the incident at that hour in the morning. Tann knew, however, that Roland Montfort, the Elysium's administrator, might not see it that way. Not that Montfort would have wanted to be woken up himself—he would just have wanted his so-called Chief Security Officer to be woken up, so that Tann could "assume the burden of his responsibilities". All things considered, Tann thought, as he used his keycard again to gain access to the building, it might have been better if Sam *had* got him out of bed, no matter how pointless it might have been. After all, the guard had phoned the police to report the trespass and the damage, even though that was pretty pointless too. There was no way the police were going to send someone around at four o'clock in the morning to investigate a case of vandalism in a cemetery, no matter how loquaciously the various spokesmen for the Undead might complain about the seriousness of such matters and the definition of the crime.

Tann went to the locker room and donned his uniform before heading for Montfort's office, steeling himself for the possible ordeal to come. He probably wouldn't have disliked his boss if Montfort had tried just a little harder to be likeable, but the administrator made no secret nowadays of his disappointment in being stuck in the same job for the last seven years—which was presumably the corporation's way of signaling that he no longer in the fast lane to promotion. Montfort thought he had been made for better things, and that being in charge of an Elysium, even in interesting times, was an insulting underestimation of his capabilities.

When Montfort had first been appointed, the only smart memorials in the Elysium had been inorganic, and there hadn't been very many of those; he'd been seen the cemetery through years of increasingly-heated controversy as the second generation of its Undead population had been gradually introduced and integrated, and he must have felt that he'd proved himself by weathering the squall. Perhaps, Tann thought, Montfort's employers thought he'd weathered it a little too well, and were reluctant to put a novice in his place now that Seymour Conway's booing brigade were finally making a little headway in terms of claiming media interest and general sympathy.

Montfort couldn't have arrived more than fifteen minutes before Tann, but fifteen minutes was the kind of margin that could generate a considerable moral advantage in the managerial mind, and Tann was expecting to endure a few subtle insults before he and his boss got down to business, so he was more than a little relieved, when he knocked and opened the door of Montfort's office, to find that the administrator wasn't alone.

Tann recognized the man standing at Montfort's desk as Nathaniel Barrow, the not-so-devoted son of the late and allegedly much-beloved Mildred Barrow—one of the four Undead victims of the incident. Presumably, Mildred hadn't been so badly damaged that she had been unable to send texts to her children via the teepee link, either calling for help or complaining about the awful injustice of the catastrophe.

Roland Montfort was standing up too, but he was a short, slim man, while Nathaniel Barrow was built like a rugby player, with a ruddy, misshapen face strongly suggestive of long experience in the scrum; there was no doubt as to who had the more intimidating presence. The two were about the same age, in strictly chronological terms, but Nathaniel Barrow had more than a hint of the Neanderthal about him, while Montfort was a trifle effete even by the most re-fined standards of *Homo sapiens*, so they seemed to be separated by a hundred thousand years of evolution.

Tann wasn't exceptionally solidly-built himself, but he was fair-ly tall, so he could at least look the intimidating relative in the eye. He was able to defuse a little of the accumulated tension in the room by greeting the visitor by name and shaking his hand before turning to face his boss. "I'm sorry, sir," he said, dutifully. "I got here as quickly as I could when I picked up the message, but the traffic's backed up at the roundabouts, as usual. Have the police arrived yet?"

"No, they haven't, Mr. Hicks," Montfort replied, in a gentler tone than Tann had anticipated. "I've had to ask your night-shift men to stay on for a couple of hours in order to make sure that the crime scene's preserved, just in case a forensic analysis team conde-scends to show up—Sam Scarlett's standing guard there now, while Doug Marcus is trying to repair the disabled alarm system."

Tann assumed that it wouldn't be diplomatic to mention in front of Mr. Barrow that the probability of the police making a forensic analysis team available to investigate a case of vandalism in a ceme-tery was so close to zero as to be almost unimaginable. Nor would it be diplomatic to point out to Roland Montfort that trying to repair the alarm system might be considered to be interfering with the crime scene. "Thank you, sir," he said, dutifully. "I'll relieve Sam right away, so that I can get his report and take a look at the damage myself."

He didn't expect to get away so easily, and he didn't, although it was the visitor who turned on him rather than his boss.

"How could you let this happen, Mr. Hicks?" Nathaniel Barrow demanded. "You knew about the threat—there's a gang of trouble-makers hanging about outside your gate every day, waving banners accusing you of being agents of Satan. What's the point of having a security force if you can't protect the monuments?"

"I'm truly sorry, Mr. Barrow," Tann said, "but the manpower at my disposal is limited. There are only two men on duty between midnight and eight, so we have to rely on technology to protect the grounds and deter intruders. This intruder was able to disable the perimeter alarm, so it wasn't until the infrared detectors picked him up that the guard in the ops room was alerted."

"The guard did reach the scene in time to prevent more serious damage being done," Roland Montfort chipped in, obviously feeling obligated to defend his staff in the face of an external adversary, no matter how displeased with them he might be himself. "The attacker fled before inflicting irreversible damage on any of the neuronets, which is why your mother was able to text you."

Barrow sighed. "Unlike my sentimentally-inclined brother," he said, "I'm not stupid enough to think that the talking computer pro-gram inside that travesty of a headstone is my mother. It's a trav-esty, and I'm convinced that she only set it up to annoy us. Even so, I'm not at all happy to discover that her grave has been desecrated. The fact that that the perpetrator seems to have got away with it will only attract more unwelcome attention—and believe me, her survi-vors have troubles enough already. Did your man even try to appre-hend him?"

"My men don't carry weapons, Mr. Barrow," Tann told him. "The intruder was armed, at least with whatever implement he used to attack the headpieces, and might easily have been carrying a knife, or even a gun. All that the guard could reasonably do was at-tempt to get a glimpse of the intruder, in order to aid in his subse-quent identification; he was under strict orders not to get into any kind of fight."

"And *did* he get a glimpse, to aid in subsequent identification?" Nathaniel Barrow wanted to know.

"The man was wearing some kind of face-mask," Montfort was quick to put in. "There's no way he can be identified from the evidence provided by the guard or the security cameras."

"So he'll get away with it? Not that it matters much, I suppose—even if the police manage to catch up with him, he'll just claim that he was doing God's work, striking a blow against the New Blasphemy—and he'll get plenty of support. In a way, I can't blame him for thinking that way, but it's still a desecration of my mother's grave. Why did he have to single her out?"

"She wasn't singled out, Nat," Roland Montfort said, apparently attempting a level of mateyness that seemed a trifle ludicrous to Tann. "All four headpieces in her quartet were attacked."

"Do you think that makes it any better, *Roly*?" the Neanderthal replied, sharply.

There was no doubt that the big man was genuinely upset about something, but the tenor of his objections rang more than a little false. Tann suspected that Barrow was almost as unconcerned about the "desecration" of his mother's grave as he was about the damage to her sim, and guessed that the only thing that really concerned him was the possibility that any consequent publicity might show him and his siblings in a bad light. Tann had taken the trouble, when he had time to spare, to converse with Mildred Barrow's sim, as he did with most of the Undead, and she had told him, in common with almost all of her peers, that all her children, and Nathaniel in particular, resented her for making provision for her preservation after death. According to her, Nathaniel and his sister flatly refused to consider that the sim animating the memorial was really their mother, or anything resembling a human being, and that her younger son, who had been more sympathetic, was now wavering under their pressure.

Perhaps the sim's anxiety was mostly Undead Paranoia—a condition increasingly being talked about as a vulnerability typical of the species—but it fitted in well enough with the logic of the situation. How many would-be heirs would be only too glad to sacrifice their inheritance in order that their dead parent could maintain a semblance of continued existence and continued influence over their lives? Some, presumably—but not many. Would Nathaniel Barrow have been less disappointed, Tann couldn't help wondering, if the vandal who had attacked his mother's headpiece had completed the job before Sam Scarlett arrived on the scene? Not that the task could really have been regarded as complete, even if the neuronet *in situ* had been irreparably damaged, so long as a back-up copy of the sim still survived, and provided that Mildred Barrow had taken out adequate insurance before popping her clogs.

"I understand your outrage, Mr. Barrow," Tann assured the distressed relative, deploying his own talent for insincerity, "and I can assure you that everything possible will be done to identify the perpetrator of the crime and guarantee his prosecution. If you'll excuse me, so that I can get on with that...."

He turned as if to leave, but he suspected that it wouldn't be so easy, and it wasn't. "Just a minute, Mr. Hicks," said Roland Montfort. "We need to discuss tactics for handling the media."

"Media?" said Nathaniel Barrow, anxiously. "TV and Web news, you mean?"

"It's not a big enough story to make headline news, thankfully," Montfort was quick to add, "but it's bound to be reported, and we need to make sure that it's reported responsibly."

"Why should it be *reported* it all?" Barrow asked, his eyes narrowing "Can't you keep it quiet? Surely the police aren't going to make a big fuss about it?"

"If we try to keep it quiet, Nat," Montfort told him, "that will only attract suspicion that we have something to hide. The facts are bound to be placed on public record—the point is to prevent them from being sensationalized. Although the incident isn't serious in itself, thankfully, the controversy regarding the Undead has heated up considerably now that smart monuments contrived in stone and silicon have been superseded by organic variants. As you pointed out yourself, if the perpetrator ever gets to court, he's likely to come out with a load of nonsense about taking up arms against the New Blasphemy. There's a danger that this might be blown up out of all proportion—which might be exactly what the attacker wants, and is certainly exactly what we don't want. That's why your men have to be careful, Mr. Hicks. We don't want anyone to start a snowball rolling."

"Don't worry, Mr. Montfort," Tann said, although he knew that there wasn't anything he could do that would stop someone like Sam Scarlett shooting his mouth off, if the mood took him. "I'll make sure that all my men are well aware of the need for diplomacy. Short factual comments only, courteous but controlled."

"If you ask me," Nathaniel Barrow said, although it seemed perfectly obvious to Tann that no one would have, "it's the other side that might want to make propaganda capital out of this—the nuts trying to claim human rights for the Undead. Mother's nearest neighbor is the sim of some old hedge-fund swindler, who's trying to claw back his property as well as maintaining a pathetic illusion of continued existence. They're the ones who are likely to blow this up out of all proportion."

"I doubt it, Nat," said Montfort. "The damage isn't that serious—it's not the sort of stuff out of which *causes célèbres* can be built. It can't be plausibly represented as grievous bodily harm, let alone murder. The spokespeople for the Undead will wait for something meatier. It's bound to come, sooner rather than later—but hopefully not from Virgil's Elysium."

"I hope you're right about that," Barrow retorted. "I don't want Mother's name dragged into any such dispute—which it would be, if her sim were to be held up as some kind of Undead martyr."

If ever there was a contradiction in terms.... Tann thought. "I really should get out to the site," was what he said aloud.

"Yes, of course, Mr. Hicks," Roland Montfort was quick to say. "This isn't the time or the place for a philosophical discussion. The sooner you can get on with the job, the more chance we have of tidying the matter up and putting this unfortunate occurrence behind us. If you'll excuse us both, Mr. Barrow...."

The big man didn't seem to want to leave—or, at least, didn't want to be dismissed by a person as small as Roland Montfort—but he wasn't given the opportunity to be stubborn. Instead of waiting for him to leave the office, Montfort moved around the desk and took Tann by the arm, ready to hurry off with him and leave his unwelcome visitor behind. Tann didn't particularly like his arm being grabbed, but he allowed himself to be drawn out into the corridor and hustled along toward the door that let out into the sector of the grounds where almost all the smart memorials were gathered.

"I've called in the bioengineers," Montfort told him, speaking in a low voice, although they were already out of earshot of Nathaniel Barrow, who had decided that it was better to turn in the opposite direction and go about his own business. "They say they'll get here as soon as possible, but God only knows when that will be. In the meantime, we need to do what we can to protect the Elysium from bad publicity. Make sure your men understand that we have to play this down, as a trivial incident of no real consequence. With luck, it will all blow over in a day or two."

Tann suppressed a sigh. He knew that the police would dismiss the incident as unworthy of the man-hours that might be required to investigate it seriously, and that the bioengineers would consider the repair work a matter of dull routine, but that didn't necessarily mean that it would "all blow over". For one thing, there were the injured Undead themselves to be taken into account. Even if Mildred Barrow's right-hand neighbor, Bruno Holzhauser, hadn't been trying to court notoriety as champion of Undead rights, and even if Mildred's sympathetically-inclined younger son could talk her into keeping quiet for the sake of the family's good name, there were two other victims who would undoubtedly be nursing a strong sense of grievance, and had the means to exercise it. Then there were the relatives of the other dearly departed, not all of whom would take the same line as Nathaniel Barrow. Although the latter was probably not in a minority, there was obviously one person even among his own siblings who was—or had been—on the brink prepared to think of the Undead sim as their actual mother, preserved from extinction by a miracle of science and granted an artificial afterlife which, if not actually a blissful Heaven, was a long way from the torments of Hell.

Some people, Tann knew, took great comfort in that idea, quite apart from philosophical disputes about the existential status of sims—and who could blame them? Add the potentially-inquisitive media to the mix, and Tann's life seemed in to be in real danger of becoming extraordinarily stressful. Given that Lucy was about to start school, and that Meg had another baby on the way, the last thing he needed at present was to be taking home more stress than he could handle.

"Unfortunately," Montfort continued, when Tann made no reply to his earlier observation, "the area in which the damage was done is full of eyes and ears, in addition to your own security cameras. Even though the four headpieces in the affected quartet have been blinded and deafened, their neighbors weren't. Sims can be frightened—they wouldn't be sims if they weren't—and they're all in contact with the outside world. It would be better in a way, if they hadn't been fitted with teepee facilities. After all, the living don't have telepathy, so it undermines their status as sims."

"Calling it *telepathy* doesn't make it into telepathy, Mr. Montfort," Tann opined. "That's just advertising, with an eye to a future that still seems rather distant. It's just a primitive texting system, which has to be hooked up directly to the Undead's neuronets because they don't have fingers and thumbs. All they can transmit is slowly-generated text, and all they can receive is a complex sequence of twinges, only a little more sophisticated than the dots and dashes of early wireless telegraphy."

"The point is," Montfort insisted, "that it puts them in direct contact with the whole damned world. If *they* want to blow this incident up out of all proportion, there's a good chance that they can—and some of them might."

"I doubt that they will," Tann said. "Mostly, they stick to texting one another and their surviving relatives. They have an even greater stake in Virgil's Elysium remaining a haven of rest than we have, given that they're literally stuck here. Apart from a few hotheads like Holzhauser, they're mostly content to keep a low profile—especially the stone-and-silicon brigade. In any case, there's no reason for the media to start taking their complaints seriously now, when the only coverage given to them thus far has been bluster about Undead Paranoia."

"Sometimes," Montfort said, "I wish we'd stuck to the old tech. Organic headpieces have been good for business, in the short term, but the whole fad might yet turn into a PR disaster. By the way, make sure that the bioengineers don't take the damaged eyes and ears away with them when they've fitted the replacements. Some record of what they saw and heard before the blows landed ought to be recoverable from the retinas and eardrums, even if the sims are too traumatized to remember the attack consciously, as it were. The police might want to bag them as evidence, even though there's probably no useful information to be gained."

"I'll make sure that everything is in order, Mr. Montfort," Tann assured him, blandly, although he knew full well that the bioengineers would be able to extract the records on site, so that the actual hardware would become irrelevant. "I'll preserve all the evidence I can, just in case."

"The intruder should never have got as far as he did, though," Montfort added, his tone emphasizing that Tann wasn't entirely off the hook, even if Nathaniel Barrow's presence when he had arrived had saved him from a serious ticking off. "The whole point of having an expert security team, with all the technological apparatus at your disposal, is to make sure that things like this cannot and do not happen."

Expert? Tann thought. *We're just eyes and ears ourselves, more for show than effect—but at least we aren't nursing delusions about what we might have been, if the company had only recognized our true potential.* "We do our best, sir," he said, aloud, "but the perimeter is nearly a mile long, and most of it is comprised of—or at least disguised as—a decorative hedge. The only way to make certain that no one can get in or out of a space this size is to surround it with high walls topped with razor-wire, which wouldn't fit very well with the Elysium's image. Glorified tripwires can't really do the trick—any smart teenager could download instructions from the Web allowing him to disable our alarms, and he wouldn't even have to be smart to put on a mask to protect himself against the cameras."

"You had two men on duty," Montfort said, stubbornly. "With all the equipment at their disposal, they should have been able to nip the incident in the bud."

Tann knew that there was no point telling his boss that he was being unreasonable, or reminding him that he had been loyally defending the security team only a few minutes before. The administrator was just venting a little of his frustration. At least Montfort had let go of Tann's arm—and he dropped back now, intent on returning to his desk while Tann took charge of the legwork.

"Report to me immediately if you find anything," Montfort said, as Tann marched on without looking back.

"Yes sir," said Tann, making no attempt to conceal his lack of enthusiasm. "You can depend on me."

CHAPTER TWO

As he passed each smart memorial, Tann paused to say hello and to ask their inhabitants how they were. It wasn't that he expected or hoped to obtain any useful information from them, or even that he wanted to emphasize that he was on their side, a friend if the need arose. It simply seemed like the polite thing to do. Being in charge of their security surely meant more than merely trying to prevent maniacs from smashing them up.

"Is this likely to happen with increasing frequency now, Mr. Hicks?" asked one of the sims embedded in an inorganic monument—a solemn rectangular block, far more dignified than an effigy of a human or an angel. "Are we all in danger?"

Thanks to their teepee links, the sims had access of a sort to the Web, including the TV channels' back-up services. They could keep up with the ongoing debates about the existential status of their own peculiar kind, and could measure the rising temperature of the argument as well as any living individual.

"I doubt it, Mr. Hahn," Tann replied. "Violence of this kind if essentially pointless, even as a publicity stunt. In any case, it's the organic headpieces that will bear the brunt of any supposedly-righteous wrath." The idea of embedding AI sims in stone monuments didn't seem to offend people's sensibilities as much as incorporating them into neuronets continued in organic structures equipped with hearts and lungs as well as eyes and ears. In the opinion of those who believed in blasphemy, that was the crucial step too far—by comparison, Mr. Hahn and his fellow members of the Old Undead seemed as user-friendly nowadays as a desktop console or an ATM.

"That doesn't console me, Mr. Hicks," Hahn said, contriving a sigh even though he was speaking through a microphone that was ill-adapted for the purpose. "The new people are my kin, whether they choose to look down on me or not, and no matter how much I might disapprove of their morals. I can't help wishing that they'd show a bit more restraint, though—their conduct reflects on all of us."

Tann was anxious to get on, but thought that he owed it to Hahn's sim—who was one of the oldest Undead inhabitants of the Elysium—to set his mind at rest. "I'm sure that there's nothing to worry about, Mr. Hahn," he said. "No serious damage has been done, and everything will be back to normal in a day or two."

It was the wrong line to take. "No serious damage?" Hahn objected. "From your viewpoint, perhaps—but from mine, this was a case of grievous bodily harm, if not attempted murder. I'm perfectly well aware of the fact that I'm not the person I'm modeled on, but that doesn't mean that I'm not a person. *Cogito ergo sum*, and all that. If that's all it takes, I'm as human as the next man—even if the next man is you, Mr. Hicks. No offense."

"None taken," Tann assured him. "I won't insult your intelligence by telling you that I know how you feel, but I do sympathize, and it's my duty to do my utmost to preserve you from harm. I know that you're a real person, even if you began life as a software mimic of the late Mr. Hahn, and no matter how slow Parliament has been to get to grips with the realities of the artificial afterlife. I really do feel for the injured parties. We're all in this together."

"I'm not getting at you, Mr., Hicks—I know that you're on the side of the angels. It's just…but I'm keeping you, and you need to see the extent of the damage, don't you? Perhaps we can talk later."

"We certainly can, Mr. Hahn," Tann assured him, as he took immediate advantage of the permission move on, accelerating his pace a little lest he be indefinitely delayed in reaching the crime scene. His greetings became perfunctory, although he knew that he would have to take more care when he finally got around to talking to the headpieces closest to the affected quartet, whose residents might have seen or heard something useful.

He hadn't been lying to Hahn's monument. He *did* feel for the injured parties—but he wasn't entirely unsympathetic, either, to the law's opinion that what had happened *wasn't* attempted murder, or even the infliction of grievous bodily harm, given that any damage inflicted on a headpiece was fully reparable. Organic memorials weren't as heavily armored as the stone-and-silicon versions, but they were resilient constructions, with considerable powers of self-repair, as well as the possibility of total replacement. A neuronet was more resistant to damage than the brains nature provided for the living, and its software was backed up, ready to be decanted into a replacement, if necessary. That, a least, was the official story.

In fact, Tann wasn't entirely sure how resilient the neuronets in the organic memorials were, and nor did anyone else, simply because that resilience had not yet been tested to the limit *in the field*, as it were. He was aware, though, that the back-up copies of the so-called mindfields of the inhabitants of Virgil's Elysium were the impressions made while the people in question were still alive. If the neuronets had to be extensively regenerated, let alone replaced and recharged, all the experiences the entombed individuals had undergone since their "resurrection" would be lost—which would defeat the object of choosing that manner of perpetuation, given that the whole point of organic memorials, at least according to their loudest champions, was to allow the Undead to continue to "grow" and "evolve" as individuals, resuming the path of mental development that had been so rudely cut off at the point of death. If the present Mr. Hahn were to be considered as a real person—as he presumably had to be, if the principle of *cogito ergo sum* were to be taken seriously—then any replacement derived from a back-up copy would be a different person. The present Mr. Hahn would be just as dead as his original model—however dead one considered that to be. No murderer of a living individual had yet been released by a court on the grounds that his victim's consciousness had been recorded, in order that the latter could join the ever-increasing ranks of the Undead.

So it isn't *just a case of trivial vandalism*, Tann reminded himself, as he approached the affected quartet of organic headpieces, *even if it's not attempted murder. I have to take it seriously, for the victims' sake, even if no one else will. I have to seek some sort of justice for them, even if no one else is sufficiently interested.*

Presumably in accordance with Roland Montfort's instructions, Sam Scarlett had strung yellow tape around the damaged quartet, looping the tape around the trunks of the slender silver birch trees that were discreetly positioned on the crest of the shallow rise where the four graves were located, in order to provide the complex with shade. Tann ducked under the tape, and greeted the guard with as much warmth as he could muster.

"I've talked to the sims in the surrounding quartets," Sam was quick to say, having observed Tann's greeting rituals. "They didn't see anything much—too dark. The intruder was careful; he wore a monomol oversuit as well as a mask, so as not to leave any trace. This wasn't a publicity stunt—he wanted to avoid being caught. That's good, right? Mr. Montfort seems keen to keep the whole thing hushed up"

"Thanks, Sam," Tann said, a trifle abstractedly. He wanted to survey the scene before getting caught up in discussion and speculation.

The situation of the damaged memorials seemed to leave little doubt that whoever had carried out the attack had targeted Mildred Barrow and her three companions specifically. Only a minority of the graves the intruder had passed by in reaching these had smart tombstones of any sort, but there were at least a dozen with organic superstructures. If the vandal had been prepared to settle for attacking the Undead at random, or even the biotechnologically-supported Undead, he would have had no need to come so far, no matter what his direction of approach had been.

There were four headpieces in the group, each one aligned with a point of the compass; that was the conventional arrangement at Virgil's Elysium, where matters of order and symmetry were taken seriously. Mildred Barrow was at the southernmost angle of the quadrilateral. The northern tip was occupied by Sarah Torquati, similarly beloved if the inscription on her plaque could be trusted, although Tann couldn't recall ever having seen any devoted Torquati children clustering eagerly around the grave. The eastern point was occupied by Bruno Holzhauser, who got more visitors than most, although Tann had got the impression, from a distance, that they weren't relatives. The western extremity was the tenancy of Richard Treguern, who was by far the chattiest of the four when Tann made his rounds, and was also the only one of the four, if Tann's impressions could be trusted, whose surviving relative was fully prepared to make the attempt to continue a meaningful relationship in defiance of the dictates of death—or, at least, prepared to mount a pretence to that effect.

The four headpieces were all conventional in shape and size—which is to say that they resembled life-sized busts of their living predecessors. They had heads and torsos but no arms—a lack that annoyed some of them considerably, although the energy required by movable arms and gripping hands would have imposed much heavier demands on the nutritional mechanisms supplying their hearts, lungs and neuronets—demands that were currently considered economically unreasonable. Tann sometimes thought of the headpieces as "Venus de Milos", not least because they tended to be prettified portraits—but the masked intruder had certainly put an end to the prettification of his four victims, even if the damage he had inflicted had been mainly superficial.

All of the headpieces had been blinded, their artificial eyes comprehensively smashed, along with the outer parts of their ears. Their mouths had been brutally assaulted too, undoubtedly causing considerable damage to their vocal apparatus, and their skulls had been caved in, in an obvious attempt to wreck the neuronets within. On the other hand, their chests were relatively unaffected; no concerted attempt had been made to spoil the females' modestly-swathed breasts or destroy their hearts. Relatively little blood had been shed; unlike head-wounds suffered by the living, those sustained by the Undead did not tend to bleed copiously, being swiftly and efficiently sealed by rapidly-growing artificial scar-tissue.

"We must be a terrible sight, Mr. Hicks," said Richard Treguern—causing Tann to start slightly, not having realized that any of the four could still speak. Evidently, Treguern could hear as well as speak, or he would not have known that Tann was there; he was certainly blind.

"The attacker certainly didn't pull his punches, Mr. Treguern," Tann replied, "but you'll be as handsome as ever in a few days' time. The bioengineers will replace any parts damaged beyond repair—which obviously doesn't include your neuronet. How are you feeling?" He knew that the Undead were able to suppress pain by an effort of consciousness, without requiring analgesic support, but he also knew that there was more to feeling well than a mere absence of pain.

"Not so bad," Treguern replied. "The others seem to have come off worse. Sarah can still hear, but apart from that, we only have the teepee—which is horribly slow, when you're in a panic, no matter how expert we've become in its use, for want of anything better to do. I don't think any of us has suffered serious brain damage, although Mildred still seems to be in shock, and none of us has much memory of the attack. We won't be much help to you, I'm afraid—we're all a trifle traumatized."

"There wasn't a lot to see, Mr. Treguern. It was dark, and the man was masked. Don't worry about it. The police will probably take a formal statement if they have time, but for the moment, I'm just trying to measure the extent of the damage."

"It was probably someone Bruno's wound up, wasn't it?" Treguern said. "Sarah thinks it was one of the kids, but it can't have been, can it? They couldn't have done something like this—not even that brute Nat Barrow. That Seymour Conway, on the other hand…."

"Let's not jump to any conclusions, Mr. Treguern. We have no idea who it was, as yet."

Tann was not unduly surprised by Treguern's conjectural leap, but nor was he surprised that Sarah Torquati had jumped to a different conclusion. The biotechnologically-supported Undead routinely generated more resentment among their surviving relatives than those preserved in smart stone-and-silicon—just as the latter tended to generate far more resentment than the recently-dead who had been content to observe the principle of ashes to ashes and dust to dust, and had not made provision in their wills for imitations of their consciousness to be artificially preserved. Although much of the rhetoric deployed in the controversy was concerned with alleged blasphemy and the hollowness or otherwise of the imitations in question, it all came down to money in the end. Cremation and the creation of inert memorials was cheap; the inorganic preservation of imitative consciousness was expensive, and the organic preservation of imitative consciousness was more expensive still. The children of the deceased, viewed as heirs apparent, had good reason to resent the expenditure of money that might have become theirs on the maintenance of an illusion of continued existence.

But why, Tann wondered, would a relative of one of the four members of the quartet have attacked the other three as well? Surely that suggested, as it obviously had to Richard Treguern, that it must be someone with a more general animosity against the Undead? On the other hand, that wouldn't explain the specific targeting of this quartet. It was not impossible, though, that whatever the specific motive might have been, the other three members of the group had been battered purely and simply to confuse the issue—to obscure the identity of the primary target, and hence the likely identity of the grudge-holding attacker.

Tann studied the extent of the damage that each headpiece had suffered with minute care. All four seemed to him to have been assaulted with a kind of controlled fury. The blows that had been struck first, presumably with an axe or a heavy hammer, had obviously been aimed specifically at the simulated faces' eyes, ears and mouths, but many had been hurried blows, which hadn't always hit the targets squarely. Relatively few of the subsequent blows had been calculated to drive deeply into the artificial flesh behind the superficial structures, aiming to disrupt, if not to destroy, the neuronets that served as the memorials' brains.

Tann estimated that there must have been at least sixty blows struck in all, almost evenly distributed about the four tombstones—*almost*, but not quite. If one of the four graves *had* been the prime target, and the others had been attacked merely in order to obscure that fact, the attacker had done a fairly thorough job, even though he hadn't bothered to move on to other memorial groups. Tann could see, however, that one of the four headpieces did seem to have been subjected to greater violence than the other three, at least in terms of the blows aimed to inflict deeper wounds.

Tann looked back at Sam Scarlett, who was watching him play Sherlock Holmes with a slightly disdainful smile. "I noticed the same thing," Sam said. "Mildred was hit the hardest, and sustained the worst damage. Might have been pure chance, though."

"Right," said Tann. Mischievously, he added: "You mustn't feel that this is your fault, Sam. I know you're embarrassed about it, or you'd have called me sooner, but there really wasn't anything you could have done. You were quite right not to chase the bastard down, given that he might have done the same to you that he did to the headpieces. Your brain's not so easily replaceable."

Sam scowled, but there was nothing in the speech to which he could object.

Was it possible, Tann wondered, that Nathaniel Barrow's presence in Montfort's office when he arrived had been no coincidence? Might Barrow have been spying on the nascent investigation, trying to ascertain where the finger of suspicion was likely to point? "Where, exactly, did the intruder gain entry?" he asked Scarlett.

"Over on the west side, where there are bushes on the far of the hedge, shielding him from the road. He made a beeline for this group. It was too dark to get any clear images through the ordinary camera eyes, but it looks as if we wouldn't have got much useful info in broad daylight. He was masked, and won't have left any fibers behind."

"Are you quite certain that it was a *he*?"

"Can't be absolutely certain, but that'd be my bet—Doug's too. He wasn't a big man—not as tall as you or me, more like Mr. Montfort's size—but he was certainly masculine in his build and movements."

Not Nathaniel Barrow, then, Tann thought. *He'd have been identifiable by his bulk alone.* "Could you make out the weapon he used?" he asked, aloud.

"Claw-hammer. Big enough, but not giant-sized. He used both parts of the head. Must have put some real power into the blows—the polymer in those lenses doesn't shatter like glass or squish like real eyeballs, but he's done a pretty good job of smashing it up."

"Has Doug made contact with Barrow, Holzhauser and Torquati via the teepee?"

"Yes—he phoned me to confirm that they were feeling okay, although Mr. Treguern had already told me. Ms. Torquati can hear us too, but she can only squawk in reply to questions. The bioengineers are supposed to coming out as soon as possible, although Mr. Montfort might not want them to go to work. He told me to preserve the scene, in case the police want to send a forensic team. They won't, of course."

"Probably not," Tann agreed. "It's awkward, though—from their viewpoint, this sort of thing is politically sensitive. They risk being damned if they don't make an effort, but double-damned if they do. We can't blame them for sticking rigidly to the letter of the law, given that their whole *raison d'être* is to enforce the law as it exists. On the other hand, it might be a good idea to wait until their responders confirm that it's okay for the bioengineers to get to work."

"Headpieces are supposed to be able to heal on their own, given time," Sam observed, glancing sideways at the headpiece in which Richard Treguern's sim was doubtless still listening. "We might not need the bioengineers at all."

"They'll all need new eyes," Tann opined, "and the two who can't hear will probably need new ears. I don't know about the neuronets. Look, collect some envelopes from the office, will you, and start collecting fragments of anything and everything, so that we can at least put on a show of having gathered up evidence for the police to send to their labs. Bring a portable camera, too. Take close-up photographs of everything, as it stands. Look for footprints between here and the hedge—any physical evidence whatsoever of the vandal's presence. It probably won't do us a damn bit of good, but we have to make the effort." *Or at least put on a show*, he repeated, silently.

"Yes, boss," said Sam, sourly.

"And Mr. Montfort asked me to spread the word that everyone's to be extra careful if the media get involved. He doesn't want anything being said that might encourage sensationalization."

"I'll tell Doug—and Frank and Sadiq, now that they'll have clocked on."

As Sam strode off, Tann went back to the westernmost head-piece and studied the ruined face at close range for a second time. He had to stoop slightly to do so. In principle, the headpieces could have been any size at all, and the clients had a wide range of choice, but no one interred in Virgil's Elysium had opted for the Easter Island look, and everyone had opted for physical as well as mental simulation with regard to the faces. All four of the vandalized memorials had artificial faces placed at much the same head height that the individuals in question had manifested in life—perhaps with an extra inch or two added on for vanity's sake, just as their features had been subtly improved, in the great tradition of court painters and cosmetic surgeons.

"Sam's gone, Mr. Treguern," Tann said, leaning forward slightly and speaking in a low tone, even though he had reason to believe that most of the other headpieces wouldn't have been able to hear him anyway. "We're alone now. We can talk privately."

"That's nice, Mr. Hicks," the simulation program mimicking Richard Treguern's personality replied, a little gruffly, "but I can't tell you anything confidentially that I haven't already said publicly. I really don't remember what happened. I was asleep, and didn't wake up until my eyes were being smashed, by which time it was too late to start paying close attention. It was an unpleasant experience, as you can imagine. I'm not hurting, but I'm feeling a bit dizzy."

As software entities, sims had no need to sleep, but as human simulations, they would not have been deemed sufficiently accurate had they not preserved that human privilege. They even dreamed, or claimed that they did.

"That's understandable, Mr. Treguern," Tann said, politely. "But you're in a better position than I am to have noticed something—anything—that might give us a clue as to the motive for the crime. You're observant, and you've apparently become quite an expert in using the teepee. If anyone can put me on the right track, it's you." *Flattery*, he thought, *will get you anywhere.*

"I heard you mention that Mildred got the worst of it," Treguern replied, warily, "but I can't believe that's significant. Her kids aren't nearly as bad as Sarah's—her two never visit, but their teepee traffic is quite open about their trying to get her *switched off*, as they put it.

Mildred's argue a lot, but Mildred's doing her level best to get them to accept her. She's almost got the younger son on her side, although that seems to have annoyed the other two. I quite liked him, until Mildred started trying to fix him up with my Pet. I couldn't have that, could I? Anyway, I still think it must have been Bruno who was the prime target, and the only reason he got away lightly is that the attacker overdid the business of trying to make it look as if he wasn't."

"I need something more than vague suspicions, Mr. Treguern," Tann said, patiently. "Is there anything specific you can tell me that might help to identify the guilty party—anything that actually constitutes evidence."

"No," Treguern admitted, although he sounded a trifle uncertain about it. "The only person whose innocence I'm sure of is my Pet. She might not want me to come home, but she wouldn't take a hammer to me—anyway, it was a man, so your assistant says." Treguern had spoken to Tann in the past about his longing to "go home", and his daughter Petronilla's reluctance to entertain any such possibility.

"You're probably right," Tann told the sim, resignedly. "There are plenty of people around who simply don't approve of your existence—who consider the Undead to be an insult to the natural order, a literally blasphemous presence in the world. There's no shortage of potential suspects in that direction, whether or not Bruno was the prime target."

"I know," Treguern said. "We might be imprisoned in tombstones, Mr. Hicks, but we hear the news. Things like this happen to people like us all the time. If we had arms, you know, we'd have been able to fight back, perhaps even overpower the attacker and hold him fast until your man arrived. We really ought to have hands, if we're to be true simulations of *Homo faber*."

"Maybe someday," Tann said, "once they've solved the energy problem. The inorganic Undead don't have access to truly effective robot bodies yet, and we're probably twenty or thirty years away from even the most rudimentary artificial androids. You only have to be patient, though—you're Undead. You might be able to live forever, even if you do get beaten up occasionally."

"If I have to live forever in a bloody tombstone," Treguern replied, glumly, "I'll go completely crazy. Even with company, and Pet, and access to the Web, and the ability to text anyone in the world through the teepee, I'm still *trapped*. I don't approve of some of the games the others get up to with the teepee, but I understand why they do it. I need hands, Mr. Hicks—or at least to go home. You understand that, don't you? Maybe it would have been better if the crazy guy with the claw-hammer had succeeded in ripping up my neuronet—at least then I could have started again from scratch."

"Don't say things like that, Mr. Treguern," Tann said, now speaking with sincerity. "There's already too much talk about Undead Paranoia, and other mental illnesses to which sims are increasingly suspected of being unduly prone. Don't give your enemies the satisfaction."

"I am careful," Treguern's sim assured him. "But you're a friend, aren't you, Mr. Hicks? I can be frank with you."

"Yes," Tann assured him.

"Anyway," Treguern continued, "it's only a matter of time. This was a botched job, wasn't it? He probably lost his bottle when he heard your man coming. Next time...."

"There's no reason to think that there will be a next time, Mr. Treguern. Incidents of this sort are rare—although I can understand why you might take a particular interest in news items of this sort, and thus imagine that they're not as rare as they are."

"Besides which," Treguern added, valiantly going along with the argument, "this wasn't a random incident, was it, Mr. Hicks. This quartet was singled out for attack, among all the others. There was *some* kind of personal motive. Bruno texts TV people a dozen times a day, you know, wanting them to take his silly lawsuit seriously and *give him a voice*. Bound to attract trouble eventually."

"Has Bruno said anything to you about that, over the teepee?" Tann asked. "Does he have any specific suspects in mind?" He would have to talk to Bruno himself, of course, but in much the same way that he'd thought that he might get more out of Treguern by talking to him confidentially, he assumed that Treguern might have got more out of Bruno Holzhauser than Holzhauser would be willing to say to him.

"No," the sim reported, "but he never has much to say to us—too busy talking to outsiders. Sarah's been banging on about her children trying to have her switched off, but she always does. I don't think she suspects them of being behind this, but she's worried that they might be able to use it somehow. Personally, I don't see that what's happened would help their case at all, even if they can find a lawyer daft enough to take it on. Bruno's already got a lawyer, of course, to argue his case for his continuing right to own property, but if you ask me, she's the one who ought to be reckoned mentally incompetent. He's got no chance, has he?"

"It's difficult to imagine a court giving AIs the right to own property, at present," Tann admitted. "That would open up a real can of worms—but you never know. We live in a fast-changing world. The AIs assisting solicitors are said to be better at the job than their masters, and it might be only a matter of time before we see AIs serving as judges. That would really shake things up. I can't stay and chat any longer, though, Mr. Treguern. I need to check with your neighbors, in case any of them saw or heard anything useful. I hope you feel better once the bioengineers have fitted your new eyes."

"I hope so too," Treguern replied, mournfully. "The view won't have changed, though—and Pet will still be annoyed with me because I want to come home, and Mildred will be on at me again about how good her Jakey and my Pet would be together."

Tan was already moving away. "Speak to you later, Mr. Treguern," he said—but he paused before leaving the space mapped out by the quartet, figuring that he ought to try to interview Sarah Torquati before moving on to other quartets, even if her ability to reply was impaired.

Richard Treguern was still talking, but the tone of his voice suggested that he knew that he was probably talking to himself. "Nobody knows what *settling down* means until he finds himself reborn as a cross between a statue and a tree," he muttered. "Dora and I only had the one child; it's not as if my kids would have to argue about which of them would have to put up with me, or whether they could share custody. I don't need to be a tombstone. I don't need to live in a godawful artificial paradise. I don't need to have friends of my own sort to keep me company. What I need is to *go home*…and a pair of arms…."

Tann couldn't help wondering whether Richard Treguern's sim might be capable of hiring a hit man to smash him up, in order to win some sympathy from his model's daughter and persuade her that he really might be better off in her own back garden. It seemed unlikely. The Undead Treguern knew as well as he did that the real point at issue was whether Petronilla Treguern would be better off with a sim of her late father perennially on hand, clamoring for her attention—but that didn't prevent the sim from nursing a sense of grievance. That, Tann thought, was either the biggest flaw in the simulation process or the most deadly accuracy. It was as difficult to generalize about the Undead as it was to generalize about the living, but one thing that an awful lot of them seemed to have in common was that they were past masters at nursing grudges against individuals, institutions and the world in general.

CHAPTER THREE

Sam Scarlett returned while Tann was still hesitating. He was carrying a camera and bearing an assortment of envelopes and plastic specimen-tubes. Tann nodded to him, and gestured for him to get on with the work of evidence-collection; then he moved over to the northernmost grave and stood in front of the headpiece, leaning forward in the same quasi-confidential manner that he had employed in addressing Richard Treguern's sim. Again he spoke quietly.

"I understand that you have difficulty making yourself understood, Ms. Torquati, although you can hear me pretty well," he said. "Is that correct."

He assumed that the squawk he received in reply was an affirmative one.

"Thanks, Ms. Torquati," he said. "Now, would you mind saying *no*, so that I can find out whether I can tell the difference?"

The negative squawk was, indeed, sufficiently different from the affirmative one for there to be little chance of confusion.

"That's good," Tann said. "Now, I'm going to ask questions that you can answer yes or no, so that we don't get into difficulties. With luck, the bioengineering team will be able to fix you up this afternoon, if your vocal apparatus hasn't healed in the interim, so that we can have a longer chat then—please be patient with me in the meantime. Now, did you wake up in time to see anything of the attack before your eyes were smashed?"

"No."

"Do you know of anyone who might have wanted to do this to you—I mean, to you specifically?"

"Yes."

Tann grimaced, but tried to control the expression, even though he knew full well that Sarah Torquati's sim couldn't see him. "Are you referring to one your children, Ms Torquati?"

"Yes."

"Is your reason for identifying your son as a suspect the fact that he and his sister have applied to have you...discontinued?"

This time, Sarah Torquati could not content herself with a one-word answer, although she did try to be brief.

"Ms. Torquati, I think what you just said is *They hate me*. Is that correct?"

"Yes."

"Well, Ms. Torquati, I'll be talking to your children later, and I'll certainly try to follow up that line of enquiry. I don't want to neglect any other possibilities, though, so I have to ask you whether you know of any reason why anyone might have had a specific reason for attacking one of your companions?"

"Yes."

"Do you mean Mr. Treguern?"

"No."

"Mr. Holzhauser?"

This time, the reply was two syllables long.

"Was that a *maybe*, Ms. Torquati?"

"Yes."

"Well, we'll have to talk about that later via the teepee. What about Ms. Barrow?"

There was a hesitation, followed by another blurred "Maybe".

"I'm sorry—do you mean that you *do* know of a reason why someone might attack Mildred like this?"

Another hesitation, then a "No." Sarah's sim had apparently changed her mind. There was a supplementary blur of sound that had more than three syllables, and didn't seem to be a name, but it was incomprehensible.

"I see," Tann said, although he didn't really see at all. "Thank you, Ms. Torquati." As he stood up he met Sam's eyes, and shook his head slightly to indicate that he had not discovered anything that was manifestly significant. He scanned the scene once more, in search of inspiration, but nothing leapt to his eye that could possibly qualify as a clue. "Thanks, Sam," he said. "Sorry about the extra hours added to your shift."

"No problem," Sam muttered. "Could do with the overtime. I'll stay as long as you like."

"I'll let you know. Keep up the good work. I'll talk to some of the neighbors before I check in with Montfort—more for their sake than in the hope of getting any useful information. I expect the boss will want to give me another token dressing-down before I start texting the other two victims and phoning their various relatives in the hope of being able to interrogate them. That won't be fun."

Sam nodded, not very sympathetically, and tried not to yawn as he got on with the job of compiling the evidential record that, in all probability, no one would ever make a serious attempt to examine and analyze.

Tann was correct in his estimation that none of the headpieces in neighboring quartets had any useful information to give him, but they delayed him for some time regardless, because he was also correct in his estimation that they would be in need of some reassurance. Like Mr. Hahn, several of them were afraid that it might be their turn next. He offered all of them the same reassurances, with the result that his words soon began to ring hollow in his own ears.

Afterwards, he reported his lack of progress back to Roland Montfort, who had apparently been on the telephone throughout the interval that Tann had spent outside, fielding all manner of enquiries from various sources. The effort of all that careful diplomacy was obviously beginning to tell on him.

"Do you know how much your perimeter security system costs, Mr. Hicks?" Montfort asked him, wearily.

"Of course I do," Tann told him. "I told you when it was installed that it wouldn't stop anyone who was sufficiently determined to get in. It's always done its job as well as could be expected, by alerting us to careless intruders. This one was a planned operation, mounted by someone who knew how to elude the alarms, and probably had a pretty good idea how much time they'd have at their disposal before Sam and Doug were alerted by the infrareds."

"Are you saying that this was some kind of inside job?"

"Not in the sense that there was any staff involvement. Whoever did it had probably visited the cemetery before, though, probably more than once, in order to familiarize themselves with the layout. He knew exactly where to find the quartet he was targeting, and how to reach it before there was any possibility of an effective response."

"We get a hundred visitors or more every day. There are more than three thousand graves on site—more than two hundred and fifty with smart tombstones of one sort or another. You'll have to narrow it down a lot further than that. I presume you mean someone who visits that particular group—one of the relatives."

"Not necessarily a relative, but it might be someone with a personal connection of some sort to one of the sims in that quartet."

"We have people here with higher celebrity ratings. Apart from Holzhauser, no one in that group was even significantly rich, let alone famous."

"Which might have magnified the resentment felt against the individual who paid for the manufacture and maintenance of the sim," Tann pointed out. "Have you printed out the relevant financial records, in case the police want to look at them?"

"Yes, but there's nothing in them that might provide a clue as the motive for the attack. I doubt that the police will do more than glance at them."

"From their viewpoint, Mr. Montfort, the whole affair is hardly worth a glance. In fact, it would probably be a diplomatic gaffe for them to take a particular interest. They won't want to appear to be taking sides in what's shaping up to be an angry dispute, if they can possibly avoid it. The only thing that might make them think twice about getting seriously involved is Holzhauser's lawyer, but she's not likely to make trouble of that sort."

"I should hope not," Montfort said, with some asperity. "That's the last thing we need."

"In the context of our own public relations, though," Tann reminded him, "we do have to be seen to be taking this seriously. The sims are anxious, and it isn't only the organics who are worried that they might be attacked next. The Undead might not be eligible to vote, but they're becoming numerous enough now to constitute a significant pressure group. We have to satisfy them, as well as their various outside contacts, that we're doing our best."

"That's why the board finances the security system, and why it pays your team's wages," Montfort said, defensively. "Whatever status they may have in law, we have to be seen to be looking after our sims *as if* they were people, or the whole economic basis of Virgil's Elysium will come under threat."

Tann could see that his boss was genuinely fearful. Whatever lingering possibility Montfort still had of promotion to the upper echelons of the corporation were presumably dwindling to zero before his mind's eye, while the possibility that he might get fired was being magnified in inverse proportion. "It could be worse, Mr. Montfort," Tann said, soothingly. "So far as I can tell, no permanent damage has been done. The bioengineers will accelerate the self-repair processes, patching in replacement tissues where necessary, and the sims will be probably be right as rain, without the necessity of rebooting the neuronets—unless you want the engineers to hold off on treating Ms. Torquati, in case her kids manage to get the switch-off order they've applied for."

"They won't get one this side of Christmas, if at all," Montfort said, dourly. "In the meantime, she's just as entitled to be fixed as the other three. I can't afford to offer the slightest evidence of neglect. Do you think Torquati's kids might be responsible for this?"

"She seems to—but no, I don't. This kind of publicity can't work to their advantage, so they're highly unlikely to have done anything of this sort. She and Richard Treguern both reckon that at least two of Mildred Barrow's kids have got it in for her too, but that's just the way their anxieties are running. May I take a quick look at those financial records?"

Montfort seemed reluctant, but had no grounds for a refusal. He picked up a file from his desk and passed it to Tann. "It's all in order," he said, as he did so. "All four paid for their own sims to be manufactured while they were still alive, and made provision in their wills for their permanent upkeep in organic matrices—although I wouldn't bet on any of the trusts, except for Holzhauser's, being able to keep up payments for more than a few decades, if that. The Torquati children are the only ones mounting any kind of formal challenge to the trust arrangements, although they can't expect to make a substantial profit, and might well emerge losers if they're not careful—legal expenses could cancel out any potential gain, and then some. Nat Barrow gets a little steamed up about things, but that's always been his way. He wouldn't bring the lawyers in, much less do anything as pointless as vandalize a grave—and it definitely wasn't him on the security tapes."

Tann scanned the various sets of figures for himself. The fee structures showed a remarkable lack of consistency, but that wasn't unusual, given the variability of costs and the fact that the technology was still developing at a rapid pace. He couldn't see anything remotely suspicious. "Shall I begin trying to talk to the relatives?" he asked. "They'll all have been notified by teepee texts, but it's only polite to contact them ourselves—or would you rather handle that?"

"Half of them have already called me," Montfort said, grimly. "If they're all going to be considered as suspects, though, it might be a good idea for you to talk to them, and see what impressions you get. Do you need the night-shift people to stay on, now that Frank and Sadiq are here?"

"Yes. Sam's gathering what physical evidence there is, and Doug's still trying to get the alarm systems back up to speed. I need Sadiq on the gate, in case the demo threatens to get out of hand, and Frank in the ops room. Sam and Doug can probably go home in a couple of hours, though, if nothing else turns up."

"Good," Montfort said. "Go fishing. Tell me if you find anything interesting."

Tann handed back the financial records, and then went back to his own office. He wasn't feeling overly confident about the potential results of his interviews, and not looking forward to them at all.

First of all, he texted Bruno Holzhauser over the teepee. It always seemed incongruous to Tann that organic sim telepathy should operate by means of the same texting system that had been developed for use by inorganic sims, but that seemed to be the only way that it could conveniently be done at present. It wasn't possible for the Undead's neuronets to transmit their own conscious verbalizations directly, because there was no easy way to encode them for transmission, but it was both feasible and cheap for them to trigger simple electronic signals that could be transmitted wirelessly to the Elysium's transmitter and translated into text at the receiving end. Something more suited to organic sims would doubtless be on the market soon, but in the meantime, everyone concerned simply had to make do.

THIS IS TANNEGUY HICKS, MR. HOLZHAUSER, he typed. I'M SORRY FOR THE DELAY IN GETTING IN TOUCH. RICHARD TREGUERN TOLD ME THAT YOU AND MILDRED BARROW ARE FUNDAMENTALLY OKAY, EVEN THOUGH YOU'VE LOST YOUR EYES AND EARS.

I KNEW THAT, Holzhauser replied, with typical curtness.

DO YOU HAVE ANY IDEA WHO MIGHT HAVE DONE THIS, MR. HOLZHAUSER?

I CAN'T GIVE YOU A NAME. THE POSSIBLE MOTIVES ARE OBVIOUS. THERE ARE PLENTY OF PEOPLE WHO WANT TO SHUT ME UP.

Tann hesitated over the possibility of inviting the sim to elaborate, but decided that it would only unleash a tirade, and would probably take far too long. Given that the motives in question *were* obvious, it would be a waste of time.

TRUE, he typed. THANKS. I'LL BE IN TOUCH AGAIN. It didn't seem worthwhile to ask whether Holzhauser had anything else to say. If he had, he would have said it—he wasn't the kind of person to procrastinate or wait to be asked. Besides which, he was probably busy communicating with the outside world—or trying to—and would only regard further conversation with Tann as an unwelcome distraction.

Apparently, Mildred Barrow was also busy communicating with someone else; she didn't reply to his enquiry signal, although he got a BUSY signal, which confirmed that she was still conscious and active.

Tann hesitated, and then decided that it was probably best to start making enquiries of the children. He decided that Richard Treguern's daughter, Petronilla, ought to be the first name on his list, but as he reached out to tap out her number on the desktop telephone, Sadiq Ashir put his head around the door.

"Sorry to interrupt, boss," he said. "I thought you ought to know that more people are gathering outside the gates—mostly anti-sim demonstrators, but some counter-demonstrators too. No media yet, but it's only a matter of time, especially if the slanging match gets serious. Frank says that we haven't made the headlines, but that the basic information is out on the Web, so it's probable that the crowd will get continue to get bigger. Doug's finished fixing the perimeter alarms, and he's relieved me at the gate while he waits for your approval to go home. Shall I let him go?"

"Ask him to wait a little while longer," Tann said, prudently. "Someone will have to stay on the gate all day, though, if only to keep an eye on the crowd. Keep your ears open, too—it's not impossible that the guilty party will start bragging to his friends, especially if TV cameras turn up."

"You think last night's attack was political?"

"It doesn't look as if it was planned that way," Tann told him, "but now that it's happened, it's certainly become political. We might have to call in reinforcements if things turn ugly, so it's probably a good idea to keep Doug and Sam around. Let me know as immediately if the situation looks like getting out of hand."

"We've got time yet," Sadiq assured him, before pulling back. "Conway and his fellow publicity-hunters will save their best efforts for when the TV cameras arrive."

Tann nodded, and completed tapping out Petronilla Treguern's phone number as the guard returned to his duties. He was on video, but she didn't reciprocate; to judge by the background noise, she was at work, in some kind of open-plan office.

"Miss Treguern," he said, "this is Tanneguy Hicks from Virgil's Elysium."

"It's okay," she said. "My Dad's already texted me to give me the whole story—every ghastly detail, and then some. Thank God he's all right, except for his eyes. Some of the others weren't so lucky, I gather."

"At present, we think that the damage is purely superficial," Tann assured her. "The neuronets supporting the sims are more resistant to damage than the perpetrator probably imagined. It will take time to ascertain whether there's any memory loss, though."

"According to Dad, they're all deaf, dumb and blind, except for him, who's just blind. Even that's a bit more than superficial. Dad says it's the kind of thing that could tip Mr. Holzhauser over the edge—mind you, Dad thinks everyone's a bit mad except for him, the living as well as the Undead. He thinks I'm completely batty, and he's still trying to run my life for me, even though he's dead. Thanks for calling, though."

"Do you have any idea who might have wanted to do something like this, Miss Treguern?"

"Me? Good God, no. I don't know any of the anti-Undead brigade, and I don't really know any of the other people who visit the quartet, although I've seen the Barrow children there. I've talked to Jacob in private a few times, because his mother keeps trying to get us together, even though Dad doesn't approve. He's a nice boy, really—not like his brute of a brother—so I've tried to let him down gently. Dad's pleased about that, but it really doesn't make it any more likely that I'm going to start campaigning to move him into my back garden. The trouble with life as a glorified tombstone is that it's all time and no action, so they all try to live vicariously, getting their kicks by interfering with the lives of their surviving relatives. I'll drop in to see Dad as soon as I can, but it'll probably be tomorrow at the earliest, maybe the day after. Got to go now. Bye."

She rang off without giving Tann the chance to ask another question.

Tann shook his head sorrowfully and looked up the number of Sarah Torquati's son, Geoffrey. He too was at work, and he too, inevitably, had already heard the news via the teepee. Tann was barely through his introduction before Geoffrey Torquati interrupted to say: "No, I didn't do it, and neither did Izzy. We're trying to get the idiot sham that claims to be our mother closed down—we certainly wouldn't waste our time smashing its cameras and mikes. I don't know how Mother ever got it into her head that training a program to imitate her would be a good idea, but it certainly wasn't either of us who put it there, and she certainly can't have been laboring under the misapprehension that it would delight or comfort us. So far as I'm concerned, I wouldn't dignify that *thing* by attacking it."

"Do you have any idea who might have attacked any of the other tombstones in the group?" Tann asked, feeling that he was just going through the motions, with no real prospect of obtaining any useful information.

"No, I don't—and I really couldn't give a damn who it was."

Geoffrey's sister Isabella was markedly less rude but no more helpful. "I really don't know anything about the other stones in the quartet," she said. "The sim sometimes tries to talk to me about them over the teepee, much as Mother used to rabbit on about her neighbors when she was alive, but I'm afraid that I never used to listen then, and I'm certainly not going to start now."

Jacob and Helena Barrow had also been notified of what had happened, but in their case the initial texts had presumably been elaborately supplemented with verbal discourse from Nathaniel.

"We're all very worried," Jacob told him, with more apparent sincerity than his brother had contrived. He was on picturephone, and Tann could see what Petronilla Treguern meant about the stark contrast between him and Nathaniel. "Mother's sim really doesn't need this. It could be quite traumatic. Mother had a difficult time before she died, you know, and that affected the sim during the re-cording process, so it wouldn't be at all surprising if the sim began to develop mental problems. There's a lot of talk about Undead Paranoia, isn't there?"

"Yes," Tann admitted, "But I'm sure that your mother...." He was glad when he was interrupted, because he wasn't really sure at all.

"If Mother was going to get herself recorded at all," Jacob went on, "she really should have done it earlier, when she was more *herself*. Sometimes, I wish I were a bit tougher, like Nat. He's able to think of the sim simply as a *thing*, whose resemblance or otherwise to Mum isn't of any significance, but I can't help thinking about Mum, and all my childhood memories, and finding the whole busi-ness slightly disturbing. It's caused some friction between Nat and me—he can be a bit of a bully sometimes, you know, and he knows how to hurt people. I texted the sim a few minutes ago, but I haven't had any reply. Helena's had no luck either. Have you managed to get through to her since she sent out her first cry for help?"

"The night-shift checked that she was okay," Tann said, evasively. "I'll check again now."

He didn't put the promise on the back-burner; he immediately sent another message to Mildred Barrow, asking how she felt.

I FEEL FINE, IN MYSELF, MR. HICKS, the reply came back, after only a few seconds' delay. HOW ARE THE OTHERS?

SUPERFICIAL DAMAGE, FOR THE MOST PART, Tann typed. RICHARD TREGUERN SAYS THAT YOU WERE IN SHOCK AFTER THE ATTACK. ARE YOU AWARE OF ANY MEMORY LOSS OR OTHER SYMPTOMS?

RICHARD'S ALWAYS TRYING TO MAKE OUT THAT THINGS ARE WORSE THAN THEY ARE. HE'S A BIT OF A DRAMA QUEEN, AND FAR TOO FOND OF SALACIOUS GOSSIP. I WAS A LITTLE DAZED AND CONFUSED, BUT I'M ALL RIGHT NOW.

YOUR CHILDREN ARE WORRIED. JACOB SAYS THAT HAVEN'T CONTACTED THEM SINCE YOU FIRST TOLD THEM WHAT HAPPENED.

FAT LOT THEY CARE, the answer came back. NOT THAT I THINK THEY MIGHT BE RESPONSIBLE. EVEN NAT WOULDN'T DO SOMETHING LIKE THIS. IT MUST HAVE BEEN SOME URBAN TERRORIST WITH A THING ABOUT THE UNDEAD. HAVE YOU SEEN WHAT PEOPLE ARE SAYING ABOUT US? THEY'RE CLAIMING THAT WE'RE ALL MENTALLY ILL. I'M NOT, AND NO MATTER HOW MUCH I DISAPPROVE OF SOME OF THEIR ANTICS, NOR IS ANY OF THE OTHER THREE. CAN YOU PROTECT US FROM FURTHER ATTACKS, MR. HICKS?

Good question, Tann thought. I'LL DO MY VERY BEST, MRS. BARROW, he typed.

BECAUSE NAT'S NOT JUST BEING MEAN WHEN HE SAYS THAT THE TRUST CAN'T POSSIBLY AFFORD TO PAY FOR EXTRA SECURITY, the sim continued. I WASN'T RICH LIKE MR. HOLZHAUSER, OR AN HEIRESS LIKE SARAH.

Tan recalled that the financial records had shown that Mildred Barrow had got a much better deal than the other three members of her quartet, and he could easily believe that the trust she'd set up for her upkeep couldn't stretch to any additional expenses. She probably had no more idea than he did what might happen if the trust couldn't meet future bills—thus far, the question of whether, and, if so, under what circumstances the Undead could be terminated had not yet been investigated in court.

THERE'S NO QUESTION AT PRESENT OF THE UNDEAD BEING ASKED TO FINANCE ANY EXTRA SECURITY, he typed, uncomfortably aware of the emptiness of any implied promise. Rapidly, he typed: DO YOU HAVE ANY INFORMATION THAT MIGHT ENABLE US TO IDENTIFY THE PERPETRATOR OF THE ATTACK?

NO, was the reply. JUST THAT IT WASN'T THE CHILDREN, NO MATTER WHAT THE OTHERS MIGHT THINK. THEY MIGHT NOT LIKE ME, AND THEY CAN'T QUITE ACCEPT ME AS THEIR MOTHER, BUT THEY WOULDN'T DO SOMETHING LIKE THIS.

THANK YOU, MRS. BARROW, Tann typed. I'LL LET YOU KNOW IF THERE'S ANY FURTHER NEWS.

He hesitated before phoning Helena Barrow, but decided that he might as well complete the set. She was perfectly happy to use a video link, even though she was at work; she had a self-enclosed office, decorated so austerely that it was impossible to deduce from the visual evidence exactly what it was that she did for a living. She was obviously intermediate in age between her two brothers, some five or six years younger than Nathaniel and about ten years older than Jacob. She was intermediate in size too, being very solidly built for a woman. Tann found himself wondering whether Sam Scarlett might conceivably have mistaken her for a man if she were wearing a mask and a body-stocking.

"Is Mother's headpiece all right?" was Helena's first question, although her tone lacked urgency.

"She seems to be," Tann told her. "I just had a teepee conversation with her, and she seems perfectly lucid."

"Really? She doesn't reply to my texts. I suppose she suspects that we had something to do with this, although I hope she had the decency not to tell you that."

"Why would she think that?" Tann asked, warily.

"She's got it into her head that we'd like to switch her off. I think she got it from one of the other headpieces in her quartet— some other imitation of a woman whose kids won't countenance the idea that she's anything but a hollow travesty of their actual mother. Mother always thought that Nat and I didn't love her when she was alive, even though neither of us ever did anything to make her think that, so it's not surprising that her sim thinks the same. We all drop in to visit the grave when we can—we're pretty regular, I think, but...well, it wasn't *our* idea to set up a sim in an organic tombstone, and no matter where you stand on the reality of artificial intelligence, it isn't *really* our mother, is she? I mean, how much can you really owe a lump of artificial wood with a fancy biocomputer inside it?"

"Do you have any idea who might have been responsible for the damage?" Tann asked, dutifully.

"This other woman's kids sound like a pretty vile lot," Helena Barrow said, "but I've never met them, and I dare say that mother's given her much the same impression of us, so I can't judge. She speaks highly of Petronilla what's-her-name, but that's because she's trying to fix something up between her and Jakey. If what she says about Petronilla's devotion to her Daddy is even half true, though, it's extremely unlikely to have been her. Who's the fourth angle of the square? I've been told more than once, but I can't quite bring it to mind."

"A man named Bruno Holzhauser."

"I remember—the sim who's trying to lay claim to his model's property. God only knows why—he still can't take it with him, because he isn't going anywhere, is he?"

It was a joke whose like Tann had heard before. "Thanks for your help, Ms. Barrow," he said. "If I learn anything, I'll be sure to let you know." He didn't feel conscience-stricken about not having told her that Mildred Barrow's sim had, in fact, denied any possibility that she or either of her brothers might be responsible for the attack.

According to the records, Bruno Holzhauser's heir apparent— whose inheritance was currently frozen in a legal limbo, while proceedings continued at the law's customary snail's pace—was a nephew named Carl Kohler. Tann hesitated again, but mustered the resolution to stick to the plan.

Carl, who seemed to be at home rather than at work, was also perfectly happy to be seen as well as heard. He turned out to be the first person Tann had called who had not previously been notified of the incident by teepee text-message. "Thanks for letting me know," he said. "For the record, I didn't do it. I was at home in bed—which isn't much of an alibi, I suppose, although I'd be very suspicious of anyone who had a better one, given the time at which you say it happened."

"No one is accusing you of anything, Mr. Kohler," Tann said. "Four headpieces were vandalized; there's no particular reason to think that your uncle was the primary target—unless you can think of one."

"Unless clinical insanity qualifies in itself, no," the young man replied. "He's doing his level best to make more enemies, though. I suppose the anti-Undead crazies might well have put him on their special blacklist, because of this silly legal business, but he doesn't have a cat in hell's chance of winning. That really doesn't bother me, you know, even though there's so much money at stake. I'm comfortable for the present. It'll be nice if and when I get it, but I'm not in any hurry—and I can't see that this is going to help me, or hurt him more than superficially, at all. Is there anyone else in the quartet that might be a target? I only saw the other graves a couple of times, and never really paid them much attention, but I guess you'd have to be a little crazy to want to be simulated after you're gone by an AI embedded in a tombstone."

"I'm not at liberty to discuss our other clients," Tann said, disingenuously. "I'll call again if I have any news of your uncle."

After ringing off, he texted a message to Sarah Torquati, asking how she was feeling.

IMPATIENT, was the reply. WHEN DO I GET MY EYES AND EARS BACK?

SOON, Tann typed. DO YOU HAVE ANY IDEA WHO MIGHT HAVE DONE THIS, APART FROM YOUR KIDS?

NOT REALLY, was the reply. SOMEBODY CRAZY AND STUPID. BRUNO'S BEEN STIRRING THINGS UP, OR TRYING

TO. HE COULD EASILY HAVE ANNOYED SOMEONE, BUT I HAVE NO IDEA WHO. THERE'S SOMETHING GOING ON BETWEEN THE BARROW KIDS, BUT I DON'T KNOW EXACTLY WHAT, AND I'M SURE IT'S NOT IMPORTANT. IF I WERE YOU, I'D CONCENTRATE MY ATTENTION ON BRUNO'S ENEMIES.

Tann hesitated over the possibility of asking another question, but eventually decided that it would be a waste of effort. He'd had enough of vague paranoid suspicions, for the time being. Instead, he decided to go to the ops room to see how things were developing at the main gate.

CHAPTER FOUR

Frank Corkindale had two cameras trained on the crowd, but its members didn't seem particularly unruly. As anti-Undead demos went, this one was still very low-key, with hardly a banner raised in anger. There were about thirty-five people in the main group, but they weren't getting excited yet. The news media obviously didn't consider it to be a big story; no vans had yet arrived with personnel and equipment.

The police, however, *had* arrived; over the CCTV link, Tann saw two uniformed officers get out on a marked car that had drawn up on the other side of the road without any siren screech. They ambled toward the gate, alongside the car park, at a leisurely pace. Both officers were female, although that was no longer supposed to be an indication that the dispatcher thought the crime unworthy of serious attention. Tann watched as Sadiq let them in, having presumably sent Doug Marcus home. None of the demonstrators tried to force a way in while the gate was ajar.

"We'd better let Montfort know that the cops are here, Frank," Tann said. "Leave it to me—I'll go down to meet them, and take them in personally."

"Don't blame you," Frank said. "The taller one's quite tasty, and I wouldn't kick the other one out of bed."

Tann sighed. "They'll be safe with me," he said. "I'm a married man."

"So am I," said Frank, glumly. "Montfort's not—but they're probably not his type." Tann had heard similar snide remarks before, but he had no reason to think that there was any basis to them and wouldn't have approved if there had been.

"Be careful, Frank," he said. "You're in the ops room, remember. Eyes and ears in every wall." He was already heading for the door as he spoke.

"Sure thing, boss," Frank called after him. "Make sure the pretty ladies give us a crime number, for insurance purposes, before they beat a hasty retreat and do their level best to forget the whole thing."

"There's not a lot the cops can do without assigning far more manpower than it's worth," Tann told him, before he closed the ops-room door behind him. He went on, silently: *And the same goes for us—except that we've got to try, for the sake of Virgil's public image.* For a moment, as he jogged along in order to intercept the policemen, he wondered whether it was conceivable that the attack might actually have been designed to hurt the Elysium's image, on behalf of a rival with better security, but there was no obvious candidate that might benefit from such a move.

Tann greeted the two policewomen, who looked him up and down in a skeptical fashion that seemed a trifle insulting. He was suddenly very conscious of the fact that his own uniform, although fabricated in a shade of blue that was only slightly less dark than theirs, was essentially an imitative travesty—except, of course, for the legend CHIEF SECURITY OFFICER inscribed in red letters over his right breast. "The cavalry has arrived," said the shorter of the two, who wore the slightly more malicious smirk. "You can let the professionals take over now."

Tann introduced himself, and suggested that the three of them should drop in on Roland Montfort before going out to the crime scene. The policewomen introduced themselves as Police Constables Anderson and York, Anderson being the taller one, whom Frank Corkindale had identified as the better-looking of the two. They were both brunettes in their late twenties, some five or six years younger than Tann, but they seemed to be seasoned officers, not probationers or Community Support Officers sent out for tokenistic reasons, and they certainly seemed to think of themselves as competent investigators. They agreed that it would be best to take a look at the damage as soon as they'd looked in on Roland Montfort to let him know that they'd arrived, for the sake of politeness.

Montfort made no attempt to delay them; he was engrossed in an incoming phone call, and didn't protest when Tann merely put his head around the office door to tell him that he was taking the police out to the crime scene. "I'll catch you up," he promised.

"The crowd outside your gate seems reasonably well-behaved," P.C. Anderson observed, as they left the administration block. "If the anti-Undead brigade had carried out the attack, you'd expect a bit more excitement than that."

"I would," Tann agreed. "I'd also expect the damage to be spread around a lot more. Once the alarm had been bypassed, anti-Undead protesters could have got a dozen people in as easily as one, with time to crack the headpieces of half a hundred sims. Instead, one lone intruder went to town on four of them—no serious damage, it seems, but enough to make sure that they were all blind. He'd probably have deafened more than two if ears were as vulnerable as eyes, but he might not have realized that they aren't. He certainly landed some solid blows, though—with feeling, it seems."

"What about the brains?" P.C. York asked.

"He does seem to have aimed some blows specifically at the neuronets in all four cases," Tann confirmed.

"Any one of them take more damage than the others?" Anderson asked, shrewdly.

"It looks to me as if the guy with the hammer tried a little harder, in that respect, to damage Mildred Barrow's sim," Tann confirmed, "but I might be inferring too much from appearances—it's perfectly possible that the blows were randomly distributed between the four victims."

Neither policewoman objected to his use of the term "victims", although their official attitude had to be that the real victims of the crime were the Virgil's Elysium Corporation—the notional owner, or at least the custodian, of the damaged headpieces—the trust funds established to pay for the upkeep of the headpieces, and the insurance companies that would have to fork out for the repairs.

When they reached the quartet the policewomen took a few moments to feign admiration of Sam's evidence collection, with suitably ironic smiles, before looking around themselves, with as much care as could be expected.

Tann watched them go through the motions, stationing himself next to Richard Treguern's headpiece.

"They sound sexy," Treguern muttered. "I do love a woman in uniform. Which one do you fancy?"

"You can't see them, Mr. Treguern," Tann pointed out.

"Just making conversation," Treguern said, in the same low tone. "You could give me a description. Just because arms aren't the only useful thing I don't have, it doesn't mean that I can't fantasize. The imagination is the most important sex organ of all, and once you've got the habit, you don't need the testosterone."

Tann reflected that he had never heard Mr. Hahn talk like that. There was supposed to be little or no difference, in programming terms, between sims embedded in inorganic matrices and sims incarnate in organic ones, but it certainly seemed that possession of actual flesh, however meager in its resources, made a marked difference to the attitudes of the newer sims. Rumor had it that it made a difference to their behavior too, but even Richard Treguern's tendency to gossip drew the line about going into detail about exactly what it was about his neighbors' behavior that aroused his disapproval—and Mildred Barrow's too, apparently.

"They're police officers looking for evidence, not strippers putting on a performance," Tann whispered, feeling a little like a naughty schoolboy engaging in smutty talk behind a teacher's back.

The policewomen obviously didn't think that it was worth their while to look very hard. After less than five minutes they were ready to head back. They were about to set forth when Roland Montfort came running to join them, evidently having found the time to tear himself away from his desktop console. "You aren't going to blow this matter up out of all proportion, I hope," he said to P.C. Anderson, presumably addressing her because she was slightly taller than her companion, rather than because he thought her the more attractive of the two.

"We are taking it seriously, sir," P.C. Anderson told him. "We'll do what we can to catch the person or persons responsible. I'm sure that your security team will be a great help. They seem to have done an excellent job of collecting physical evidence, and I'm sure that the tapes from your security cameras will provide useful evidence, if you'll forward copies to our tech team."

"Did you get anything useful out of the relatives, Mr. Hicks?" Montfort demanded of Tann.

Tann glanced at the headstones in an exaggerated fashion, to remind the manager that they weren't all deaf, and then drew Montfort and the two policewomen aside. "Nothing concrete," he murmured. "The only one who doesn't seem at all unhappy that the artificial shade of her dear departed parent is still around is Richard Treguern's daughter—but in all fairness, Richard has always seemed to me to be the only one of them that anyone would be glad still to have around. The only one with big money at stake is Carl Kohler, Holzhauser's nephew, but he doesn't have any obvious motive for doing something as manifestly pointless as this. It seems to me more likely that it's a personal thing—someone lashing out in frustration."

"At all four headpieces?" said P.C. York, skeptically.

"No, just at one," Tann said. "He probably attacked the others in the same way so that it wouldn't be obvious which one was the real target. If he didn't try quite as hard with the secondary targets, though, the odds are that the actual target was one of the more thorough jobs: Holzhauser or Barrow, with Barrow the marginal favorite."

"But you don't think Carl Kohler's behind it?" Roland Montfort said.

"No—but do I think it was personal, and I do think those two headpieces are the more likely targets," Tann said, carefully. "That doesn't mean that the children are the only suspects, even in Mildred's case."

"I looked at the visitors' book," Montfort told him, "but hardly anyone bothers to sign it. We can check the tapes for pictures of visitors, but it'll take forever. We have to keep in mind the fact that the sims can and do communicate electronically with the outside world, though. Even if the motive is personal, it could have been generated that way."

"You mean that some kind of grudge might have arisen from on-line sexual relationships?" P.C. Anderson suggested, "You think that one of their partners might have got a trifle upset if they found out they'd been having it off with a tombstone?"

Tann was slightly startled by that, in spite of all the rumors and the conversation he'd just had with Richard Treguern, but he found it interesting that the P.C. had jumped so swiftly to that particular conclusion. Montfort seemed slightly discomfited by the suggestion, as well he might. "There could be other scenarios that would work just as plausibly," the director said. "Bruno Holzhauser's sim has apparently been making a royal nuisance of himself while seeking publicity for his lawsuit. We don't have the authority to commandeer the sims' communication records, unfortunately." He glanced sideways at Tann as he spoke, as if looking for moral support.

"And we don't have the authority to let *you* look at any records we might commandeer," P.C. Anderson said, blandly.

"I don't suppose you can spare the time to look through them yourselves," Tann put in. "That's a shame."

"Such is life," said P.C. York. "I'm sorry we can't let you help out—it would make our job easier if we could."

"That's okay," Tann said, having formed a strong suspicion that the supposedly-sealed records might find their way to him somehow. "I understand the difficulty. If you need to talk to Sam Scarlett and Frank Corkindale about the evidence we've collected, you'll probably find them both in the ops room. Might I have a few moments with Mr. Montfort, if you can find your way there for yourselves?"

The two policewomen were only too happy to oblige.

"Are they going to create difficulties for us?" Montfort demanded.

"They seem quite prepared to do everything they can to avoid making a fuss," Tann assured him. "They really can't spare the manpower to treat it as a serious crime, given that there are real murders happening practically every day, and the financing of forensic science is always three steps behind the demand. They aren't giving us the brush-off, but I think they'll be perfectly happy to let us handle things our own way. Sam will hand over the evidence he's collected, and they'll take it in to the lab, just in case, but they won't be keen to invest any real effort in an investigation, unless we can give them good grounds for making an arrest."

Montfort seemed to take some comfort from this news.

"I'll have to send Doug home very soon, sir," Tann added. "He's due back on at midnight, and he needs to get some sleep. Is there any news from the bioengineers?"

"They say that they're giving it top priority," Montfort replied, in a wearily skeptical tone. "They reckon that they'll be here by two o'clock at the latest."

"Probably four at the earliest, then," Tann opined. "It doesn't matter—it's probably a two-day job anyhow. It's not just a matter of a few injections and patching in bits of new tissue; there's a complex adjustment and adaptation process. It's unfortunate that the artificial eyes are the easiest sense-organs to disable, and that their replacements take time to settle in. As soon as the policewomen have gone, I'll start reviewing all our video and audio tapes from last night, to see if there's anything I can pick up."

"Are there likely to be any DNA traces in the material that Scarlett has collected?"

"Dozens, probably—but none that are likely to belong to our intruder. If he took the trouble to put on a monomol one-piece from the neck down, he's unlikely to have been careless with his saliva and dandruff. He came prepared to leave no trace, unlike all the innocent people who've passed this way in the last couple of weeks. You do understand, I suppose, that even if we can figure out who did it, it might not be possible to mount a prosecution unless he actually confesses to the crime?"

"Quite frankly," the Elysium manager said, "I'd rather he didn't. Part of me would like this one to be caught, in order to set an example to others, but the other part just wants the whole thing to pass quietly into oblivion."

"If we can initiate a prosecution," Tann pointed out, "it would prevent people from thinking that all of our much-advertised security is just for show. I'd prefer people to think that it was real, and effective—wouldn't you?"

"Of course," Montfort agreed, dutifully but without overmuch enthusiasm. He probably didn't think that his job was actually at stake, but he was definitely worried.

Tann was worried too; he didn't suppose he'd get the sack if the intruder wasn't caught, but any prestige that might be attached to his position was certainly at stake. If he could solve the mystery, with or without a little help from the police, he'd come across as a detective. If he couldn't, he'd look more like a glorified janitor. He wanted to be seen as a man of substance, if only for Lucy's sake, and that of his as-yet-unborn second child. "If you don't mind my asking, sir," he said, as Montfort retreated again, "do you intend to become a resident of Virgil's Elysium yourself, some day?"

"Of course I do," the administrator replied curling his lip slightly to imply that he might be being sarcastic. "Company loyalty demands it—and I'll be able to take advantage of the staff discount."

As Tann reached the office complex again, twenty or thirty paces behind Roland Montfort, P.C. Anderson came out, looking for the two of them in order to say goodbye. "I think we have everything we need," she said. "I've given your ops room man a crime number for reference purposes. We'll get back to you if the lab finds anything. In the meantime, I wish you the best of luck with your own enquiries." She sounded reasonably sincere.

"Thanks," Tann said, figuring that he was probably going to need it.

When he got back to his own office, intending to review the security tapes of the incident, but not expecting to see anything therein that Sam Scarlett had missed, he found a woman waiting outside the door. Given the severe cut of her clothing, the perfect sleekness of her blonde hair, her somewhat aristocratic bearing, and the fact that she had been allowed through the gate, he deduced immediately that she was a solicitor.

"Tanneguy Hicks?" she enquired.

"That's me," Tann confirmed. "How can I help you?"

"I'm Mirella Coleridge. I represent…well, in a technical sense, I represent the Organization for the Protection and Advancement of Artificial Intelligences, but I have special responsibility for a number of individual cases, including that of Bruno Holzhauser's simulacrum."

Tann invited her into the office and offered her a chair before sitting down at his desk. "You're the person entrusted with trying to assert his right to the property his model owned while alive," he guessed. "A rather thankless task, I suppose, given the present state of the law."

"Not entirely thankless," she assured him, "and not entirely hopeless either, if that's what you're trying to imply. The law is in a perpetual state of flux, and attempts to guide its evolution are at least as important as attempts to negotiate its present application."

"But the principal battle's being fought in the U.S.A.," Tann observed. "That's where the basic issues are being hammered out in front of the cameras. The British courts won't even take it on at present."

"The American cases are being fought on the basis of rights issues arising from Constitutional law," Ms. Coleridge told him. "The debate there revolves around the issue of whether an AI, if proven to be genuinely self-aware, has to be considered human, and hence entitled to the privileges and responsibilities of citizenship. What we're attempting to do is employ a very different avenue of approach, merely proving that an AI, irrespective of whether it's human, or even provably self-aware, is an entity capable of holding property within the law. There are, you see, already numerous entities that are neither human nor self-aware, but which are entitled to hold property—corporations, trust funds and so on. Although corporations require directors and trust funds trustees, it's not actually specified in law that only humans can hold those positions, and it wouldn't be so great a step, legally speaking, to establish that sims of the sort contained in Virgil's Elysium are, in effect, already at least equal in status and influence to the nominated trustees administering the funds set up to support them. We don't actually have to prove that Mr. Holzhauser's sim is authentically self-aware, let alone human, in order to establish his right to own property—we just have to establish that he qualifies as one of the several kinds of entities capable of fulfilling that function in law."

"Wow," said Tann. "Beyond all the jargon, though, what the organization paying you wants to do is win human rights, or quasi-human rights, for AIs."

"Ultimately, yes," she agreed, smiling, "but it's impossible to calculate, at present, what process of incremental steps will get us to that destination. Who would have thought twenty years ago—or even ten—that the most significant population of advanced mimics of human mentality would be situated in graveyards?"

"Elysiums, please," said Tann, smiling back. "Or Havens—we don't quite have the nerve, as yet, to put the extra vowel in and call them Heavens."

Mirella Coleridge seemed to have tired of the preliminary banter. "Do you have any idea who attacked Bruno Holzhauser's headpiece, Mr. Hicks?" she asked, abruptly.

"No," he replied, with equal bluntness, "but I'm still investigating. There's no reason, as yet, to think that Holzhauser's sim was the primary target; Mildred Barrow's headpiece was attacked with even greater violence, if the evidence of my not-so-expert eye can be trusted."

"Are you implying that what happened to Bruno was merely collateral damage?"

Tann took note of the easy fashion in which the solicitor has slipped into first name terms in referring to the sim. "No," he said, "I'm just saying that, whatever the motive for the attack might have been, Mildred came off even worse."

The blonde woman smiled again, evidently approving of Tann's own use of a familiar name. "And what, in your not-so-inexpert judgment, was the probable motive for the attack?" she asked, keeping her tone light although her gaze was perfectly serious.

"I think it was personal," Tann said. "A vandal wouldn't have focused the attack so narrowly, passing dozens of other headpieces, all of them more conveniently placed, to get to the four he smashed. We get our fair share of demonstrators here, as you doubtless observed at the main gate, protesting against the implied blasphemy of our alleged attempts to pretend that we can raise the dead and preserve the souls of the dear departed in graven images, but they're a pretty anemic shower. If someone wanted to mount a big publicity stunt they'd target Highgate or Kensal Green—they wouldn't come this far out into the Thames Valley."

"I did notice that your demonstrators seemed a trifle confused," the solicitor admitted. "I don't suppose they'll know what attitude to take to last night's event until the media offer some suggestions, although I dare say they're ready to hail the perpetrator as a hero—the first man in Berkshire to strike a telling blow against the unholy legions of the Undead. You did say that it was a man, acting alone, didn't you?"

Tann realized that he had indeed said as much, without quite meaning to, but there seemed to be no reason why he should keep any of the details of his investigation secret, especially as Mirella Coleridge was likely to be more willing than the police, and perhaps more able, to offer tangible support.

"He won't be much of a martyr if we do catch him," Tann observed. "He's unlikely to face any penalty worse than a fine, although it would be nice if the magistrate gave him a community service order requiring him to help out in the cemetery."

"The Elysium, you mean," she reminded him, flashing another smile. "And you reckon that Mildred Barrow was most likely the prime target, the damage inflicted on the others being mere obfuscation?"

"Not necessarily," Tann countered. "If the blows really were intended to disable Mildred's neuronet, they seem to have failed—I talked to her via the teepee, and she seemed quite *compos mentis*, although Richard Treguern told me that she was in shock earlier, and she's probably not in a position to be certain whether or not she's suffered any amnesia as a result of the attack. The others seem mentally unimpaired too, although it's difficult to be sure."

"If she was the primary target, do you have any suspects?"

"Not really. She says that her model's children don't like her— the two older ones, at least—but that they wouldn't take a hammer to her. It definitely wasn't her older son who carried out the attack, although I suppose he could have organized a hit."

"A hit? You mean that the perpetrator could have been hired to do the job?"

"Of course he could. It's not the sort of thing a relative would be likely to do himself, is it? If it were planned in cold blood, that is."

"One can't expect prospective heirs to be overjoyed at the prospect of losing a substantial part of their inheritance in perpetuity," Ms. Coleridge said, in a level tone. "It's in their economic interest to take the view that the sims are instruments of deceit and mockery. How can they avoid being even more resentful when the sims insist on taking a continuing interest in their lives, making demands on their time and attention?"

"Mildred is alleged to have been trying to play the matchmaker with her younger son and Richard Treguern's daughter," Tann told her, wondering how significant the tidbit of information might be. "That could have added an extra measure to the resentment in question."

"That's interesting," the solicitor said, a trifle off-handedly. "Let me see—Treguern was in retail, wasn't he? Made his money out of smart clothing? Bruno was in the city, of course, and grew rich gambling with other people's money. Sarah Torquati inherited her money from wealthy parents, never did much in the way of paid work, although she liked to pride herself on her charitable endeavors. Barrow was a self-made woman, though, involved in consultancy work in sports science. Torquati died a widow, Treguern a widower, Bruno never married, and Mildred Barrow was a long-time divorcee whose ex-husband remarried long before her death. Have I got all that right?"

"So far as I know," Tann confirmed. "You've been doing your homework."

"Of course. How well would you say that the four members of the group got on with one another? Any friction?"

"There was no trouble between them that ever required my attention, but I don't have a lot of time to chat to the inmates, and there's way too much gossip for me to keep track of it. I really wouldn't know very much about their personal relationships."

"But you do have audio tapes of their conversations? And their teepee texts?"

"Audio tapes exist," Tann confirmed, "and teepee transcripts—but I don't have access to them. They're automatically sealed, and it requires a court order to open them—the police can get one easily enough, but I don't have the status."

"Really? Does that automatic protection imply that the directors of Virgil's Elysium have formally recognized their inmates' right to privacy?"

"No. It's supposedly a matter of protecting the privacy of the relatives and the sims' other correspondents. *You* might be able to get a court order granting you access to the records, if you think they'd be useful to your own case. They might be useful in proving 'authentic self-awareness', although no one seriously doubts any longer that sims are capable of conscious thought. The police will probably requisition them, although I'm not sure that they'll have time to go through them properly."

"Which might encourage them to let you have a look in their stead, on the sly?" the solicitor observed, rhetorically.

Tann made no comment.

"You say that you don't have a lot of time to chat to the inmates—but you do chat to them. You also said that Mildred Barrow seemed quite *compos mentis* to you when you checked up on her via teepee. In your informed opinion, then, are all four of the victims of the attack of sound mind?"

"Well, I couldn't swear to it," Tann hedged. "First of all, I'm no psychologist, and secondly, I'm not sure whether one can really speak of sims being *of sound mind* in the same way that one can of humans. The opposition in Bruno's case is claiming that he's incompetent to administer property, I believe, but I don't see how they'd go about proving that. He seems rational enough to me, but who am I to judge? They're all a little paranoid, but—as you pointed out yourself—that's entirely justified by the logic of their situation. Sarah's kids are trying to have her switched off, so they really are out to get her."

"That's an interesting case too, in legal terms," the solicitor confirmed. "Not likely to go before a judge any time soon, though—it's an even hotter potato than mine. Do you think that Sarah Torquati's children might have decided to take a short cut, and make an attempt switch her off themselves?"

"I doubt it—you'd be in a better position than I am to judge whether it would be easier, in legal terms, to prevent her sim being reloaded into the headpiece than to have an existing sim legally obliterated. If that was the plan, though, the hit man screwed it up. Sarah not only wasn't obliterated, she's still capable of making herself understood in term of audible speech, albeit vaguely."

"Do *you* think he screwed up?" the solicitor was quick to ask. "Or did he do exactly as much damage as he intended?"

Tann thought about it for a few seconds before saying: "I think he screwed up. I think he's an amateur who didn't really know what he was doing, and got too nervous to carry his plan through to its ultimate objective before fleeing the scene."

"Do you think he'll come back for a second bite at the cherry, then?"

Tann thought about that too. "I don't know," he said, pensively. "If he does, though, I'd sure as hell better catch him, or I'm going to look like an incompetent idiot."

His visitor paused, as if running through her mental agenda to make sure she hadn't forgotten anything. Then, she said: "Do *you* think the Undead deserve recognition as human beings, Mr. Hicks?"

Tann was slightly taken aback, although it fit the pattern of the interrogation. "It doesn't really matter what I think, does it?" he said, eventually.

"Yesterday, it didn't," Ms. Coleridge confirmed, a trifle brutally. "Tomorrow, it might. We don't know where this is heading yet, or how rapidly—but you can bet your boots that someone will try to make something of it, and if they succeed...."

"You, you mean," Tann said, rudely.

"Among others," she replied, frankly. "Well, *do* you?"

It took Tann a moment or so to catch up, and realize that she still wanted to know whether he thought the Undead qualified as human. "I've no idea," he said, honestly. "Ten years ago, all the talk about AIs being candidates for human status was focused on the programs supervising on-line multi-player games—surrogate gods in their own pocket universes—and the systems trading on the principal stock and currency exchanges. As you said, nobody would have predicted then that attention would shift to sims located in glorified gravestones, and maybe there'll be a new set of contenders next year, or the year after. To be honest, it doesn't really matter to me whether they're *authentically self-aware*, or however tomorrow's favorite catch-phrase will put it. They're just *there*, and it's my job to look after them as best I can—which includes trying to put their minds at rest when they get scared. If I can find out who did this, I will, but that's all I can do—deciding exactly what the culprit is guilty of, and how he ought to be punished, isn't really my business."

"Of course it's your business," the solicitor objected, "and it's simply not true that you have no idea. You might have the wrong idea, but you have an idea. Everybody does."

"Okay," Tann said. "My heart says yes, my head no—which is only to be expected. Given the extent to which we anthropomorphize our pets and our cars, how can we help responding in much the same way, emotionally, to entities that can talk to us as if they were human beings and send us texts to boot? But when we consider the matter rationally, how can we avoid knowing that anthropomorphizing is exactly what we're doing, projecting our own self-awareness on to the programs when we know perfectly well that they're only constructs, designed and built in labs? I certainly can't believe that the recording processes used in constructing the simulations are really capturing or duplicating souls, for later decantation into an authentic afterlife. The headpieces are exactly what their name proclaims them to be: memorials. They provide the illusion that some of our dearly-departed relatives aren't entirely gone, that some echo of them remains to remind us of who they were and what they meant to us. It's slightly unfortunate, though, that the sims cherish that illusion far more than its supposed beneficiaries."

"So you won't be setting up a trust fund to perpetuate yourself in this way?" the solicitor asked, mischievously.

"Not on my salary," Tann countered, glibly. "Although there is a staff discount available, according to Mr. Montfort."

The solicitor stood up. "Thank you, Mr. Hicks," she said. "You've been very helpful. I hope we'll be able to discuss the matter further, as more facts emerge and the situation evolves. If I discover anything relevant to your investigation I will, of course, let you know immediately."

"Thanks," said Tann. "I'm not sure that anything we find out is going to help your case, though—even if it turns out that Bruno Holzhauser *was* the prime target, and his property the prize at stake."

"Perhaps not," she agreed, "but you never can tell, when you're adrift in uncharted waters. Here's my card."

She handed him a handsomely-embossed smartcard. Tann threw it into a drawer as he got up to escort his visitor to the door.

Roland Montfort was hovering outside in the corridor, but he wasn't waiting to talk to Tann. The administrator immediately buttonholed the solicitor and steered her in the direction of his own office.

Out of your league, mate, Tann thought, *even if she is your type.* He returned conscientiously to his desk and slotted the first of the disks containing camera footage of the invader's progress into his computer.

CHAPTER FIVE

As Sam Scarlett had said, the ordinary cameras had picked up nothing but darkness, and the infrared ones merely displayed a vaguely human shape making a beeline for the four vandalized graves. The way the figure moved did strongly suggest that it was a man rather than a woman, but Tann wasn't prepared to take that for granted on the basis of a mere impression. The image became noticeably brighter as the attack actually began, and the silhouette of the claw-hammer was easily discernible on several occasions against the dimly glowing figures of the headpieces. Tann tried with all his might to deduce from the pattern of the frantic flailing which of the four headpieces was the primary target but could not do it.

Perhaps he will come back for another go, Tann thought, *if he's crazy enough—and there's certainly nothing here to indicate that he isn't. Better if he doesn't, though. If he got away a second time, my neck might be on the chopping-block—and I really can't see any way to make sure that he couldn't.*

He went back out into the grounds then, to see whether the bioengineers had arrived. They hadn't. He checked the main gate to see how the protest was going, but it still seemed to be hesitant and confused. No one had yet arrived, in person or via a phonescreen, to rouse the rabble to a proper pitch of indignation and to give them a specific focus for their complaints. Seymour Conway seemed to be as hungry for more information as Tann was, but Tann didn't give him any. He wandered back to the crime scene before returning to his office, in order to provide the anxious Undead with a few words of reassurance, and to have another conversation with Richard Treguern's sim.

"How are you feeling, Mr. Treguern?" he asked.

"How am I supposed to be feeling?" the injured headpiece replied. "I don't know—maybe that part of my neuronet has been torn or crushed. I'm not in pain, of course, but I hate not being able to see. Will the replacements work immediately, when the finally get round to installing them?"

"I don't think so," Tann told him, "but you'll get used to them soon enough. Mr. Treguern, I'd like you to cast your mind back, if you can, and review the events of the last week or so. Has anything happened in the vicinity of the quartet that struck you as odd?"

"Pet didn't seem quite herself when she last came to see me, if that's what you mean—although she never does seem quite herself nowadays. She went off to talk with Jacob Barrow, in a rather shifty fashion, but I expect they're both a bit pissed off with the old witch and wanted to have a chat about how to deal with her matchmaking ploys." Treguern kept his voice low, as if he suspected that Mildred Barrow's apparent loss of hearing might be a ruse.

"Did you see anyone hanging around that you didn't recognize?" Tann asked.

"There are always people passing by," the headpiece replied. "They look at us, you know—staring, as if we were freaks. That's one of the reasons why I want to go home. I don't like it here. I never wanted to come here in the first place, but Pet wanted me out of the way—out of sight and out of mind."

"Actually, Mr. Treguern, your daughter didn't have much of a choice in the matter," Tann told him, dutifully. "The old regulations for disposing of bodies are still in force, even though the situation is much more complicated now. The law always takes time to catch up with technological innovation. You can't *go home*, as you put it, unless and until the law is changed. For now, you can only stay in a licensed burial ground. It doesn't make sense, I know, but while your ashes are integrated into your organic structure, you're considered to be a corpse of sorts, subject to the regulations pertaining to corpses."

"Bloody nonsense. Holzhauser's got the right idea—get himself declared a person, so that he can spend his own money. Don't like the man much, but he'll be doing all of us a favor if he wins. I can just imagine the faces of Mildred's and Sarah's kids when they find that Mummy's clawing *all* the cash back. Sarah's got designs on Holzhauser, you know."

Tann hadn't known. "What sort of designs?" he asked.

"Marriage," Treguern specified. "Daft, I know—and not a white marriage either." He hesitated, but then went on: "They're at it all the time, by teepee, although neither of them seems to be at all exclusive. Can't blame them. Nothing much else to do, is there? I can't wait for the day to come when I can be something more than a head on a pole again—a fully-fledged android, able to go where I want and do what I want. A fully functional android, mind; I don't want any censorious mentality interfering with my anatomy."

"Of course not," said Tann, suppressing an impulse to laugh out loud. He couldn't help wondering, though, whether the datum regarding the "affair" between Sarah and Bruno might somehow be important. What if the attack *had* been some sort of crime of passion? He hoped that P.C. Anderson wouldn't be long delayed in slipping him a bootleg copy of the four victims' teepee communications, although the thought that many of them might belong in the XXX domain was more nauseating than titillating.

"I can only look eastwards, mind," Treguern reminded him. "I get to see lots of sunrises, but no sunsets. If anything sinister happens, it's more likely to be going on behind me than in front of me. Best ask Mildred when she can hear and talk again—no point teepee-texting; you'd wear your fingers out trying to keep up on a keyboard."

"Thanks, Mr. Treguern," Tann said, wondering as he moved on to Sarah Torquati's headpiece how anyone could possibly refrain from anthropomorphizing an AI like that, no matter how convinced intellectually they might be that the sim was only a program, devoid of "true" self-consciousness.

"Are you feeling any better, Ms. Torquati?" he asked the headpiece at the northernmost point of the quartet.

A croak emerged from the damaged vocal apparatus. It seemed to be optimistically affirmative in its inflection. Evidently, air was still making its way in and out of the headpiece's lungs, and the circulation of the blood within the body-cum-pedestal was still healthy.

"That's good," Tann said. "In case it's of any interest, the others all seem to be in reasonably good condition, although we won't know for sure until the bioengineers get here. I've talked to Bruno and Mildred via the teepee."

Three blurred syllables reverberated uneasily, which Tann took to be: "So have I." Of course she had. She probably knew far more about their condition and opinions than he did.

"Do you still think that it might have been one of your children who did this to you?" Tann asked.

"Yes."

"Geoffrey?"

"No."

Isabella, then—but not in person. "But Bruno Holzhauser's the one who's trying to stir things up," Tann said. "He's the one who's threatening to upset the whole apple-cart, if he wins his lawsuit. Isn't he a more likely target than you or Mildred Barrow?"

"Maybe." The blurred syllables seemed rather guarded, but that might have been an auditory illusion.

There seemed little point in asking for more details until he could talk to her again in clearer terms, by text if not audibly, so Tann paused for thought instead, but Sarah added another remark off her own bat.

"Did you say *No kids*, Ms. Torquati?" Tann asked.

"Yes."

"He does have a nephew, though."

The reply had three syllables—probably "Not the same."

"Okay—thanks, Ms. Torquati. Keep in touch with the others, will you? You all need to keep your spirits up until the bioengineers get through. You'll be able to see again, and speak normally, in a day or two.

Sarah Torquati's reply had two syllables, which might or might not have been "Bullshit." She knew what time it was, and how long ago the engineers would have been summoned. No wonder she and her fellows often felt neglected and unloved.

Tann went back to the office. Again, he found someone waiting for him. This time, he recognized Petronilla Treguern. She was still in her twenties, and probably hadn't yet needed the service of cosmetic engineers to dispose of a single crease or blemish. She had long jet black hair and dark, soulful eyes. "I managed to get away after all," she said. "I thought I ought to see you before going to see…my father."

"He's been bashed up pretty badly," Tann told her. "He can still hear and speak, but it might be a little distressing for you."

"He'll be all the more insistent that he wants to come home," she said, mournfully. "I've tried to explain that he can't, but he won't have it. I think he wants me to sneak in and dig him up, roots and all, and carry him off."

"I tried to explain too," Tann told her. "No matter what the ads might say, sims don't have the same mental flexibility as living people; their thinking tends to get stuck in a rut." *In more ways than one, apparently*, he didn't add,

"Dad's sim wasn't the real target, was he?" she said.

"I can't be sure, but I don't think so. Would you like me to come out to the quartet with you?"

"No, that's all right. I'm not going to faint or anything. Have any of Mildred's children been yet—she's the one who was the most badly hurt, wasn't she?"

"Nathaniel came early this morning; I expect the others haven't been able get away from work yet."

Petronilla frowned. "I would have thought Jacob was more likely to hurry to his mother's side," she said. "I hope…Sarah Torquati's kids won't come at all, though. Bruno Holzhauser has a nephew, apparently, but I've never met him."

"He's not a regular visitor either."

"Not surprising, in the circumstances," she judged, as she turned away and walked along the corridor. She didn't seem any less anxious and concerned for having talked to Tann. Even so, she said: "Thanks, Mr. Hicks," speaking over her shoulder as she moved away. Tann estimated that Richard Treguern must have been pushing fifty when she was born, if not a little older. How he must have doted on her, while he was alive! And how he must be trying to dote on her still, now that he was dead!

Tann went into his office and checked his desktop in-box. There was a massive file in it that appeared to have emerged from nowhere, as if by virtue of some random cosmic accident. It contained the teepee records of the four members of the afflicted quartet, going back several months. It would take weeks to read it all, but Tann figured that he might be lucky enough to pick out something relevant by skimming, and could at least get some notion of the victims' links to one another, and to the outside world. He locked his office door, lest anyone catch him indulging in a barely legal endeavor, and got stuck in.

He hadn't found anything significant by the time that the bioengineers finally arrived—at four o'clock on the dot, just as the official shift ended. Tann had to stay late in any case, in order to demonstrate his commitment to cracking the case, so it was no hardship to accompany the engineers to the quartet, in order that they could make a start on repairing the damage.

The senior engineer was a veteran named Sterling Dodgson, who had supervised most of the installations at Virgil's Elysium and carried out almost all of the necessary repairs. He had been in the business long before anyone had even thought of muscling in on the monument business with organic headpieces, and inevitably regarded such ventures as blots on the landscape of a noble art. His assistant, on this occasion, was a morose apprentice he introduced simply as "Jack". Jack's sullen expression evidently owed more to the necessity of working under Dodgson's supervision than to any distaste for the work to be done; he seemed genuinely upset by the sight of the ruined faces, and started his healing labors with a fine fervor while this boss proceeded and a markedly slower pace.

"Have to replace all eight of the eyes," Dodgson reported to Tann. "Too delicate by half—designed to maximize optical efficiency rather than resistance to wear and tear. Ears and vocal apparatus are sturdier, but we'll still have to replace about half the units. You are insured against this kind of vandalism, I hope?"

Tann wasn't unduly worried about the exact extent of the insurance that Roland Montfort and the sims might carry. "None of the sims remember seeing anything of the attack," he said to Dodgson, "but that doesn't mean that nothing registered on their retinas, right?"

"Neuronets probably went into shock," the bioengineer relied, laconically. "Sim consciousness isn't as prone to hysterical disturbance as the natural kind, but it has its frailties. The old story about human retinas retaining the last image formed before death is a myth, but artificial eyes are cleverer—we should be able to play back the last few seconds before the final disruption for most of the eyes, although I doubt we'll get anything at all from these two."

These two were Sarah Torquati's eyes. They didn't look any worse to Tann than the others, but he readily deferred to the expert opinion. "Mr. Montfort says that you're not to take the parts you're replacing away with you, in case the police want to send them to the lab," he remarked.

Dodgson rolled his eyes in complaint against the administrator's stupidity. "It's okay," he said. "I'll rip the data right here, and send copies to the cops and your office. The actual objects are just waste for recycling."

"Orders," said Tan, shrugging his shoulders to indicate his helplessness. "I'll give them back next time you call, so that you can recycle the materials."

Dodgson shrugged too, to indicate that he'd been around enough to understand the ways of the world. "The new ears will set in fairly quickly," he said. "The sims should get their hearing back by morning. The eyes will take a little longer, but some visual function will return during the day. The vocal apparatus will have to heal *in situ*, though—it'll be at least three days before this one can talk again." *This one* was Mildred Barrow.

"The old gal got hit worse than the others," Jack reported, pausing in his work. "Her neuronet's got some bad rips. Might be some serious damage to her mental faculties."

"I don't think so," Tann told the youth. "I talked to her via teepee, and she seemed okay."

"Teepee's not entirely reliable in that respect," Dodgson told him. "Like your mobile phone, the output mechanism is programmed to anticipate and guess what the user is trying to say, so the message sometimes comes out more coherent than it really is— unless, of course, the system makes a wrong guess, in which case it comes out more incoherent, for lack of swift correction."

"The teepee connection is buried deep," Jack added. "The weapon didn't reach it. What was it—some hind of crowbar?"

"A claw-hammer," Tann told him. "The attacker used the rear end of the head to tear up the insides after he'd smashed the eyes and ears with the flat end."

"Ouch," said Jack, sympathetically. "If she seemed okay over the teepee, it's probably worth letting the net heal on its own rather than putting in patches—it'll give a smoother result, if it works. The other affected organs have protected themselves reasonably well—no damage to any of the hearts, lungs or stomachs, although the blood-replenishment system has run their energy reserves down to next-to-nothing. You were right to top up their metabolites, but they'll need a boost to put their repair mech into overdrive."

It was actually Sam Scarlett who had given the headpieces an extra injection of nutrients and supplements, but Tann didn't bother to point that out.

"I'll prescribe a special diet for the next week," Dodgson said. "You'll have to be careful, though—these things can get addicted just like people can, and you don't want any of them turning into junkies."

"We can hear you, you know," Richard Treguern put in. "I can, anyway, and so can Sarah. We're texting progress reports to the others."

"That's okay," said the senior bioengineer wearily. "I don't say anything behind your backs that I wouldn't say to your faces. Unlike you."

A few hours before, Tann might not have understood the full significance of that remark, but he did now. Having spent a couple of hours skimming through the records of the quartet's supposedly-secret teepee communications, he had a better appreciation of the private lives of the undead. They weren't necessarily complimentary about the living when talking in the normal fashion, but the gloves really came off when they were communicating under cover—which seemed a little ungrateful to Tann, given that the undead owed their existence entirely to the ingenuity and effort of the living.

"You're going to be fine, sir," Jack said, standing up and turning to face Treguern, even though Treguern couldn't see him. "In a week, you'll be as good as new. The ladies to your right and left might take a little longer, but the other gentleman will be right as rain."

"Unless the bastard comes back," said Treguern.

Sarah Torquati added a plaintive squawk that was presumably an endorsement of the sentiment.

"We're going to do everything possible to make sure that doesn't happen, Mr. Treguern," Tann said, trying to sound more confident than he was.

Treguern wasn't fooled. "We have access to the Web," he reminded the Chief Security Officer. "We know exactly how long the perimeter is, and how many men you have. The alarms might have been reset, but that isn't going to make your response times any faster, is it? We want a twenty-four hour guard—an *armed* guard."

"You know that we're not licensed to carry weapons, Mr. Treguern—and you know perfectly well that if I put one man on duty here around the clock, other important duties would go undone. I simply don't have enough personnel to have three people on shift twenty-four hours a day."

"So hire some more," Treguern said, "and get a license to allow them to carry guns. Suppose the freak comes back with a shotgun, or a can of accelerant and a lighter?"

"It's not that easy to hire more guards and acquire firearms licenses, Mr. Treguern."

"Actually," the sim said, "it is. Bruno's already texted his lawyer instructing her to hire a properly licensed guard, and to sue the pants off his trustees if they won't stump up the money. *He*'s looking out for us, even if you aren't."

"Virgil's Elysium can't allow that, Mr. Treguern. The corporation can't have armed freelancers operating on its property—it's too dangerous. Bruno shouldn't have done that without consulting with me first."

"Well, he did," was Treguern's answer to that—after which he fell silent, probably engaged in teepee communication with his neighbors.

"Did I mention that they get paranoid, too—just like people, only more so," Sterling Dodgson observed, following his policy of not bothering to keep his voice down for fear of offending delicate ears.

You can hardly blame them for being paranoid, Tann thought, *given that there really are people out to destroy them, and that the law offers them no more protection than a rose bush.* "Do you have any idea who might have done this, Mr. Dodgson?" he asked aloud, for form's sake, before leaving the engineers to get on with it.

"Sure," said Dodgson. "Chuck a stone into that crowd of jerks gathered outside your gates. If you don't hit the guy who actually did it, you'll hit someone who could just as easily be these folks' next unwelcome visitor."

"Seymour Conway claims that his acolytes follow the rules of peaceful protest, and that they observe a strict code of non-violence," Tann said, although it didn't sound convincing even to him.

"You might find that their definition of non-violence is a little elastic, sir," Jack put in. "They might feel that taking a hammer to a headpiece doesn't count as violence, because a sim is only masquerading as a person."

"But they don't seem to know whether to approve or disapprove of what's happened," Tann replied. "They won't permit us interrogate them, because they have a strict policy of non-cooperation too, but the guys who've taken turns at the gate say that they seem just as puzzled as we are." He knew how weak the argument was; it only required one wolf in sheep's clothing to be hiding among the flock.

"That may be true of the people gathered there this morning," Dodgson told him, "but they were just the local nut jobs. Now the news is out that there might be scope for a bit of aggro, there'll be boot boys spoiling for action heading out from London and Slough. They might not have made any trouble yet, but it's odds on that they will. That gate's not going to hold them, you know—it was designed for show, not for defense."

The bioengineer seemed almost to be licking his lips in anticipation. Tann had to hope that the old man was exaggerating in the interests of melodrama. "The situation is under control," he lied, as he moved away in order to let them complete their work without any further distraction, and to avoid clocking up too much fruitless overtime. It was already past five.

On the way back to the office he phoned Mirella Coleridge.

"Mr. Hicks," she said, sounding pleased to hear from him. "Any developments?"

"Not at my end," he said, "except that I've got hundreds of hours of teepee transcripts to trawl through. You wouldn't believe some of the things that sims get up to—or perhaps you would, given that Bruno Holzhauser has recently instructed you to hire him an armed guard."

"I told him that it wouldn't be easy," the solicitor replied, with a slight sigh. "I rather hoped that the trustees would veto the expenditure, so that I wouldn't even have to try to run it past you and Mr. Montfort."

"And did they?"

"Not yet. They're in conference. I have a suspicion that they might actually agree to it."

"We can't," Tann said—but he couldn't help feeling slightly queasy, given that it would add to the Elysium's responsibility if there were a further incident. "How do you feel about it, Ms. Coleridge?"

"I'm neutral—but from the viewpoint of jurisprudence, I could see how it might set an interesting precedent."

"It implies that Holzhauser is convinced that he was the prime target of the attack."

"Not necessarily. Even if he were sure that the damage he'd suffered was collateral, he wouldn't want a repeat, would he? Will the bioengineers be able to extract any useful evidence from the damaged sense-organs?"

"They reckon that they can pick up sense-data not consciously remembered by the sims—but it's unlikely to be useful, given that it was dark and the attacker was masked. It's not going to give us a close-up of his face, unfortunately."

"And you're still no closer to identifying a likely personal motive?"

"Not yet—but I still have a lot of texts to trawl through. Something might catch my eye eventually. I'll carry on with that at home, if I can, but I really do have to go home soon. My wife's pregnant. I'm only the Elysium's Chief Security Officer, you know, not a real detective."

"You don't have to make excuses to me, Mr. Hicks. I'm grateful that you took the trouble to call. I'll call you if I find anything— but not in the dead of night. You'll need your sleep if you're to make a fresh start in the morning."

Tann still had numerous checks to make before he clocked off, and he also had to report his relative lack of progress to Roland Montfort, who seemed to have no pressing reason to return to his own home and evidently disapproved of the fact that Tann had.

"I've put a third man on for the midnight shift," Tann told him, "but I can't do that repeatedly unless we take on extra manpower. If we were to hire an extra man of our own, though, that might take the wind out of Holzhauser's campaign to hire a guard with a gun."

"I'll put it to the board," Montfort said, "but I can't see them going for it—this business has already put a big strain on the budget. The insurance company is quibbling, which makes matters even worse."

Tann checked his watch; it was nearly seven o'clock. "I'll be in at six-thirty," he said, on the grounds that coming in half an hour early would at least be showing willing. "Nothing significant is likely to happen before then." *Famous last words*, he couldn't help thinking.

CHAPTER SIX

It turned out that Tann's anxieties were far from groundless, although what actually happened came as a shock, all the more surprising because it reached him through the medium of broadcast news, labeled as a "breaking story" when it went out at ten o'clock.

Having virtually ignored the incident all through the day, the media vultures had finally decided to descend upon it in force—a decision apparently prompted by a combination of three unconnected circumstances. For one thing, they now had close-range footage of the assault, which could only have been obtained from the eyes that Sterling Dodgson and Jack had replaced. For another, they had at least some of the teepee transcripts that the police had surreptitiously forwarded to Tann in order that he could help out with their drudge-work. Thirdly, and perhaps most importantly—although the news editor would probably have axed the material on the grounds of lack of objectivity had the artificial-eye footage not added a useful visual dimension to the story—they had a series of text messages sent to them by Bruno Holzhauser's sim, alleging that he was the victim of a "murder conspiracy" designed to prevent him from carrying forward his legal battle for the right of the Undead: a conspiracy whose members cared so little about those same rights that its protagonists were willing to smash up "innocent mothers of ungrateful children" in a reckless fashion, simply because their headpieces were situated in close proximity to his. The texts in question would not have been such a tempting prospect had the news editor not had the others to hand, which permitted the newsreaders to question the description of Mildred Barrow and Sarah Torquati as "innocent", in a slyly teasing manner that promised further revelations.

"Oh shit!" Tann murmured, reflexively putting up his hands to cover his face as he slumped forward on the settee.

"Is that bad?" Meg asked, innocently, putting a hand on his shoulder in a gesture of moral support.

"Yes," he said, "it's very bad. The bastards are going to blow it up out of all proportion. There's nothing really there, but they think they can make something of it—and I'm going to get the blame."

"Why? What have you done?"

"Not a damn thing. The video footage must have come from one of the bioengineers, but I'll be held responsible for letting them leak it, even though there was nothing I could do to prevent it. The teepee transcripts probably leaked from the cop shop, but they aren't ever going to admit that, and I'm in possession of a set of bootleg copies, which I've even brought home from the office. Not only are the police likely to point the finger in my direction, in order to shield themselves, but they'll probably claim that I obtained the transcripts illegally. As for Bruno bloody Holzhauser, when the Elysium tries to come down on him for violating his tenancy agreement, he's going to tell anyone who'll listen that he was forced into it because I refused to let his trustees post an armed guard on the quartet. I'm going to be everybody's favorite scapegoat, cast as the villain of the piece."

"Oh," said Meg, somehow packing a wealth of meaning into the syllable, suggestive of the fact that she really didn't need any extra stress at this point in her pregnancy. She was evidently claiming a privileged position at the head of the scapegoat-hunting queue. After a pause, she said: "Is it true about the sims? Have they really been getting up to no good?"

"It depends what you mean by *no good*," Tann said. "Imagine what it would be like to be trapped in a motionless body without arms or legs, like a quadriplegic who can't even turn your head. You can see and hear and talk—at least until some crazy bastard takes it into his tiny mind to smash your head in—but you're locked in place, at the angles of a square with twelve meter sides, so the only people you can really talk to in private, as it were, are the people who condescend to visit you—except that even the people who do condescend to visit you are either openly or covertly resentful of your existence, and would rather you had never been created. The only relief you have from that situation is called telepathy, but that's a mere mockery, because it's just a matter of sending and receiving signals that aren't much more sophisticated than Morse code. You master it, of course—in fact, you become so skilled in its usage that you can mimic the best text-message addicts in the living world—and you use it to its maximum potential...which is probably greater than its inventors anticipated, in some ways, just as your own potential as simulated human intelligences is greater, in some ways, than your inventors anticipated. How could you possibly refrain from milking it for all it's worth?"

"Yes," said Meg, dubiously, "but *text-message sex*? You might expect that from a few living weirdoes, but not from sims intended to serve as memorials to the dead, for the solace and consolation of the living."

"If they really are intended for the solace and consolation of the living," Tann observed, "the system seems flawed, to say the least. For the most part, the living barely put on a show of toleration—which must hurt the Undead, given that they're designed to think of the living in question as their loved ones, their cherished offspring. And why not text-message sex, given that every other kind is denied them, although they're carefully equipped with the relevant desires and sentiments, in the interest of making them better mimics of human consciousness?"

"But they're not actually *human*, are they?" Meg said. "You've often said so yourself."

"So I have," Tann admitted. "The more I talk to them, though, the less sure I am of that. What I am sure of, though, is that if they aren't human, it's certainly no kindness to them to make them think they are. An AI sim running a telephone system, or a cyberspatial game, or even a smart car, knows what it is and what it's supposed to be. If it's capable of thinking *cogito ergo sum*, then it's also capable of being content with its unhuman lot—but how can sims designed as mimics of human personalities be happy, if they're imprisoned for life in the headpieces of graves? It didn't seem such a bad idea when it was just the old kind, incarnate in stone-and-silicon, but if you ask me, the new generation of organics has shown us what a bad idea it really is."

"I didn't know you felt so strongly about it," Meg observed.

Tann paused for a moment, in slight bewilderment, before saying: "Neither did I. I guess it's a side-effect of the job, and its associated responsibilities."

"But what can you or anyone else do about it?" Meg asked. "Do you want them all switched off, and laid to rest in cyberspatial tombs of their own?"

Tan had to think about that for a moment or two; then he said: "No—that's not an answer. I suppose that, at the very least, I'd like Richard Treguern to get his wish—a pair of arms, in the short term, with an eventual promise of authentic freedom of movement."

"For *tombstones?*"

"No," Tann repeated, after another momentary pause for that. "Not unless they want to continue to serve in that capacity. If a tombstone is self-aware and smart, then it ought to have the freedom to choose not to be a tombstone."

"It's a pity Lucy's asleep in bed," Meg observed. "She has no idea that her father is capable of such zealous fervor. On the other hand, perhaps it's as well that she is asleep—we wouldn't want to frighten her." It was said lightly, but Tann couldn't help feeling that he was being criticized, and in a rather unfair manner.

"This is going to change things for us, Meg," he said, softly, nodding his head at the TV screen. "This is going to make my job ten times harder, if it doesn't make it so impractical that the corporation will simply abolish it. Any minute now, the acid rain's going to start coming down on my poor hatless head."

Almost on cue, the phone buzzed. The tone had been set to QUIET in order not to disturb Lucy, but it sounded ominously loud to Tann. He didn't dare refuse the call, because the indicator said that it was the police.

It was P.C. Anderson, on picturephone. Tann put his own phone into visual mode too. "Are you watching the news?" the policewoman asked.

Tann confirmed that he was.

"Is the leak at your end?"

"No," Tann said—but a sudden surge of honesty compelled him to add: "Unless someone's been in my office since I left work, and got through my password-protection." He was thinking about Frank Corkindale, although he didn't want to name anyone.

"It could happen to any of us," P.C. Anderson said, more philosophically than Tann had expected and feared. "My inspector's going to have to make a statement now. He won't like being dragged into it, and he won't like our being forced to mount an all-out investigation, but we can't afford any more PR disasters this month. What time will you be in tomorrow morning?"

"Six-thirty."

"Right. Katy and I will meet you there, and you can fill us in. It would be really nice if we had something to report. I don't suppose the footage the TV people have is likely to give us any new leads?"

"Judging by what they actually showed, no. One masked maniac wielding a claw-hammer looks like any other. All the footage tells me is that he was in even more of a hurry than I thought—probably panicky, unless he got *really* carried away by righteous wrath. The sims won't tell us anything more, even if they could—all of them except for Holzhauser are probably afraid that their kids might have done it, even if Torquati is the only one prepared to say so. If they weren't paranoid before, they will be now."

"Do you think it's one of the children?"

"I don't know for sure—but it doesn't seem likely, unless there's something I'm missing. It would take a special kind of trigger to make a child smash up even a sim of a parent, and the attack would surely have been more focused if it had been that kind of crime of passion. Barrow only sustained slightly more damage than the others, which was as likely due to chance as planning. Whatever we might think of Holzhauser's recklessness, he has a point—it really does look as if the attacker has something against the Undead in general, and might well have singled out this particular quartet because of his presence within it."

"Right. Let's hope we can make some progress in the morning—preferably in time to generate a lunch-time news-break." She didn't sound hopeful.

As soon as the policewoman rang off, the phone buzzed again. By now, there were three callers queued up, and Tann figured that there would probably be more by the time he'd done his duty by a second caller. He refused one call from an unidentified source that was almost certainly a media reporter, and only hesitated momentarily before taking Roland Montfort's call ahead of Mirella Coleridge's.

"It's not my fault," Tann told his boss.

Fortunately, circumstances had now developed beyond the point at which the administrator's primary aim was to lay the blame on someone else. "I know," Montfort said. "It's that bastard bioengineer and Holzhauser's crazy sim. It wouldn't surprise me if they were in it together. Do you have any evidence to suggest that Holzhauser might have set up the whole thing just to get his paranoid ravings on to the prime-time news?"

"No." Tann said, curtly, "and I hope you won't repeat that within earshot of any media personnel. Holzhauser's lawyer would have us for breakfast. She's waiting for me to take her call now. I'll be in at six-thirty, as I said—at least there'll be a proper police investigation now; the two who called yesterday will be waiting for me at the gate." *You have to be careful what you wish for*, he added, silently, although he didn't dare say it aloud to Montfort, *in case you get it.*

"All right," the administrator said. "You handle the police and Holzhauser's lawyer; I'll handle the media as best I can. If anyone from Web news calls you, it's *no comment* and you tell them to talk to me, okay?"

"Fine," Tann said.

Mirella Coleridge took a more apologetic line. "I'm sorry about Bruno's outburst, Mr. Hicks," she said. "If he'd channeled it through me, I'd have softened it up considerably, but he didn't. He's the client; I'm just the employee. I'm all in favor of drumming up publicity for his suit, but it's not true that all publicity is good publicity, and the hints they're dropping suggest that they're going to go after him with ammunition drawn from the teepee transcripts. How bad will that be, do you think?"

"I've only skimmed through them," Tann said, "but pretty bad, if they decide to hit below the belt, so to speak." The newsreader hadn't used the word *necrophilia* and Tann wasn't about to do it either, but the solicitor knew as well as he did that sex always sells, especially unnatural sex.

"Who would have thought it?" she said, with a sigh. "Undead sims in textual orgies! I bet nobody anticipated that one when the first designs for organic memorials came off the drawing-board."

What Tann had just told Meg was still echoing in his consciousness. "They don't have any hands, Ms. Coleridge," he observed. "They get frustrated as well as bored, imprisoned in their motionless heads. They haven't got any sex-organs either, in the vulgar sense—but that doesn't stop them thinking, or wanting, or fantasizing. That's the way they're made."

"That's the line I'll have to take, on Bruno's behalf," the solicitor said. "I'm not looking forward to it. Some billable hours turn out to be a lot stickier than others."

When that conversation had finished in its turn, Tann switched the phone off and put it on the sideboard.

"I'm not so sure that it would be a good idea to give sims sex-organs," Meg immediately put in, resting her right hand on her swollen belly. "Do you want them to have the freedom to have babies, too…the freedom to found families?"

"When we put AIs in an organic envelope," Tann told her, "it seems that we rendered them vulnerable to all the frailties of the flesh, even if they haven't got the right anatomy to indulge in the everyday sins of the flesh. We created this mess, Meg—us, the living, not them. It's not the Undead's fault. Given that they can text through their teepee systems, and that they can use their imagination freely, this was inevitable—if we didn't see it coming, it's because we were stupid or willfully blind. It wouldn't be so bad, I suppose, if Bruno, Sarah and their intimate circle of Undead friends had stuck to texting one another, but it isn't at all surprising that they wanted to go further afield. The scandal would have kicked off soon enough anyway, I guess—it's just my bad luck that it was an unrelated incident in Virgil's Elysium that pushed the button."

"*Was* it unrelated?" Meg asked. "Mightn't it have been some-one's discovery of the smutty details of the sex lives of the Undead that triggered the attack?"

"That's a good question," Tan admitted. "Maybe so. That might help to explain the peculiar nature of the attack—but I can't help hoping that whoever did it had a slightly better motive than sexual bigotry…or necrophiliac jealousy. Mind you, it was the first thing P.C. Anderson thought of, so she'd obviously seen transcripts of the sort that were forwarded to me before. She must have known that there was a nasty carbuncle in formation, almost ready to burst. The police must have been keeping quiet about it, just as they used to keep quiet about the prevalence of autoerotic asphyxiation, and its tendency to make accidental deaths look like suicides. Are people going to think that I had some responsibility to keep tabs on this, and maybe even rein it in? Surely they can't…can they?"

"Of course not," Meg said, plumping for loyalty rather than scapegoating this time. "You're not to blame for any of this. You just happened to get caught in the net, the way dolphins used to do in tuna nets."

Given that dolphins were on the brink of extinction, it wasn't a comforting comparison. "I need some sleep," Tann said. "Tomorrow is going to be a very long day."

CHAPTER SEVEN

The crowd outside the gate had swelled substantially, in spite of the earliness of the hour, and seemed much more excited than before. It was now clearly divided into two substantial rival camps, but the supporters of "Undead rights" were still far outnumbered by those demanding the removal of all organic headpieces from Virgil's Elysium, England or the world.

Fortunately, P.C. Anderson and P.C. York were waiting in their patrol car, ready to leap out and help clear a way through the crowd for Tann, once he had quit his vehicle. Once inside the gate, they walked with him to the administration block.

"Still no reporters out there," P.C. Anderson observed. "Not so much as a hand-held camera. They'll be here by lunchtime, though."

"That's not my problem," Tann told them. "It's Roland Montfort's job to take care of PR."

"It's not our problem either," P.C. York put in, "but that'll only make sure that the inspector will be on our backs all the way. He hasn't even put a D.S. on the case to take the pressure off. Officially, it's still just vandalism. Nobody wants to take the paranoid sim seriously—but we've been up nearly all night, looking at evidence and following procedure. Neither of us got more than a couple of hours' sleep."

"Let's hope that the paranoid sim doesn't turn out to be right," Tann said. "Have you made any progress?"

"Quite a bit," Anderson told him, "but not quite enough to lead to an arrest, unfortunately. Tired or not, we need to keep going. At least you're fresh. We just have to press on tiredly, until we can join up all the dots and see the whole picture."

"The problem is that we don't actually have much in the way of relevant evidence to look at," Tann said, glumly. "All I can really do is keep on trawling through the teepee transcripts, in the hope that I might turn up something more nutritious than junk fodder for salacious gossip."

"At least you've got us to help you now," said P.C. Anderson, "and at least it'll keep us busy. We could do it just as easily at the station, of course, but it's better for us to have an on-site presence. We need to be seen to be doing something, even if we're just going through the motions. We'll probably need to talk to your victims again."

"Be my guest," Tann said. "You'll still have to use the teepee to talk to Barrow and Holzhauser, though, and Torquati too if you want to get any sense out of her. Their new eyes will probably be usable within the next few hours, and their ears probably work already, but their vocal apparatus won't heal for a couple more days, according to Mr. Dodgson."

"We'd better have a word with him too," P.C. York put in, stifling a yawn. "He might know how those retinal images found their way into the media's grubby hands—although I don't suppose he'll be in any hurry to tell us, if he does."

"You'll probably have to do follow-up interviews with the relatives too," Tann observed, with some slightly malicious pleasure. "Good luck with that."

After Tann had donned his uniform, checked with his staff and determined the rotas for the rest of the day, he and the two policewomen divided up the relevant tasks; he was delegated to continue his examination of the transcripts, while Anderson went out to the quartet and York questioned the victims who were incapable of speech through the teepee. That required York to sit at Tann's desk, but his office was big enough to hold two computer-stations, so he wasn't unduly inconvenienced; he swiftly improvised a second network link for himself.

The relatives didn't wait to be interviewed by the police, however; by seven-thirty, calls were queuing up on the Elysium switchboard, and Tann was obliged to come to Roland Montfort's rescue.

The first call he took was from Sarah Torquati's daughter Isabella.

"You can't win now," she said. "They're all going to be switched off, not just that vile thing pretending to be my mother. In fact, you need to take that one off-line right away, in order that mother's reputation isn't further besmirched. Geoff and I will get a court order if need be."

"It's not the prerogative of the staff of Virgil's Elysium to make decisions of that sort," Tan told her. "We will, of course, obey any court order that we receive. The police will want to talk to you, by the way—later this morning or this afternoon."

"Why? Surely they can't think that we had anything to do with the...incident. People are saying that it must have been one of these perverts who's being talking dirty to sims like my mother's—someone who didn't realize what they were talking to, in the beginning, but eventually realized that they were being conned."

"What people?" Tann asked. "Who's saying that?"

"Everybody. It's the principal topic of water-cooler gossip. Why did my mother's sim have to be caught up in it? Why couldn't it have been some other nest of vipers?"

"I don't know, Ms. Torquati," Tann said, unsympathetically. "Was it just chance, do you suppose, or was there a particular reason?"

"Aren't you the one who's supposed to be trying to figure that out?"

"Only one of them," Tann was now able to retort. "The professionals are on the job now. As I said, the police will be in touch later."

The second caller he selected from the queue was Carl Kohler. "Mr. Kohler," he said, not having to feign more interest than Isabella Torquati had been able to awaken in him. "This is Tanneguy Hicks. What can I do for you?"

"I can't get through to Bruno's sim. Is he all right? Has something happened to him?"

Tann felt a twinge of anxiety, in case something had and he didn't know about it. "I expect that he's cut his teepee connection temporarily," Tann said. "Having sown the media wind, he must be in danger of reaping the whirlwind. Don't worry—the bioengineers said that he'll be fine, in physical terms."

Kohler sighed. "He was always a bit fragile mentally," he said. "His death hasn't done his sim any favors in that regard. Getting smashed up might have tipped him over the edge. Sims are more vulnerable to that kind of breakdown than the living, it's said. Can you do anything to shield him, Mr. Hicks? I know that he's made his own bed, and will have to lie in it, but if you could help to turn away some of the flak, I'd be grateful."

"Do *you* have any reason to think that the attack was aimed at him, Mr. Kohler—or that it was his presence in the quartet that drew the attacker to it?"

"No reason based on evidence—but it can't have been a coincidence, can it?"

"It could," Tann said. *Except*, he thought, *that if it wasn't Holzhauser's presence in the quartet that led to it being targeted, exactly whose was it?*

"Please," said Kohler, "if you manage to talk to my uncle's sim, one way or another—and you're surely the person he's most likely to talk to—tell him to text me. I'm concerned about him."

"I'll do that," Tann promised.

As soon as the connection was broken he sent a text to Holzhauser, not really expecting a reply. Kohler was correct, though; Tann was one person with whom the sim was eager to communicate.

WHAT NEWS? Holzhauser asked.

NOTHING SUBSTANTIAL, Tann replied. YOUR INTERVENTION HAS MADE THE INVESTIGATION MORE DIFFICULT.

SORRY. DO I GET MY ARMED GUARD?

NO. THE LAST THING WE NEED IS SOMEONE GETTING SHOT.

NOT IF IT'S THE LUNATIC. HE'LL BE BACK TO FINISH THE JOB, IF YOU DON'T STOP HIM.

THERE'S NO REASON TO THINK SO, Tann typed, wishing that he could contrive a reassuring tone. YOUR NEPHEW CALLED. HE WANTS YOU TO CALL HIM, TO TELL HIM THAT YOU'RE OKAY.

HE'D RATHER I WASN'T—NOT THAT I THINK HE DID THIS. IT'S NOT HIS STYLE. THE BARROW BROTHERS ARE MORE LIKELY CANDIDATES FOR RADICALIZATION. DO THEY HAVE ALIBIS?

WE HAVE NO REASON TO THINK THAT THEY'RE IN-VOLVED, Tann typed, diplomatically. WE'RE EXPLORING ALL POSSIBILITIES. *We have to*, he thought, *in the absence of any authentic leads.*

IF I DIE, Holzhauser countered. MY LAWYER WILL HOLD YOU RESPONSIBLE. BETTER GET YOUR ASS IN GEAR, HICKS.

"You've already died," Tann murmured. "That's the problem, you daft old git." I'LL GET BUSY, THEN was what he actually typed. He didn't, though; there were more calls coming in—far more, obviously, than Roland Montfort could handle, or dared to ignore.

The next one Tann took was from Nathaniel Barrow.

"I've just had a text from Mother," Barrow said. "She's frightened. She says that she's being harassed."

"Harassed? By whom?"

"Some policewoman asking her impertinent questions. Aren't you supposed to be protecting the victims of the attack?"

"I'm working with the police on the investigation. I'm sorry if your mother considers P.C. York's questions to be impertinent, but we're still trying to discover the motive for the attack, and we have to follow up any lines of enquiry that present themselves."

"My mother is one of the victims here," Nathaniel Barrow continued. "She shouldn't be put in the pillory because of her private business. She's been sensitive about that sort of thing ever since Dad divorced her, even though we managed to keep the scandal out of the media then. You shouldn't have given that information to the vultures. We're thinking seriously about suing the cemetery for violation of trust."

Tann took note of the fact that Nathaniel Barrow was now talking about the sim as if she really were his mother, but nobly refrained from calling attention to the fact. It was on the tip of Tan's tongue to issue a formal denial that he or anyone else at Virgil's

Elysium had given any information to the media, but he was interrupted before voicing the statement by a screeching alarm. He slammed down the phone and whirled around to meet P.C. York's bewildered gaze.

"It's the perimeter alarm," he said, groaning. "Someone's broken through the hedge—it's probably nothing, but...."

He didn't need to say any more. The policewoman, who suddenly seemed wide awake, had already risen to her feet and was running to the door. She stood aside after going through it in order to let Tann lead the way. As they exited the building Tann raised his pocket picturephone to his face and demanded a status report from his staff.

"They're getting noisy at the main gate," reported the guard on duty there, "but there's no breach here. They're just acting up because someone with a TV camera has arrived."

"The breach is on the far side," the man on duty in the ops room reported. "The cameras show two masked men running through the grounds. One of them's carrying a chainsaw, the other an axe. They're heading straight for the quartet that was attacked before."

Tan groaned again. He glanced sideways at P.C. York to check that she'd heard, and couldn't help measuring her from top to toe. She was five foot five and reasonably sturdy, but the only weapons she was carrying were an asp and a pepper-spray. She didn't even have a Taser. Her lack of weaponry wasn't preventing her from traveling at top speed, though; she knew that her colleague needed reinforcements immediately. Tann had to stretch his stride to keep up with her. P.C. Anderson, he recalled, was an inch or two taller, but also slimmer. He didn't remember her being equipped any differently. For his own part, he had no weapons at all—not so much as a truncheon.

Sam Scarlett, who had been patrolling the grounds, was also running toward the threatened quartet from a thirty-degree angle. He did have a truncheon, and already had it in his hand, but Tann couldn't imagine it having much effect in a duel with an axe-man, let alone someone carrying a chainsaw.

Because the injured quartet was closer to the offices than the perimeter, all four of its would-be defenders were able to gather there before the two masked men reached it, and they were able to form a defensive line before the man with the chainsaw flicked the switch of its electric motor. Tann didn't dare hope that its battery might be too low to sustain it for more than a couple of minutes.

The masked men hesitated, presumably not having expected to find a police presence in addition to Tann's men, and perhaps a trifle more reluctant because the two police officers were both female. If they were maniacs, they didn't seem to be unscrupulous maniacs.

"I've called for back-up," P.C. Anderson said, ostensibly speaking to her colleague, although her words were clearly intended to reach the two invaders. "There'll be an Armed Response Vehicle here in twenty minutes—ten if the roads are clear."

This is Bracknell, Tann thought. *The roads are never clear. Better give the A.R.V. half an hour.*

Anderson was now looking directly at the two masked men, then, and said: "If armed police arrive to find a threat situation, or if any one of us has been injured, they'll shoot to kill."

"Better stand clear, then," growled the man with the axe. "You wouldn't want our blood on your conscience, would you?"

"Put down the weapons," Anderson commanded, in a tone especially trained for that purpose.

"They're not weapons," objected the man with the chainsaw. "They're tools. We're here to clear out some weeds."

"You can't have any doubt, now," the second intruder added, "that the trees with human faces are abominations that must be destroyed. You watch the news."

"They're not trees," Tann couldn't resist putting in. "Technically, they're xenoplastic hybrids of tissues ultimately derived from both plants and animals, including human tissues."

"Monsters," said the man with the axe. "Chimeras. Insults to the handiwork of God. Demonic mimics of human voices."

"Et cetera, et cetera," said Anderson. "They're still under our protection, whether as people or property, and we're still obliged to defend them. Now, put down the...tools and put your hands behind your heads. You're both under arrest for criminal trespass and threatening behavior."

The man with the buzzing chainsaw stepped forward, extending the instrument in front of him.

Anderson didn't flinch. "I'm not going to give you another warning," she said. "Drop the chainsaw, or the charge will be assault with a deadly weapon, which will see you banged up for at least five years."

"Just get out of the way," said the man with the axe, with feigned weariness. He didn't move forward—but P.C. York did, and a jet of pepper-spray hit the axe-man in the face.

If the mask had had clear plastic over its eyeholes, the stinging spray would have been useless, but the eyeholes were actual holes. Tann hadn't realized that the spray-gun had such a long range, and neither had its victim. The axe-man squealed, more in rage than pain—but he didn't drop the axe.

Tann made the curtest of gestures to Sam Scarlett, bidding him to help Anderson if necessary, before he hurled himself forward in support of York, who now seemed more threatened than threatening. As the axe-man moved blindly toward her, perhaps all the more dangerous because he couldn't see where the swinging head of his weapon was going, Tann dived underneath the swirling blade, tackling him around the thighs and head-butting him in the groin.

The axe-man folded up, and Tann felt the blade and haft of the axe come down on his back—but the edge of the blade was horizontal rather than vertical, and the heavy head of the implement only bruised his coccyx. Then York joined in the fight, swiping sideways with her asp at the man's forearm. Tann thought he could hear one of the bones break. At any rate, the momentum of the axe carried it out of the suddenly-relaxed grip, and the weapon was rendered harmless.

York was already turning around to face the man with the chainsaw. Tann came to his feet as rapidly as he could to complete a semicircle, while the axe-man stayed down, unable even to groan for want of breath.

All in all, Tann thought, the man still standing probably had the advantage, provided that he shut his eyes in time if Anderson fired her pepper-spray. A horizontal sweep of the buzzing chainsaw was capable of doing far more damage than the sweep of an axe, even against four opponents—but it had to be obvious to the man wielding the saw that he could not attain his objective without committing murder. No matter how little conscience he had about attacking sim-bearing headpieces, he still had compunctions with regard to mowing down living human beings.

Making a disgusted noise, the intruder switched off the chain-saw, and lowered it to the ground. Then he took off his mask. Tann had never seen his face before. His complexion was ruddy, making his blond eyebrows and pale blue eyes stand out, but his gaze was more tearful than steely. Tann couldn't tell whether the moistness was due to rage or frustration

"I'll take my day in court," the zealot said. "At least the media are interested now—and people will find out exactly how disgusting those loathsome things are."

"Wanker," was P.C. Anderson's immediate verdict—although her training caused her to mutter it, so that it was barely audible even to Tann.

"I don't suppose, by any chance, that you'd care to confess to the attack with the claw-hammer too?" Tann asked.

"If that had been me," the blond man replied, disgustedly, "I wouldn't have used a piddling little hammer, and I wouldn't have stopped until I was certain they'd been destroyed."

"You ran past plenty of potential targets," Anderson said, obviously keen to claim her share of the interrogation. "Why?"

"Like I said—I came to finish a botched job. Thanks to the lunatic who started whining to the TV people, they're famous now—the smut-talking talking heads everyone loves to hate. We won't be the last, you know."

If it wasn't personal before, Tann thought, *it is now. Righteous indignation or not, these idiots were looking for the media spotlight that Bruno Holzhauser finally contrived to claim. If we're not careful—and maybe even if we are—this affair is going to escalate so fast that it will get completely out of hand before the shift finishes.*

In the meantime, P.C. York had hauled the axe-man to his feet. "Better get an ambulance in, Jess, for form's sake," she said to Anderson. "Got to do things by the book."

Anderson was already phoning in the requisition. When she'd finished, she handcuffed the blond man, who put up no resistance. Already, he seemed to be posing for the flying cameras that had not yet put in an appearance, as if waiting for a close-up.

"Well," said Anderson, grimly, "I think your texting head might just have got his round-the-clock armed guard, courtesy of the tax-payer. The D.I. will be spitting feathers, but he can't fail to respond to this. The cretin's right—there probably will be others, if we give them half a chance."

"It's not our fault," York pointed out.

"It's not anyone's fault," Tann said. "The situation's taken on its own momentum—and we can't stop it."

"If you'd given us arms and hands in the first place," Richard Treguern called out, from behind him, "we could have nipped it in the bud by grabbing hold of the first maniac and holding him till you arrived." Still blind, the sim had no way of knowing exactly what had happened, but he had heard enough to deduce the essentials.

"Sure," said Tann. "Do you still want to go home, Mr. Treguern, to stand alone, exposed and unarmed in your own suburban garden?"

"I could have gone home long ago, if you and your kind hadn't screwed this whole thing up," Treguern retorted. "It's your fault that I need an armed guard—yours and Bruno's. It's a pity the imbecile can't hear me yet—I'd give him a piece of my mind. Can't do that properly by bloody teepee—too bloody slow."

"Don't be too sure that he can't hear you," Tann said, lingering behind while the two policewomen set off to march their prisoners back to the office block. "Replacement ears set in a good deal faster than replacement eyes—Mr. Dodgson said that Bruno's new ones should be working by now."

"Don't care," was Treguern's gruff response. "Hate the bastard anyway—don't care who knows it. Nobody likes the bugger. If the Hooray Henry with the hammer really did come for him, we'd have cheered him on, if he'd only let the rest of us alone, and wouldn't have shopped him even if he had shown his face."

Tann had been about to set off to follow the policewomen, but he stopped dead. "What do you mean, *Hooray Henry*?" he said.

"It's an expression," Treguern retorted, after a pause. "A bit before your time, maybe—but I'm an old man, or the ghost of one."

"It's not so far before my time that I don't understand the implication," Tann retorted. "Did you hear the man with the hammer say something during the attack, Mr. Treguern—something that allowed you to draw an inference from his accent?"

Treguern hesitated. "I don't know," he said, eventually. "Maybe—I can't remember. You've got Holzhauser's old ears as well as his eyes, though. If he did…."

Tann set off for the offices at a run. He hadn't had time to check any recordings that might have been recovered from the smashed ears, and he was willing to bet that the bioengineers hadn't even bothered, being more intent on ripping off something that they could sell to the TV news.

He found the recordings waiting in line for someone to take notice of them, and played them back. There wasn't much on Holzhauser's tape—mostly grunts and the clash of the hammer striking again and again, but on Mildred Barrow's tape there was something else: a muttered comment coming from her left as a blow was delivered to her head. Richard Treguern's headpiece was to the left of Mildred's, which was why he'd been able to hear it too, even though he no longer remembered having done so.

Contrary to Tann's initial expectation, there was no identifiable accent marking the six syllables, which were difficult to comprehend. He had to play them back three times before he was even moderately sure of what he had heard. So far as he could tell, the man wielding the hammer had pronounced a name, albeit a highly unlikely one: "Florrie Atatona."

"Who the hell is Florrie Atatona?" he muttered "and why would her name make Richard Treguern think about Hooray Henrys?"

He hesitated briefly as to whether it might be better to call one of the Barrow children, but he eventually decided to go straight to the source.

Mildred Barrow responded to his initial text immediately. WHAT HAPPENED? She demanded. RICHARD SAYS THERE'S BEEN ANOTHER ATTACK. I STILL CAN'T HEAR PROP-

ERLY, AND CAN'T SEE MUCH AT ALL, SO IT WAS ALL JUST NOISE AND A BLUR TO ME.

THERE WAS A SECOND INCIDENT, Tann confirmed. THANKS TO THE POLICE, IT WAS CONTAINED. DOES THE NAME FLORRIE ATATONA MEAN ANYTHING TO YOU?

NO.

ARE YOU SURE? I THINK IT'S WHAT THE ATTACKER SAID AS HE SMASHED YOUR HEADPIECE.

After a long pause, the answer came back. IT'S NOT SIGNIFI-CANT. FORGET IT. She broke the connection.

That puzzled Tann—and it had the opposite effect to the one apparently intended. The sim's evasion had to be more significant than any actual answer she could have given. It implied that she did know who the mysterious Florrie Atatona was, but didn't want to tell him.

Swiftly, he typed the name into a search engine; it produced no hits.

There seemed to be only one thing to do; if the name had meant something, even subconsciously, to Richard Treguern, the he was the most likely person to recognize it. Tann's fingers hesitated over the keyboard, but the teepee seemed too cumbersome a means of communication. Instead, he ran back to the quartet, and took up a position close enough to Treguern's headpiece in order to speak without being overheard.

"It's Tanneguy Hicks again, Mr. Treguern. Does the name Florrie Atatona mean anything to you?"

"It means enough for me to know that it isn't a name," Treguern replied, a trifle scornfully. "It's Latin. *Floreat Etona*—the motto of Eton College. Not that I went there myself, of course. Grammar school boy, me, and proud of it."

Tann realized that he'd misspelled the phrase when he'd texted it to Mildred Barrow—but she had apparently understood it anyway, after a few moments' thought, and had probably understood its significance in the context of the attack. Tann wondered whether either or both of her boys had gone to Eton. The school was less than twenty miles away from Virgil's Elysium, as the crow flew—not exactly local, but that hardly mattered, given that it took boarders.

"It's famous in another context too, of course," Richard Treguern added. "Apart from the Hooray Henrys of Eton with their stupid boating song."

"What context?" Tann asked.

"*Peter Pan*, you dummy," Treguern told him, as if it ought to have been perfectly obvious. "Captain Hook's last words, before he gets eaten by the crocodile."

Really? Tann thought. He was almost ready to believe that the datum might be relevant, given that the situation seemed to have become positively bizarre. Aloud, he said: "Why on Earth would someone attacking a group of the Undead be quoting Captain Hook's last words?"

"How should I know?" the sim retorted. "You're the detective—and I'm no pirate."

Perhaps I misheard, Tann thought. *Perhaps it only sounded like* Floreat Etona. *Perhaps it really was a name, but I mistook one of the syllables, preventing the search engine from dredging it up.* He cudgeled his brain, trying to conjure up a plausible alternative rendering, but he came up blank. "Damn it!" he said. "Thanks, Mr. Treguern—I guess it's back to the drawing-board."

He set off in the direction of the administration block. Roland Montfort came out to meet him, evidently having somehow become aware of his hasty expedition.

"Have you found something?" Montfort asked.

"I don't know," Tann told him. "I picked up something from the audio-tape recovered from one of the ears the bioengineers replaced. The man with the hammer muttered something as he was smashing Mildred Barrow's headpiece. I think she recognized it, but she denied it. I'd told her it was a name, but Richard Treguern identified it as a Latin motto."

"A *Latin motto*?" Montfort queried.

"Yes. *Floreat Etona*. Eton College—and the famous last words of Captain Hook, apparently." Tann stopped abruptly as soon as he had pronounced the last brief sentence. Roland Montfort had actually gone pale, with astonishing suddenness. He looked as if he might be about to suffer a panic attack.

The two men stared at one another, neither of them saying anything, until Tann finally plucked up the courage to ask: "Does that mean something to you, Mr. Montfort?"

"No," said Montfort.

Tann couldn't remember ever having heard a more blatant lie. "Where did you go to school, Mr. Montfort?" he asked, blandly.

"Reading," Montfort replied.

Reading was even closer to Virgil's Elysium than Windsor, where Eton College was located. Tann knew enough about the town to be aware that Montfort probably meant the prestigious Reading School, rather than merely a school in the town of Reading. It wasn't quite in the same league as Eton, but its pupils might conceivably make a grammar school boy like Richard Treguern think of Hooray Henrys.

"Come on, Mr. Montfort—let me in on the secret," Tann ventured. "Mildred Barrow clammed up too, but she obviously knows something I don't, just as you obviously do. If you want me to figure out who did this, you need to tell me."

"On due reflection," Montfort said, frostily, having apparently collected himself. "It might be best to leave this to the professionals, now that the police are fully involved. You might as well return to your normal duties, Mr. Hicks."

Tann could hardly believe his ears. "You're joking," he said. "Do you think this attack was aimed at *you*, Mr. Montfort? If you do, you'd better tell me—because the police, as you said yourself, are fully involved now...and they really are professionals. If there's a secret to be discovered, they'll winkle it out."

"Don't tell them," Montfort said, his tone uneasily suspended between a command and a plea. "Don't tell them what you've just told me." He hesitated, finally coming down on the side of command. "That's an order. If you value your job, keep quiet. Let the police do what they need to do, in their own way. Just *bow out*, will you?"

Fat chance, Tann thought—but he did value his job, and he knew that he was going to have to handle the matter carefully. It didn't help that he still didn't have a clue what *Floreat Etona* might signify, in the context of the assault on the four headpieces. "I think you ought to tell me what's going on, Mr. Montfort," he said. "I'm not your enemy."

Montfort was, however, far too well aware that Tann wasn't his friend either. "I've given you an order, Mr. Hicks," he repeated. "Go back to your normal routines. Let the police handle the investigation as they see fit. Try not to confuse them with irrelevant details."

"As you wish, Mr. Montfort," Tann said, after the slightest of pauses. "You're the boss, after all." As he continued on his way back to his office, however, he couldn't help wondering whether that might not be the case for very long.

CHAPTER EIGHT

Tann's first impulse, on settling back down at his improvised desk, was to text Mildred Barrow and resume his interrogation as subtly as he could, but he thought that might qualify as an overly provocative move.

Instead, he began a rapid investigation of the files held on the Elysium's network relating to the biographies of the four members of the quartet that had been attacked. None of them appeared to have any close relative who had been to Eton, but one datum that would have had no significance had he glimpsed it before did leap out at him now.

Nathaniel Barrow had attended Reading School. Although Tann could only guess at Roland Montfort's age, he judged that even if the two of them had not been in the same year, their careers at the school must have overlapped to a considerable extent. He noted, too, that Jacob Barrow had *not* been to Reading, even though his mother had still been living at the same address in Caversham when he had reached the appropriate age.

It only took a few further clicks to discover that one of Mildred Barrow's appointments as a consultant sports scientist had been at Reading School, although the position had been terminated immediately after Jacob's birth, a few years before her divorce from Andrew Barrow. Andrew Barrow had also been connected with the school while Nathaniel was a pupil there, helping to coach the rugby team.

Tann realized that Roland Montfort had not just been attempting an inappropriate mateyness when he had addressed Nathaniel Barrow as "Nat" the day before. He had been attempting to recall the terms of an ancient friendship. Tann wished that he had paid more attention to the exact fashion in which Nathaniel had emphasized the name "Roly" when he had flung it back in Montfort's face with seeming contempt.

Tann couldn't help wondering, now, about the precise significance of Nathaniel Barrow's presence in Montfort's office when he had turned up for work the day before. Perhaps his assumption that Nathaniel had dropped in to check on his mother's condition had been too ready. Perhaps Montfort and his visitor had suspected even then who might be responsible for the attack, and what the motive for it might be—but Tann thought that hypothesis too tenuous to be worth following. Montfort did not have the Machiavellian acumen necessary to encourage his Chief Security Officer to investigate the affair, however feebly, if his real desire had been to cover it up completely. No, Montfort had surely had no inkling then of the *Floreat Etona* connection, whatever it might be. On the other hand, Nathaniel....

"This is crazy," Tann muttered, just as P.C. York came back into the room.

"The A.R.V.'s gone again," she said, "and the van's collected the two crazies. Special Duties will assign a squad to guard the targets, one man at a time, working in four-hour shifts. He'll be armed with an automatic rifle. Let's hope that discourages further intrusion rather than prompting future intruders to bring guns of their own. What's crazy?"

"I just checked the audio tapes made from the damaged artificial ears," Tann told her. He only hesitated briefly over Montfort's belated instruction not to confuse the policed with irrelevant details; he wasn't about to start withholding evidence when he didn't know himself what its implications might be. "As the guy with the claw-hammer struck one of his blows," he told the policewoman, "against Mildred Barrow, I think, he muttered something. Check it out and see what you make of it."

He transmitted the audio file from one desktop to the other.

York listened to the tape three times over, and then said: "I can't quite make it out. What do you think he's saying?"

"*Floreat Etona,*" Tann quoted, flatly.

"What does that mean?"

"It's the motto of Eton College—and, apparently, Captain Hook's famous last words in *Peter Pan*."

"*Peter Pan*?"

"It's a play."

"I know what it is," she replied, acidly. "But what can it possibly have to do with the investigation? Come to that, what can Eton College have to do with it…unless one of our suspects was at school there?"

"None of the children were there. The phrase meant something to Mildred Barrow, though, although she wouldn't say what. It put the wind up Roland Montfort too."

"Your boss?"

"Yes."

"You think *he* might have been the target of the attack?"

"Maybe. One of them, at any rate. He ordered me to stop my investigation and leave it to you."

"Did he, now? Is that what you're doing?"

"I'm the Elysium's Chief Security Officer," Tann reminded her. "It's my job to support and cooperate with the police in any way I can."

York smiled at that, in a strangely predatory fashion. "Good," she said. "Let's…hang on a minute—did you say *Captain Hook*'s last words?"

"That's right—he's the pirate in *Peter Pan*."

The smile immediately turned back into a frown. "I know that," she said. "It just took time for the name to strike a chord. I noticed something in one of those teepee transcripts while I was scanning them last night—while I was practically falling asleep at the desk, unfortunately. The saucier dealings tend to be pseudonymous on both sides, for obvious reasons…and I'm pretty sure that I noticed *James Hook* among the pseudonyms. I didn't think anything of it at the time. Didn't you see it?"

"No," Tann said, suddenly struck by the horrible thought that he too might have seen it and thought nothing of it, to the extent that he had completely forgotten it.

"Hang on while I do a quick machine search…." York bent over the desk; the search only took a few seconds. "Yes—it crops up in a dozen different exchanges, some of them quite long—but not in correspondence involving Mildred Barrow."

"Richard Treguern?"

"No, Sarah Torquati. It isn't Torquati who uses it, though; it's the guy—presuming that he is a guy—she's talking to."

"Treguern told me that Torquati had been getting into orgiastic talk with Holzhauser. We are talking hard core smut, I assume? Could James Hook be Holzhauser?"

"No, that would be obvious—even if the dialogue were being routed by a roundabout path, for purposes of concealment. I'd rather not repeat this stuff aloud, if you don't mind, but both participants are certainly pretending—or fantasizing—that they're alive. I'll need the services of a specialist hacker to figure out who's behind the pseudonym, I'm afraid. I suppose it *could* be one of the children—or one of those idiots we just arrested. I had him, by the way."

"Who?" said Tann, mystified.

"The guy with the axe. You didn't have to dive in head first. You could have been hurt. If there's a next time, don't be so quick off the mark. Best to keep your distance in situations like that. I could have nullified the threat with the asp."

"Okay," said Tann, dubiously. "Can we get back to the issue in hand? Can you tell from the exchanges thrown up by the search whether this James Hook ever figured out that he was dealing with an Undead correspondent?"

York studied the information on her screen for several minutes, scrolling through it carefully. Tann got to his feet and tried to read over her shoulder, but there was insufficient space behind the desk for him to get into a comfortable position.

"She didn't let on," York said, eventually. "If he figured it out, he didn't let any evidence show here. We'll have to get a court order to extend our search to his records, and the IT people will have to track down his real name and other aliases. That might take until tomorrow. It's an interesting lead, though. How are we going to play it with Torquati? We'll have to talk to her again, more carefully than before. She can hear, right, but she can't talk properly? Should we go out there, or use the teepee?"

Tann couldn't help feeling that he was being hustled along, and was acutely conscious of the fact that it might be more diplomatic for him to take a back seat, however keen he was to be in on the action.

"Best use the teepee," he said. "If you go out there to ask the questions verbally, Treguern will probably be able to overhear you, and he'd be sure to text the other two. Best to keep thing confidential, for the moment."

"Okay," she said. "I gather that you want me to do it—because of your boss ordering you to drop it?"

"It doesn't really matter which of us does the typing," he said, "but we need to use your ID. Montfort knows that you're using my desk."

"Okay," she said. "I'll be sure to make it official." She texted Sarah Torquati, saying that she needed to ask a few questions related to her enquiries.

IS IT ABOUT THE SECOND INCIDENT? the sim replied. I HEARD YOU TALKING TO SOMEONE, BUT I COULDN'T MAKE OUT WHAT WAS HAPPENING.

A SECOND ATTACK WAS AVERTED, P. C. York typed. I'M SORRY TO HAVE TO ASK YOU ABOUT THIS, MS. TORQUATI, BUT WE NEED TO FIND OUT EVERYTHING WE CAN ABOUT SOMEONE WHO USES THE PSEUDONYM "JAMES HOOK" IN CORRESPONDENCE WITH YOU.

There was a long pause before the answer came back. IF YOU HAVE TRANSCRIPTS OF MY TEEPEE TRAFFIC, it said, YOU KNOW AS MUCH AS I DO.

THE PERSON USING THAT PSEUDONYM NEVER VISITED YOU? York typed.

DON'T BE RIDICULOUS was the reply.

WHAT DO YOU UNDERSTAND BY "JAMES HOOK"? the policewoman typed.

A HOOK IS SOMETHING THAT PICKS THINGS UP. It was impossible to tell for sure whether the reply was sarcastic, but Tann figured that it almost certainly was. Like everyone else, Sarah Torquati was hedging, unwilling to reveal whatever it was that she knew.

WHAT ABOUT "FLOREAT ETONA"? York asked.

DOESN'T RING A BELL.

PETER PAN?

This time, there was a pause. Finally, a reply came, in segments. GEOFFREY SAYS THAT I'M NOT ALLOWING HIM TO GROW UP, it read. HE WANTS TO KILL ME. HE SAYS THAT I'M STEALING HIS POTENTIAL. DID HE DO THIS TO ME?

WE DON'T KNOW THAT, P.C. York was quick to type. WE'RE CONTINUING OUR ENQUIRIES. "Well," she said, aloud, to Tann. "Do you think he might have done?"

"It looks like dissimulation to me," Tann said. "We went to Sarah in search of information about Hook, but she doesn't want to play ball. The chain of association leading to Geoffrey is far too tenuous. Hook's a far likelier suspect than he is."

"Unless...," York ventured.

"I think we need a little more evidence before we start speculating about accidental incest," Tann said.

"But the hammer-wielder did go for the eyes," York persisted, as if talking to herself. "Isn't that what Oedipus did?"

"Oedipus put his own eyes out," Tann reminded her—but realized, even as he said it, that he couldn't be sure that the hit man hadn't been commissioned, directly or indirectly, by one of the victims of the crime. How significant, he wondered, were Richard Treguern's continual lamentations about having no hands of his own? "This is getting silly," he hastened to add.

"Best to stick to procedure," York agreed. "I'll run the tape over to the IT people, and put in for the court order. I'd better bring Jess up to speed. All in all, this is turning out to be a more exciting day than I anticipated when I spent the better part of last night supervising an AI search of every traffic camera in east Berkshire, with a side-order of teepee pornography. We might lick the problem yet."

Tann's eyes went to the switchboard on his desk. The display told him that Roland Montfort was still a long way behind in taking calls, and the queue was now fifty or sixty long. Most of the people waiting were either unidentified or honest media vultures, but thirty-five places down there was a call waiting from Geoffrey Torquati. When York had left the room to go in search of her partner, Tann selected that one.

"I've been waiting for half an hour!" Geoffrey Torquati complained, before Tann even had time to identify himself—although that was unnecessary, given that he was using a picturephone. So was Geoffrey, which gave Tann the chance to study his features as he said: "Does the name *James Hook* mean anything to you, Mr. Torquati?" He thought it best to spring the question without warning.

"No," said the heiress's son, giving nothing away. "Why?"

"What about *Floreat Etona*?"

"No." If Geoffrey Torquati really had been the hammer-wielder, and had muttered that phrase as he attacked Mildred Barrow, he had an expert poker face. "What are you blathering about, Hicks? My sister said you stonewalled her when she phoned you demanding action. We're taking legal advice, you know."

"I know," Tann said, coldly. "Good luck with that. Why are you calling, Mr. Torquati?"

"The news is reporting that there's been a second attack. Were any of the headpieces injured?"

"You mother is perfectly safe, Mr. Torquati. The police talked to her a few minutes ago. There's nothing to worry about."

"She thinks I did it, doesn't she? I didn't. You believe me, don't you, Mr. Hicks. You must have checked up on me by now. You know I didn't do it. Mother—that thing that thinks it's my mother—is paranoid. It harasses me, you know. If it were a person, I'd take out a restraining order. You have no idea what it's like, Mr. Hicks—no idea at all. You're nursing a nest of vipers there—a nest of vipers."

"So I've been told," Tann told him, dryly. "Thanks for calling, Mr. Torquati. As I said, you have nothing to worry about." He cut the connection. He thought about taking another call, but couldn't find one that seemed worth taking. Instead, he used the same limited search procedure that P.C. York had used to find Hook to look for "Floreat Etona" among the teepee transcripts.

Unsurprisingly, the phrase didn't turn up any hits at all. "Peter Pan" produced a dozen isolated mentions, but nothing that seemed significant.

"Oh well," Tann murmured to himself. "I need to think this through properly. I could really do with a coffee."

Meg had packed him two salad sandwiches and a banana for his lunch, but he decided that it was too early for that. He went empty-handed to the block's kitchen, where there was a coffee machine. Sam Scarlett was there, sipping from a cup whose contents were obviously still hot.

"I've just been talking to Sadiq," Sam said. "The rabble-rousers are getting busy out at the main gate, but they're just putting on a show for the cameras. It's going to make the prime-time news again, though. All this stuff about the sex-lives of the Undead is just too tempting. The TV people have probably known about it for a while, just waiting for an excuse to put it out there. Just our luck, eh?"

"It wasn't just luck," Tann told him. "If Bruno Holzhauser hadn't been one of the victims, and if he hadn't been pestering the vultures for months, trying to attract their attention...."

"And he's deeply involved in the dirty talk, too," Sam supplied, practically licking his lips. "With Torquati, no less. Who'd have thought it?"

"Not me," Tann admitted. "I've been chatting to them all, in a neighborly sort of way, but I never had the slightest suspicion. I'm off the case, by the way."

"What do you mean, off the case?"

"Montfort's told me to drop it—to leave it to the police."

"Why? I thought he was keen for you to clear it up—to save face for the Elysium."

"I don't know. All I said to him was *Floreat Etona*."

"What's that?"

"It's what the man with the hammer said as he smashed Mildred Barrow's artificial face in."

"Barrow's? Not Holzhauser or Torquati's?"

"No—but he did attack all four. Maybe he had it in for more than one of them...and Mr. Montfort too."

Sam seemed amused by that idea, but he shook his head in a pantomime of bewilderment. "Montfort owes us one, though," he said. "So do those two Thames Valley Police Barbies. If we hadn't been there when the second lot came in, waving that bloody chain-saw...."

"The P.C. who talked the axe-man told me that she could have handled him without my help—that all I did was get in the way."

"Crap," Sam said. "If we hadn't been there to back them up, they could have ended up getting seriously hurt, or dead—and our four friends might have lost their heads. Not that I expect a medal, mind—our sort never get the medals." Tann was not entirely sure that he was included in the plural term.

After a pause, Tann resumed the conversation by saying: "You're right about the media, Sam. This might get ugly. The dem-onstration is bound to grow, and become more assertive. We're go-ing to be in the front line, no matter how much support the police can provide. There's no way to defuse the situation now—and the physical battering the four victims took will probably pale into in-significance by comparison with the media assault they'll have to endure. It's not just Bruno and Sarah—I'm pretty sure that Richard and Mildred are involved too. There's probably not an Undead in the Elysium who isn't...the organics, at least. Mr. Hahn and his fel-low inorganics are presumably made of sterner stuff in more ways than one."

"Well, you know what they say about all the Undead being crazy," Sam replied, philosophically. "Paranoid *and* sex-mad. It's not going to be good for business—they might even suspend the whole program. Not that I'd be sorry if the next few hundred incom-ers were all stone-and-silicon. They don't seem quite so...unnatural. Which is odd, I suppose, but true nevertheless. Not that I'll ever be able to afford any kind of artificial afterlife myself—I daren't even cling to the hope that there might be a real one, in case there's a Hell as well as a Heaven."

"The staff discount would help," Tann suggested—and then sat up, bolt upright. If his coffee cup hadn't been half-empty, he would have spilled some of the liquid in his lap.

"What?" asked Sam.

"Montfort showed me the accounts yesterday. I didn't think anything of it at the time, because all the inward payments varied, according to slight differences in timing and provision—but Mildred Barrow's trustees paid significantly less than the fees pertaining to the other three members of her quartet. It wasn't because she got second-class service—it was because she got a *discount*."

"But she's not on the staff," Sam pointed out.

"No," Tann agreed, "but her son was at school with someone who is. The families have known one another for more than twenty years. Montfort knew Mildred when she was alive."

"So what?"

"So all three of them have now figured out who's behind this, and at least part of the why."

"Which three are we talking about?" Sam asked, still bewildered.

"Mildred, Montfort, and Nathaniel. The shit really is going to hit the fan. No wonder Montfort wanted this played down. We need to help him, Sam. I should have listened to him—but I had to go and tell Katy York what I'd found. She's no fool—she and Jess Anderson will get to the bottom of it in no time, now."

"What on Earth are you talking about, boss?" Sam demanded.

"I'm talking about our jobs," Tann said. "All of them. The Elysium's in trouble."

Sam Scarlett was getting impatient, but Tann had no time to explain. He had to find Anderson and York.

They were both in his office; York was sitting behind his desk and Anderson was perched on top of it. They both looked up as he came in.

Tann sat down at the other desktop, and typed a rapid series of terms into a general search engine. The result came up in a matter of seconds. Schools were very conscientious in matters of record-keeping, and always avid to advertise their extra-curricular activities, over as long a time-span as possible.

Anderson stood up and leaned forward to look over his shoulder, but he blanked the screen.

"I told Montfort yesterday," Tann said, "that there was no way that you were ever going to get a conviction in this case, unless you got a confession, because there simply wouldn't be enough evidence. Is that true?"

"Probably," Anderson answered. "Why—do you know where we can get a confession?"

"Not exactly," Tann said, "but I think I can tell you who did it."

"We're already pretty sure that we know who did it," York told him. "The point, as you just pointed out, is to build a case that will stand up in court. It's not enough to have the indicators pointing in the right direction—you have to be able to join the dots up into a solid chain of evidence."

It wasn't the first time that the policewoman's patronizing attitude had annoyed Tann, but this time he couldn't help responding to the provocation. "So who did it, then?" he demanded, skeptically.

"Jacob Barrow, of course," was York's reply. "I thought you'd worked it out yesterday, but didn't want to tell us until you had the evidence in place to back it up."

Tann couldn't help feeling chagrined that the policewoman was dead right about the identity of the perpetrator, but dead wrong about the time it had taken him to figure it out. "How did *you* figure it out?" he asked, a trifle weakly.

"Standard police procedure," Anderson put in. "It's not true, unfortunately, that every step that everyone takes nowadays is covered by CCTV cameras, whose video records only need to be interrogated retrospectively to backtrack their movements throughout their life—but anyone who thinks that he can drive from Caversham to Bracknell in the early hours of the morning without sticking out like a sore thumb when an AI search does a routine trawl is crazy. He was smart enough not to park right outside the hedge, of course, so there's a crucial gap in the record—just enough to make us hold off on an arrest, and reserve a modicum of doubt as to whether he was acting alone—but what we had seemed to be enough to tell us what picture we were trying to complete."

"But you didn't think to mention it to me?" Tann said, knowing in his heart of hearts that there was absolutely no reason why the two policewomen should have felt any such obligation, even if they hadn't decided to pay him the compliment of assuming that he was in the same boat as they were. He was, after all, a civilian with a joke uniform and a joke job.

"As I said," York put in, with obvious insincerity, "Jess and I assumed that you'd figured it out for yourself, but that you were just playing your cards close to your manly chest."

Anderson obviously felt that they'd teased him enough. "Drop it, Katy," she said. She looked Tann straight in the eye. "What have you got, Mr. Hicks?" she asked, politely. "If you can fill in any of the gaps, we'd be grateful."

"I can certainly fill in some of the gaps," Tann told her, trying to maintain a matching politeness in his tone, but not quite succeeding, "but I'm not sure it's enough to secure a conviction in court. It's too weird—but it might be enough to obtain a confession if you confront him with it." He shut up then, and waited.

After a few seconds, York said: "Okay, you've made your point. We're sorry—and we're all ears. Spill it."

For a few seconds more, Tann remained stubbornly silent—but there was no point in trying to extend the dramatic pause indefinitely. "The Dramatic Society at Reading School puts on an annual play," he said. "It's a big occasion—all the parents come along, especially if they're the kind that likes to get involved with school activities. Twenty years ago, the play was *Peter Pan*. Captain James Hook was played by Roland Montfort—who, apparently following a common theatrical convention, also played Mr. Darling. His friend Nat Barrow only had a bit part, as one of his pirate crew. Being a rugby player, Nat probably wasn't cut out to be convincing as one of the lost boys, let alone as Peter or Wendy."

"Ah," said York. "Dot, dot, dot. The families knew one another. Mildred Barrow was divorced by her husband a few years after Jacob was born. You think that Montfort is Jacob's father. You think he was knocking off his school friend's sexy mother on the sly. *That* we can check—a simple DNA test will do the job. Is that how Jacob found out, do you think? By means of surreptitiously-gathered DNA?"

"He might well have confirmed it that way, but I strongly suspect that he was prompted to start investigating by Petronilla Treguern, whose father knew all about Sarah Torquati's colorful posthumous sex-life, and had every incentive to investigate Jacob, once Mildred started trying to throw him at Petronilla. Richard doesn't have the slightest idea what he set in motion, of course, by suggesting to Petronilla that Jacob, in his Web guise as James Hook, was exchanging flirtatiously obscene texts with Sarah, and about Sarah being similarly involved with Bruno. Richard didn't recognize the full significance of *Floreat Etona,* because he didn't know that Jacob must have been familiar with the play from an early age. Hell, his mother must have made a point of reading it to him, and calling particular attention to the character of Captain Hook. It probably gave her a nice warm feeling of remembrance. That's probably why his bullying big brother gave the game away, when things began to get nasty, and the single hit he'd already sustained became a crushing one-two. You can see why Jacob didn't confine himself to smashing in his mother's face, can't you? He wasn't just trying to obscure the fact that his mother was the prime target—he had it in for all four of them. They were *all* part of the mess in which he suddenly found himself, although none of them was aware of the whole pattern."

"It's all just speculation," Anderson pointed out. "And you're right about it being way too weird for the average juror to get his stupid head around. We need more than that."

"We can get it, though," York countered. "If Hicks is right, our hackers will be able to prove that Barrow is Hook, and Petronilla Treguern will tell us whatever she told him—she has no reason to keep quiet about it, unlike Montfort and Mildred Barrow's sim."

Anderson shook her head. "It's still got too many gaps in it. It's not enough, without a confession."

York was still thinking about it. "At least I was wrong about the incest factor," she said, reflectively. "It really would be too weird if he'd been unwittingly cozying up to his mother instead of Torquati. He can't have known who Torquati was, mind—was it pure coincidence that they...um...*hooked up?*"

"Probably not," Tann said. "Torquati denied knowing who James Hook was when you talked to her, but she would, wouldn't she? She's seen Jacob Barrow in the flesh, visiting his mother. Richard Treguern might not have fancied him overmuch as a potential mate for his daughter, but Sarah…well, she's only human, after all, and she hasn't got much opportunity to fuel her fantasies, given her situation. She's stuck in the mud, looking perpetually southwards—directly toward Mildred Barrow's sim."

"Okay," said Anderson. "We'll assume, for the sake of argument, that you're right. You deserve a pat on the head for being a clever boy. But how do we go about getting the confession? Do you think he'll crack if we simply confront him with it?"

"That does work far more often than one might think," York put in, but her tone made it obvious that she would prefer a more reliable strategy.

"He didn't confess to Petronilla Treguern, and he's had time to pull himself together now," Tann said, trying to think it through himself. "He seemed calm enough when I talked to him on the phone, but that might only mean that he was bottling up the crazy, building up the pressure in preparation for another volcanic outburst. If you could trigger something like that…but if he really is in control of himself now, he knows that his mother and his big brother aren't about to take sides against him—and we know that Montfort isn't about to, either. Sarah might, though, if you tell her the whole story…and Bruno Holzhauser will be avid to nail him, once it's explained to him. Bruno has a good lawyer, who seems keen to help out."

"We'd rather it didn't get too complicated, to be perfectly honest," P.C. Anderson told him. "And we'd rather claim all the credit for ourselves, if we can—meaning no offense to you, given that you're under orders to stay out if it anyway. Arrest and confrontation might be the best bet, in my opinion."

"Thanks for being prepared to leave me out of it and claim the credit for yourselves," said Tann, dryly. "Very generous."

"We'll know how much you helped, though," York put in, "and you'll have the satisfaction of knowing how grateful we are."

Big deal, Tann thought—but he had already put all his cards on the table, and there was no point in regretting it now. "Well," he said, "I'm glad to have been some slight assistance. Shall I leave it to you professionals, now? You can always come back to me, if you need any more help."

"Thanks," said York. "We'll do that."

That could easily have been the end of it, but it wasn't. Tann's phone suddenly began ringing—not with its customary discreet buzz but with the emergency tone. Almost simultaneously, the police-women's phones began clamoring for attention too.

Tann's caller was Sadiq, phoning from the main gate.

"The situation's gone bad, boss," Sadiq said. "The crowd have breached the gate—it just wasn't strong enough to hold them back, when they all started shoving in unison. It's the cameras that pro-voked them into it—there are half a dozen helicopter drones hover-ing over them, two police and four media. They know that the foot-age is probably going out live to the whole of Britain, if not a sub-stantial fraction of the world. It's like the peasants storming Frank-enstein's castle—except that the Undead are sitting ducks."

Tann was slightly ashamed that his first thought was: *And what the hell am I supposed to do about it?* He was already moving to-ward the door, however, and he didn't even think about stopping when P.C. York called after him: "Leave this to us, Mr. Hicks. Just stay out of our way. It's best to leave riot control to the profession-als." He was, after all, the man whose primary responsibility it was to make sure that the Undead were safe in their graves.

CHAPTER NINE

Tann didn't head for what he thought of as the rear door of the administration block, which faced the main gate. He figured that it was already too late to make any attempt to stop Seymour Conway's acolytes there. He went out of the other door, which opened on to the Elysium's supposedly-quiet fields. He had some vague idea in his head about making a stand directly in front of the ground where the Undead lay helpless, as if he could somehow shield the likes of Mr. Hahn and Mrs. Barrow alike with his own poor frail flesh. At the back of his mind was the thought that Seymour Conway, like the reckless idiot with the chainsaw, was too scrupulous a man to hurt a living person in his haste to get to the real targets of his ire—or, if not too scrupulous, at least too media-sensitive to have a human being trampled to death in front of a buzzing swarm of avid cameras.

As he hurried toward the burial-ground, however, something else caught Tann's eye. In the distance, he could see the top of the rise where the quartet of headpieces that had been attacked on the night before last was situated. Although his view was slightly obscured by birch-trees, he could see that the quartet had visitors: at least four of them. Tann knew that that was wrong. The police had stationed a man of their own there: a Special Duties officer, probably seconded from Heathrow, who was licensed to carry a gun. The armed guard should have been sending any and all potential visitors away, no matter who they were.

The one that Tann's eyes picked out right away was Roland Montfort; the second, easily recognizable by her shiny blonde hair, was Mirella Coleridge. It took him more than ten seconds, however, to realize that the other two were Petronilla Treguern and Jacob Barrow. By that time, he was already sprinting at full speed, because he had also realized the most significant detail of all: the invisibility of the armed guard.

Special Duties officers, Tann knew, did not desert their posts. They did not take coffee breaks. If the Special Duties officer was invisible, it could only be because he was lying down—and that could only mean that someone had taken him out, presumably taking advantage of the distraction provided by a heated discussion with Roland Montfort and Mirella Coleridge as to the propriety and per-missibility of the injured members of the quartet receiving visitors, now that they could all hear again, and were at least able to form blurred visual images.

He really was keeping the crazy bottled up, Tann thought. *But the pressure was too great. He's flipped—and the bastard's done it on my bloody shift.*

Tann knew that his talent for speculation had hit the nail on the head when he got close enough to see that Jacob Barrow was hold-ing two guns, one in each hand. The one in his left hand was so small as to be almost derisory, but it had evidently been adequate as a means of shooting the guard. The other was big, black and ugly—obviously the weapon that the guard had been carrying, but had never had the chance to use.

Tann knew very little about guns, but he had seen media reports of what the guns carried by the security men at Heathrow could do, in case of a terrorist incident. They were automatic rifles, which could spray bullets around like hail. They weren't intended to be fired one-handed, but they weren't the kind of guns with which one had to take careful aim, if one's only intent was to inflict maximum damage.

There was little doubt, alas, that Jacob Barrow's intent was to do some serious damage. He might not have come with that inten-tion clear in his mind—perhaps he had only brought Roland Mont-fort out to the quartet in order to have a little family chat with his father, while his mother listened in—but once he had shot the an-noying policeman and picked up the automatic rifle, his course had been set.

Jacob was standing in the center of the square formed by the four headpieces, having taken up a position from which he could, if the whim took him, blast all four headpieces with a single circular sweep of his weapon. He was swaying and swiveling eerily, in order to keep one or other of the guns periodically pointed at each of his three hostages, who had wisely drawn apart.

In spite of the swaying and swiveling, Jacob's pose was suitably dramatic—and the directors of the helicopter drones that had been tracking the crowd that had broken through the gate had become aware of it at much the same time as Tann. There were as many flying eyes on Jacob Barrow now as there were on Seymour Conway's horde of amateur avenging angels—and when Tann risked a glance behind him, he saw that the amateur avengers were well aware of the fact.

Obedient to the logic of media coverage, the members of the crowd were slowing down in their run and stopping. They were not paying any attention to Mr. Hahn and the inorganic Undead among whom they were now distributed; their attention was focused on the celebrity quartet of potential organic martyrs, on Jacob Barrow and the automatic rifle…and, as Tann belatedly realized, on him.

Jacob Barrow wasn't the only one to have cast himself in a leading role in the unfolding drama. Without quite meaning to, Tann had run straight into the second lead, instantly upstaging Roland Montfort, Mirella Coleridge and Petronilla Treguern. His position on the ground, and the fact that he was running, had put in an irresistible claim for the attention of the flying eyes, and an automatic bid to be considered the hero of the story…or the villain, if one happened to be of the same mind as Seymour Conway.

Oh shit, Tan thought. *Meg is bound to be watching.*

That was a horrible thought in its own right, but not nearly as horrible as its corollary, which was that Lucy was probably watching too, if this really was being broadcast live. It had to be, he knew. There was nothing broadcast news editors liked better than a hostage situation—most especially of all one in which some stupid prick had decided to rush in where even avenging angels would fear to tread, instead of leaving the job to the professionals.

The real professionals, Tann knew, weren't here yet. Even if they came by helicopter instead of by road they would still be anything up to half an hour away—except for P.C. Anderson and P.C. York, who would have quite enough to do trying to exert some measure of control over the invading rabble, in the interests of converting their momentary pause into a long wait.

It really was up to him, at least for the moment.

Tann slowed down as he drew near to the quartet, and paused on the edge of the square. It wasn't just the flying eyes that were focused on him; all four of the people standing within the square were looking at him, with a mixture of puzzlement and dread.

Jacob Barrow stopped swiveling, and directed his attention squarely at Tann. That meant that he could no longer keep Mirella Coleridge in his field of vision, because she was behind him—but Tann could see that the solicitor wasn't about to tackle the gunman from behind. She was considering making a run for it—but she didn't dare, in case he turned and saw her, and the sight of her retreat triggered the violence latent in his panic.

Jacob was definitely in a state of panic. The eyes that fixed themselves on Tann left no doubt about it. This was a man who no longer had any rational course of action open to him, who felt that his entire existence had collapsed under the double blow of discovering that Roland Montfort, his brother's ex-school friend, was his real father, and that the lover on his private chat-line was the Undead headpiece situated opposite his mother's grave. Tann could see the shame and the confusion seething in his gaze, each feeding and amplifying the other.

Knowing that he had to do something, Tann strode forward to the place, which was mercifully less than a dozen feet away, where the Special Duties guard lay supine and helpless. The policeman's eyes were open, and he was breathing hoarsely, but he couldn't get up. Tann knelt down beside him, and examined the wound in his neck, just above the rim of his bullet-proof vest.

The policeman knew what had to be done; he was using his hand to pinch the flesh in the vicinity of his carotid artery, to slow the blood-loss—but he was already barely conscious. Tann leaned over the body as if to listen to the stricken man's chest to check his heart-rate and his breathing; then he looked up, straight into Jacob Barrow's maddened eyes.

"He's not dead yet," Tann said, evenly, "but he needs immediate medical attention. Put the guns down now, and you needn't be a murderer. Leave it another ten minutes, and it could well be too late."

There were many things that Jacob Barrow could have said that might have reassured Tann, but what he actually said seemed somehow to be far more ominous than any direct insult or threat.

"Tell me, Chief Security Officer Hicks," the gunman drawled. "How does a man with a surname like yours end up with a forename like *Tanneguy*?" Tann had never heard his name pronounced with such vicious contempt, and knew that Jacob was trying to diminish him, to make him into something pathetic and ridiculous—someone who could be shot without overmuch compunction.

"My maternal grandfather was French," Tann told him, speaking perfectly evenly. "He was very proud of his Breton heritage. There had been Tanneguys in his family for twenty generations, or so he said. The Hickses didn't have that sort of tradition behind them—Dad had nothing to put up in opposition to Mum's pressure. You know how things are in family circles—it's always a contest."

Jacob smiled, in a twisted sort of way. "I had no idea," he replied, "until recently. No idea at all. At least you know who you are, and it's who you always thought you were. How many of us can say that, eh?"

Tann knew that the plural implication wasn't intended to embrace Roland Montfort, Mirella Coleridge and Petronilla Treguern—it was a backhander aimed at the Undead, who were, virtually by definition, not the people they thought they were.

Tann risked a rapid sweeping glance at the three humans and the four Undead, all of whom it was his duty to protect. Petronilla, not unnaturally, was standing next to her father's headpiece, while the solicitor was beside her client's. Roland Montfort wasn't quite as close to Mildred Barrow's headpiece, but he wasn't that far away from it.

All the four of the Undead were looking at Tann, three of them through recently-replaced pairs of eyes that still seemed to be squinting uncertainly, not quite able to bring the situation into focus. Because they couldn't turn their heads, they had no choice but to look at him askance, and because their faces were essentially wooden, they couldn't muster much in the way of expressions, but Tann didn't need overmuch imagination to figure out that they were terrified, and that they were looking to him, in naked desperation, for help.

"You don't have anything against the living, Jacob," Tann said, guessing that the professionals would have taken that line if they had been handling the matter. "Let Roland, Mirella and Petronilla walk away. I'll stay, if you need a living hostage for a little while longer."

"Fuck off, Hicks," was Jacob's reply. "I've seen the movies too—but we're not working to the same script. The living and the Undead are all in this together, parts of the same unholy conspiracy. *These* living, at least—including you. You just don't get it, do you? You don't see what's happening. You can't see where the world is heading, even though you, of all people, should know."

Oh good, Tann thought. *He's going to make a speech, for the benefit of all those cameras—not to mention all the other eyes and ears in the cemetery. He's center stage, and he knows that he has to make the effort. He knows that he can't just let rip with that blasted rifle. He knows that he has to what the script demands, even if it's not the one that I was trying to work to.*

Tann was right; Jacob Barrow did, indeed, feel the need to make a speech. He probably hadn't come with any such intention, and hadn't had any such intention when he'd snapped, shot the guard, and stolen the more powerful weapon, but the logic of the situation had him in its grip now, and he was following it, just like everyone else.

Anderson and York had had some success in keeping the crowd at a safe distance—safe, that is, in the sense that they were probably out of range of potential gunfire—but their sheer numbers made it impossible for Jacob or anyone else to ignore them; there were at least three hundred of them. Many of them were standing on gravestones in order to get a better view—including smart gravestones, whose Undead inhabitants had momentarily ceased to be of interest.

Jacob Barrow had to know as well as Tann did that the only reason the members of the crowd were consenting to be held back out of rifle range was the fact that they all had their picturephones tuned to broadcast news, so that they could watch and listen along with the rest of the world to everything that the zooming drones were picking up: everything that Tann and Jacob were saying and doing, set against the backcloth of their own ominous presence and their own collective murmur. *At least* he *isn't tracking me by picturephone*, Tann thought, *or he'd probably have seen me palm the pepper-spray from the policeman's belt, just like everybody else.*

Tann knew, by virtue of that fact alone, that he was committed to using the spray. He merely had to pick his moment, and do the best he could to make sure of his aim. He too was trapped by the logic of the situation.

The moment hadn't arrived yet, though. Jacob still had his speech to make—and he was pretending that he was addressing Tann.

"You look after them," Jacob said, still fixing Tann with a stare than Tann could only assume to be a stare of insane, uncontrolled paranoia. "You talk to them. I've seen you, every time I come here. You know what they are, and what they get up to. You know what travesties they are of the people who had them made, in a futile, crazy attempt to secure themselves a perverse kind of immortality. You know full well that if any human beings are worthy of any kind of immortality, these are not among them. You know that these are greedy, avaricious egomaniacs—the very worst of human scum. You know the exact extent of their decadence and debasement—the absurd intensity with which they try to import the sins of the flesh into flesh that isn't even equipped to serve them. You know exactly how vile they are, exactly how hollow a mockery they are of the human beings that served as their models.

"What are they *for*, Mr. Tanneguy Hicks? Whose purposes are they supposed to serve? Are they really intended as a consolation to their living relatives, their survivors? Are they really intended to provide us with comfort and solace? Are they hell, Mr. Hicks? They're a reflection of the insane reluctance of certain people to die—people who can't bear the idea of being consigned to oblivion, of leaving no trace behind, of not being able to extent their evil influence just a little further, in time and in space. Their existence represents everything that's nasty in human nature, Mr. Hicks—the seven deadly sins, with a few extra twists. And that's why they need to be exterminated."

As if on cue—presumably, in fact, responding to what Seymour Conway must have immediately recognized as a cue—the distant crowd began to chant: "Kill the Undead! Kill the Undead!" The relatively discreet terminology of their banners had been cast aside in favor of something a little catchier.

"I can understand why you're disappointed in your mother, Jacob," Tann said, "but she was alive at the time, and you're not responsible, however unwittingly, for your parents' divorce. You can't hold it against Roland, either. He was sixteen, for God's sake; there was probably nothing as glamorous in the world, to him, as his friend's mother." From the corner of his eye, he saw Roland Montfort stiffen, and the ghastly pallor he had seen once before in his boss's face returned, along with the realization that all the secrets that everyone had harbored in connection with their various masquerades as Captain James Hook were doomed to exposure. Petronilla Treguern didn't look happy, either—but she kept silent. *Everybody* in the foreground, except for the two lead players, was keeping silent, including the Undead. With the exception of Richard Treguern, the Undead didn't have a choice about that, as yet, but Tann knew that they would have kept silent anyway, because they understood the logic of the situation, and the logic of the implicit script. This was a dialogue, not a free-for-all—except, of course, for the sullen chorus, whose chant was more like incidental music than diegetic narrative.

Tann had hoped to take Jacob by surprise, and perhaps cause him to drop his guard, but Jacob was presumably beyond the reach of that sort of surprise. The fact that Tanneguy Hicks knew his secret was largely irrelevant, even though he hadn't known it himself until very recently, because he knew full well that everyone would have found out soon enough, once the news of his perverted affair with Sarah Torquati broke, and the investigative acumen of the Web's best reporters was focused on him.

Unfortunately, Jacob had made his speech now, and it was time for action—-but Tann still had some faith in what he'd said earlier. Jacob's beef was with the Undead, not the living. Even though he'd shot the Special Duties Officer, Jacob's hatred was still focused primarily upon the headpieces, not their living companions. If he intended to present himself to the avid cameras as something more than a mere homicidal maniac, he had to target his mayhem.

Perhaps understandably, the first one toward whom the deadly barrel moved to take aim was Sarah Torquati: the only one without an associate present—or the one whose present associate was the maniac with the guns.

Fortunately or unfortunately, Tann only had to take two long-legged strides in order to take up a position directly between the muzzle of the gun and Sarah's headpiece. "No, Jacob," he said, gently. "I can't let you shoot her. It's my job to protect her."

This time, Jacob *was* surprised—probably not so much by the fact that Tann was acting like a fool, as by his own reflexive hesitation. Obviously, he hadn't yet diminished Tann enough to make it easy to shoot through him in order to get to Sarah.

It was time for Tann to make his own speech, although he knew that he had to be quick, because there was a policeman bleeding to death a few feet away.

"It may seem silly," Tann said, "given that they're all backed up, and no matter what you do, the headpieces will all be set up again, equipped with brand new sims—but the new sims won't be the same individuals as the ones you intend to shoot. You might think that's a good thing, since it's the present Sarah Torquati with whom you've been exchanging sexy telepathic texts, but from my viewpoint, it means that what you want to do really is *murder*, that it really is the destruction of a unique individual...or four unique individuals."

While Tann was speaking, obedient to the logic that he had just imposed on the situation, Petronilla Treguern had already taken two steps sideways, so that she was directly in line between Jacob Barrow's position and her father's headpiece. Roland Montfort was a fraction slower, but he had more to lose, image-wise, than anyone else, and he dutifully stepped into the firing-line between Mildred

Barrow and her son. Mirella Coleridge actually raised her eyes heavenwards, as if to say "Why me?"—but she knew, in her heart of hearts, exactly why she was on the spot, and even solicitors were human. She stepped forward, as boldly as she could, to form a human shield for Bruno Holzhauser. Jacob seemed to sense her movement behind him, because he began to sway and swivel again, moving both his guns in arcs akin to sectors of a circle. His stare, however, remained fixed on Tann Hicks, the spanner in his works.

"You see, Jacob," Tann said to Jacob Barrow, "we're not dealing with the sum of human evil here, but the sum of human conscience. Put down the guns."

"Fuck you," muttered Jacob, He might have fired then, and blasted Tann apart where he stood, but he was still too hesitant, still too conscious of all the eyes that were upon him, and all the ears that could hear his bad language, no mattered how much he lowered his voice.

Tann hoped that Meg was covering Lucy's ears—and her eyes too, just in case. "Before you start shooting," Tann said, calmly, "there's something you really need to take a look at."

"What?" Jacob asked, hooked without realizing it.

"This," said Tann, raising his right hand as if to show Jacob Barrow the image on a hand-held picturephone—except that what he was holding wasn't a picturephone, and he wasn't raising his hand in order to display what he held, but in order to make sure of his aim. He had never fired a pepper-spray before, and he didn't want to risk missing by firing from the hip.

Innocently, like the dupe that the implicit script had marked him out to be, Jacob looked straight into the muzzle of the little weapon—and the spray hit him squarely in the face.

Tann didn't wait for the spray to take effect—he was already lunging forward, head down. It wasn't the sort of tackle of which a rugby player like Nat Barrow would have approved; it was way too low, and Tann's head made a crunching impact with Jacob's groin—but it was all the more effective for that.

In his imagination, Tann could already hear the *rat-a-tat-tat* of automatic fire as the gun sprayed deadly fire around at random, at least for a second or two, but that was all in his mind. Although the riot of confused noises that grew around him, as the voices of those closest at hand were suddenly found and the chanting voices were suddenly broken with shock, could not possibly have been described as any kind of silence, the deadlier gun remained as mute as the slightly less deadly one that Jacob had already fired. Once Jacob had collapsed, Tann was able to roll over on to the arm that held the automatic rifle, while his free hand reached out to grapple with the one that held the pistol.

Tann still had the more dangerous weapon pinned beneath his body, and had the other one safely in his own possession, when help arrived like a tidal wave. A police helicopter had obviously unloaded its cargo; there were uniforms everywhere. The two uniforms that formed a shield over Tann belonged to P.C. Anderson and P.C. York, who somehow contrived to get him clear of the chaotic crowd, pick him up, and dust him down.

While York took possession of the pistol, Anderson murmured in his ear: "Lucky you were able to see that he hadn't taken the safety-catch off the automatic, eh? Otherwise, that stupid stunt could have gone *horribly* wrong."

Tann knew that she was helping him, feeding him a necessary prompt. He could tell by the way that Katy York was looking at him that they both knew perfectly well that he had no more idea than Jacob Barrow where the automatic rifle's safety-catch was located, or what had needed to be done to it to enable the gun to fire.

York couldn't resist saying: "We could have taken him, you know. You'd already spun it out long enough for a sniper in the copter to knock him over, if necessary. You didn't have to play the bloody hero all the way to the end. For a big guy, though, I have to admit that you can really get your head down and dirty."

"I didn't want to leave it to the professionals," Tann muttered—although he knew that York not only knew that but understood it. "It made a better story the way it panned out."

"Oh, it hasn't panned out yet," Anderson told him, in a whisper suggestive of commiseration. "This is just the beginning. You have no idea of what's in store for you, Tanny boy—no idea at all."

In fact, though, Tann had a pretty good idea of what would be in store for him, now he had shot to media stardom in a matter of minutes. He had watched TV all his life; he knew how the world worked. He had just taken the lead in the universal drama of the Defense of the Undead against the dark legions of their enemies, and it was a role he was probably going to be typecast in for the rest of his life, or at least until Lucy came of age. He felt a lot better now about the thought that Lucy might have been watching her Daddy, if Meg hadn't been able to prevent it.

"I did what I had to do," Tann said, in a perfectly normal voice. "It's my job." He didn't think it necessary to spell out that he was the Chief Security Officer of Virgil's Elysium; the title was, after all, printed on the bosom of his uniform.

CHAPTER TEN

The first grave by which Tann paused in order to say farewell was Mr. Hahn's. Hahn had already heard the news.

"So you're going to work for the Organization for the Protection and Advancement of Artificial Intelligences," the sim said. "Glad to have you on our side, Mr. Hicks. And you'll get to work with Ms. Coleridge too. I've seen her, at a distance—she's nice."

"I'm a married man," said Tann, automatically.

"I wasn't implying anything," Hahn's sim told him, in a slightly injured tone. "I leave *double entendres* to the new people."

"Sorry," Tann said. "I won't be disappearing forever. This is more an *au revoir* than a goodbye."

"We'll always be glad to see you. You've got an uphill task before you, though. The new people haven't done the rest of us any good at all, with their shenanigans. I told you, didn't I? I remember it distinctly."

"It wasn't that long ago, Mr. Hahn," Tann reminded him. "I can remember it quite distinctly myself."

"I couldn't see what you did over there on the rise," Hahn said, "because some swine was sitting on top of me chanting 'Kill the Undead!' and I don't mind admitting that I was scared. The word from those who could see, though, is that you were a real hero."

"I was lucky," Tann admitted, hoping that the sim wouldn't take him too seriously, given that that was what modest heroes were supposed to say.

"Well, we all need a bit of luck to get by," Hahn said. "The living more than the Undead—although we're going to need a fair amount of luck ourselves, now. This isn't over, is it? The danger hasn't gone away—and we won't have you to help protect us now. With all due respect to Mr. Scarlett, he isn't in your league."

"It's kind of you to say so, Mr. Hahn," Tann told him, "but Sam will grow into the job—just give him time."

"What about Mr. Montfort's replacement? Will he *grow into the job* too?"

"Of course he will. I'm sure you'll meet him soon."

"I'm not. What's become of Mr. Montfort, then?"

"A sideways move, apparently—although they haven't put him in charge of one of the other sites. He's been banished to darkest Manchester, which probably doesn't fill him with joy, but at least he didn't get the sack. Not that they had grounds, given that the crucial event that triggered the whole sorry mess happened long before he joined the firm, and his subsequent infractions were distinctly minor. Don't think too badly of his successor if you don't see much of him—he'll be a busy man."

"I'll try not to. Roll on the Robot Age, eh? Someday, we'll all be released."

"Some day," Tann promised, without bothering to add that he didn't foresee it happening any time soon. "Got to get on, Mr. Hahn—be good, now."

"Be lucky," Hahn replied.

Tan went up the slight slope to the spot where the most famous quartet in the Elysium was located. The first of the sims he went to talk to was Sarah Torquati. "How are you feeling now, Ms. Torquati?" he asked, in a low voice.

"Better," she told him, speaking normally. "Spoiling for a fight. You're going to help prevent my kids from closing me down, I hear."

"Yes I am—and I'm confident that we'll be successful. Ms. Coleridge is helping too."

"I know. I never thanked you properly for what you did when Jacob was going to shoot me, did I?"

"You thanked me by text," Tan reminded her.

"That's what I mean—I never thanked you properly. It was a brave thing to do. I wish my eyes had been fully operational, so that

I'd have a better memory of it. It's all a bit blurred, I fear—but thanks, from the bottom of my heart."

"You're welcome," Tann said, and would have passed on to Bruno Holzhauser, working his way clockwise round the formation, if Sarah Torquati's voice hadn't dropped to a murmur, while taking on a tone of sudden urgency.

"Wait!" she said. "I need to explain something. It might not do any good, and it's way too late to save me from being cast as the Jezebel of the Undead, but it's something you need to know, and something you, at least, might be able to understand. You've always talked to us, Tann—you know us better than anyone."

Tann moved closer to the headpiece. "What is it?" he asked.

"I need to explain about the sex—the teepee sex. It's not what they say it is."

"In what way?" Tann asked, not without a certain genuine curiosity.

"They keep calling it text-message sex—which it is, in a way…but it's not the same as text-message sex between two living people, even if the living partner thinks it is. To the living person, you see, it is *just words*: words that he types with his fingers, and words that he reads and translates into sounds in his mind. But we don't have fingers, and we don't have to read the replies. We have to *understand* the replies, but we don't do that by translating them into phonemes. We can understand them *directly*, as electronic stimuli—electronic stimuli that become, because of their context, intrinsically pleasurable. Do you understand what I'm trying to say, Tann? For us, teepee sex isn't just a poor substitute, the way that text-message sex seems to be for the living. For us, teepee sex *is* sex. It's all we have, and the fact that it's all in the mind, all in the imagination, shouldn't be allowed to diminish it, or to make it ridiculous, or to make it into an excuse for *shooting* us. I'm not going to tell you how beautiful it is, and make it out to be something romantic, but it's all we have, and it's not negligible. It's an intrinsic part of the way we're growing and evolving. I know that the old Undead don't experience it the same way, because their silicon matrices aren't adapted to it, and I know that old farts like Richard—and Mildred too, in spite of her own checkered past—take a holier-than-thou attitude too, but you're not like them, Tann. You can understand how terribly lonely it is to be trapped this way, and how any process of education that might help our minds to cope a little better is not merely forgivable but worthy of applause. It's your job now, isn't it, to plead on our behalf, so you need to understand. You do understand, don't you, Tann?"

After a moment's pause, Tann said: "Yes, Sarah—I think I do. I'll do what I can to help others understand—you have my word on that."

"Thanks, Tann," she whispered.

For a moment, he was afraid that she was going to continue: "And if you ever...."—but she didn't, and he didn't have to remind her that he was a married man.

He continued circling the square.

"We've got them on the run now," Holzhauser said to him. "Thanks to me, it's all out in the open."

"Yes it is, Mr. Holzhauser," Tan agreed. "Every last little thing is out in the open—largely thanks to you."

"When I get control of my money," the sim said, "you can work for me, Hicks. I'll make it worth your while. We'll see it through together, eh? The living and the Undead, shoulder to shoulder. Makes you proud, doesn't it?"

"I hope it will, Mr. Holzhauser," Tann said, as he hastened to pass on. "Look after yourself, won't you?"

"You can be damn sure that I will, given half a chance," Holzhauser's voice called after him.

"If I were looking for a son-in-law," Richard Treguern told Tann, "I certainly wouldn't be looking at Jakey Barrow any more. I thought he was quite a good kid, you know, in spite of the how's-your-father with Sarah. A fine judge of character I turned out to be. Have you seen Pet lately?"

"We've exchanged a few words. She was the one who turned the situation around, you know—if she hadn't been brave enough and quick enough to follow my lead, the others wouldn't have done it either. I'm assured that the police sniper would still have stopped Jacob before he blasted you to smithereens—assuming that he could have found the safety-catch on the automatic—but it wouldn't have been the same without the noble gestures. You should be proud of your daughter."

"I am—and you're right; there's no way that slimeball Montfort would have stepped up if Pet hadn't shamed him into it, and no way that the lawyer would have taken her turn if she hadn't been left with no other choice, save for a massive loss of face. She's a looker, and no mistake, but not as sweet as Pet, and nowhere near as gutsy. You should steer clear of her, if she starts making eyes at you."

"I'm a married man," Tann reminded him, with a slight sigh over the necessity of using the line anyway. "I've got a daughter of my own, and another on the way. I'm not looking for anything extracurricular."

"I am," Treguern replied, glumly. "It's not easy, though, in my position."

"Well, I wish you the best of luck, Mr. Treguern. I'll be seeing you again, in the not-too-distant future, I hope."

"You'll be hearing from me too," Treguern said, "at least by text. There's no escape."

Tann passed on again, and came to stand in front of Mildred Barrow.

"I'm truly sorry," she said. "For everything."

"You aren't responsible for your model's mistakes, Ms. Barrow," Tann told her. "You might have inherited her conscience, but you're quite innocent, in yourself. Jacob should have known that—but he got caught in the same paradoxical trap as the rest of us. He knew you weren't really his mother, but he had no one else to blame. How's he doing?"

"He seems to be as well as can be expected. At least he's talking to me again. He doesn't like you, though—he seems to think that it might somehow have worked out better if you hadn't interfered. I try to tell him that you saved him from far worse, but he can't see it yet. Nat and Helena still hate me, but that's only to be expected, and at least they're talking to me. Roly's the only one who won't talk to me, but he'll come around in time. I'm not saying that it was six of one and half a dozen of the other—I really did take advantage of him—but he wasn't entirely innocent, even at sixteen. He was *very* good as Captain Hook. I never saw a sexier performance. He is the sexy one in the play, you know—Peter Pan's nothing by comparison."

"It's not supposed to be a sexy play, Ms. Barrow," Tann told her. "Quite the reverse."

"I suppose not," the sim agreed, still exercising her conscience in spite of what Tann had said to her earlier. "Have you read it, then?"

"I have now. I'm reading it to my daughter. She likes Wendy, obviously—and Peter too. She's still at an age where she thinks not growing up would be quite a good idea. I'm not sure that I can persuade her otherwise, or even that I ought to try."

"To die will be an awfully big adventure," Mildred Barrow quoted, very softly. "I can't quite persuade myself of that, either—or even that I ought to try, in spite of already having embarked on the adventure in question once already. All in all, I'd rather be a vampire, if I have to be Undead at all. I'd rather be alive, of course, but that's not an option, is it?"

"I'm afraid not," Tann agreed.

"You make the best of it, Mr. Hicks—and try to love your wife. If I learned one thing from life, it's that everything works best if a man can love his wife. Trust me on that."

"I do love my wife," Tann assured her. "And I believe you when you say that it's the best way to go. I wish you the best of luck, Mildred—I really do."

"I'm truly grateful, Tann," the sim replied, as he turned to leave. "I need it. I think we all will, if we're to make anything of ourselves—but we might eventually get by, with the help of our friends among the living."

"I hope so," Tann said, setting a course for the main gate and the unknown future. "At any rate, I'm proud to be one of them."

ABOUT THE AUTHOR

BRIAN STABLEFORD was born in Yorkshire in 1948. He taught at the University of Reading for several years, but is now a full-time writer. He has written many science fiction and fantasy novels, including *The Empire of Fear*, *The Werewolves of London*, *Year Zero*, *The Curse of the Coral Bride*, *The Stones of Camelot* and *Prelude to Eternity*. Collections of his short stories include a long series of *Tales of the Biotech Revolution*, and such idiosyncratic items as *Sheena and Other Gothic Tales* and The *Innnsmouth Heritage and Other Sequels*. He has written numerous nonfiction books, including *Scientific Romance in Britain, 1890-1950*, *Glorious Perversity: The Decline and Fall of Literary Decadence*, *Science Fact and Science Fiction: An Encyclopedia* and *The Devil's Party: A Brief History of Satanic Abuse*. He has contributed hundreds of biographical and critical entries to reference books, including both editions of *The Encyclopedia of Science Fiction* and several editions of the library guide, *Anatomy of Wonder*. He has also translated numerous novels from the French language, including several by the feuilletonist Paul Féval and numerous classics of French scientific romance by such writers as Albert Robida, Maurice Renard, and J. H. Rosny the Elder.